MW00527409

The Gardener's Plot

The Gardener's Plot

A MYSTERY

Deborah J. Benoit

MINOTAUR BOOKS
NEW YORK

First published in the United States by Minotaur Books, an imprint of St. Martin's Publishing Group

THE GARDENER'S PLOT. Copyright © 2024 by Deborah J. Benoit. All rights reserved. Printed in the United States of America. For information, address St. Martin's Publishing Group, 120 Broadway, New York, NY 10271.

www.minotaurbooks.com

Spot art: flowers and leaves illustrations © c.ruxandra/ Shutterstock and Ann.and.Pen/Shutterstock; shears © Jovanovic Dejan/Shutterstock

Design by Meryl Sussman Levavi

Library of Congress Cataloging-in-Publication Data

Names: Benoit, Deborah J., author.
Title: The gardener's plot : a mystery / Deborah J. Benoit.
Description: First edition. I New York : Minotaur Books, 2024.
Identifiers: LCCN 2024025620 I ISBN 9781250334978
   (hardcover) I ISBN 9781250334985 (ebook)
Subjects: LCGFT: Detective and mystery fiction. I Novels.
Classification: LCC PS3602.E6683 G37 2024 I DDC 813/.6—dc23/
   eng/20240624
LC record available at https://lccn.loc.gov/2024025620

Our books may be purchased in bulk for promotional, educational, or business use. Please contact your local bookseller or the Macmillan Corporate and Premium Sales Department at 1-800-221-7945, extension 5442, or by email at MacmillanSpecialMarkets@macmillan.com.

First Edition: 2024

1 3 5 7 9 10 8 6 4 2

To my mother and father, who always believed. I wish you were here to share this adventure with me.

The Gardener's Plot

Chapter One

Of all the people I didn't want to run into, the person at the top of that list just happened to be in line in front of me at the Grocery Mart. By the time I realized who I'd stepped behind, it was too late. I glanced around, wishing I could spontaneously vanish. Much to my relief, Catherine Whitacker kept her perfectly coiffed head of shoulder-length auburn curls turned stiffly forward.

I'd met her back in seventh grade and had instantly landed on her blacklist. Catherine (never, ever Cathy) had always avoided speaking to anyone she didn't want to take the trouble to be nice to. Overt rudeness was not something Mrs. Henderson's daughters indulged in, but acknowledging an unwanted presence often included a soul-shredding remark—delivered in the nicest possible way, of course.

So, when I found myself in the checkout line behind her, I stood quietly, hoping she would leave without a backward glance. But luck abandoned me. Just as Catherine pulled out her wallet, recognition dawned in the clerk's eyes.

"Hey, you're Maggie Walker, aren't you?" She snapped her

gum and nodded in rhythm. "Yup, I remember you. I'm so sorry to hear about your gram's passing."

That's all it took. At the sound of my name, Catherine turned in horror-movie slow motion. When she realized the clerk was right, a saccharine smile replaced her frown.

Catherine's tone oozed faux long-lost friend. "Why, Maggie— Oh, but you go by Margaret since you left for the big city, don't you?" Tiny lines had appeared at the edges of her steely blue eyes since I'd last seen her, but her makeup was as impeccable as ever.

The clerk slid the last of Catherine's purchases across the counter and into a pristine red, white, and blue shopping bag with THINK GREEN printed across it. "Um, Mrs. Whitacker?"

Catherine's face fell into neutral as she turned. "Yes?"

"Do you have any coupons today?"

"Of course not."

"Then that'll be thirty-three ninety-seven, please."

"Of course," Catherine said, introducing a credit card to the reader. "So, Margaret—Carruthers, isn't it now?" She scribbled her signature and extended her hand for her receipt without another glance at the clerk.

"No, Walker," I said. I really didn't want to get into the whole once-I-was-Walker-then-Carruthers-now-Walker-again story in a public place—especially not with the slow smirk I could see forming on Catherine's face. I'd bet my first vine-ripened tomato she'd already heard it in one form or another anyway. I wanted to head back into the aisles, saying I'd forgotten something, but Catherine would likely interpret that as a victory, and I hadn't reached the point of surrender. Not by a long shot. If she pushed, I'd just fall back on the easy explanation: Walker is the name I write under.

"Thank you for shopping at Grocery Mart, Mrs. Whitacker," the clerk said with her best retail smile.

Catherine nodded in return. "Well, I always say, we have to support our local businesses. If we don't care for our own, who will?" She pulled her purse over her shoulder and gathered the grocery bag, but before I could contemplate a sigh of relief, Catherine turned to face me again.

"I hear you've moved into your grandmother's house. I suppose with all you've been through you'll want to sell it as soon as you can. My brother will be in touch with you." Without a pause, she was gone in a swirl of expensive perfume. Like so many times in the past, Catherine's assumptions about my intentions were dead wrong, and I'd lost an opportunity to set her straight. If that was at all possible.

❦

Back home, I couldn't recall what else the clerk had said or how much my few groceries had cost. The drive to the house was a blur, too. Somehow, with just those few words, Catherine had brought back every *Twilight Zone* moment of growing up in Marlowe, a tiny town in the Berkshires of western Massachusetts, in my grandparents' care. She was the cherry on top of a week of frustrations, the worst of which until this morning had been the certified letter from my cousin Simon. And *that* I'd been trying to ignore since its delivery the day before.

But one sight of the old, in-need-of-paint Victorian brought a smile to my face. I'd fallen in love with the big wraparound porch and gingerbread trim when my parents first brought me here as a young child. As I grew up and times got emotionally tough, I'd retreated into books in the bay window or on the porch swing. Now that I was back here and it was mine, I had plans to restore what needed to be restored in the house and the garden. Gramma had loved both. She'd lived here into her nineties but in recent years hadn't been able to keep the place in the condition I so fondly remembered. The flower gardens had become smaller each year, and the growth of the trees and underbrush of the woods that bordered the backyard inched closer to the house. Yet I had no trouble picturing it as it would be again. None at all.

I pulled my little red Wrangler around the house and to a stop in front of the garage, then headed to the back door with my paper bag of purchases. When I entered the house, I didn't see drafty windows, dated wallpaper, or the faded linoleum that covered the kitchen floor. I saw the flowery curtains and tablecloth my grandmother had sewn on her trusty Singer and, through the kitchen doorway, the shelves of books she'd collected—books she'd encouraged me to read instead of sitting staring at the television for hours on end. I'd devoured those books and many more, though I still managed to indulge my television habit.

I put the groceries on the kitchen table and closed my eyes. I felt her arms around me, reassuring me that whatever life threw at me, I'd find a way to deal with it. That included Catherine Whitacker. I hoped Gramma was right. She had been so far.

Gramma passed away last fall. When the time came to dispose of the estate's assets, the house had been appraised. Her will had specified family had a right of first refusal on the property—me first, and then any other member of the family who would like to place a bid on it. Since I wanted nothing more than to retreat to the one place my heart called home and felt certain none of my cousins—spread to the four winds as they were—would feel the same, I'd put in a bid with the real estate agent at the appraised value. She promptly told me another offer had been made and suggested I make a counteroffer. Confused, I'd called the estate lawyer. It turned out the other bidder, who seemed more interested in the location and the land the house sat on than the house, was not a relative. The house was mine under the terms of the will. I'd rolled over the net proceeds from selling my condo and a chunk of my late, almost ex-husband, Bryce's, life insurance to pay the purchase price, and now the house and land were mine. I'd moved in a month ago, certain I'd made the right decision.

As I stowed my groceries in the pantry, I thought about my cousin's letter, a belated demand for a larger share of Gramma's tiny estate. I'd stopped reading after the first page. No doubt the rest contained a recitation of the numerous messages he'd left on Gramma's—my—answering machine for the past week or so.

I sighed. It was barely nine on Friday morning and I was already tired from my encounter with Catherine and a lack of sleep the night before. I was tempted to sneak upstairs and crawl back into bed when I finished tidying up, but I had obligations, one in particular I'd been looking forward to.

I had just enough time to get where I needed to be for my meeting with Violet Bloom to cross the last of the t's and

dot any dot-less i's before tomorrow morning's opening of the
Marlowe Community Garden.

I grabbed my notebook and cell phone and stashed them
in my backpack, then headed for the front door. As I stepped
outside to get my bike, I took a deep breath and smiled into the
sunshine. It was the perfect morning for a bike ride: spring flowers scented the air, a trio of robins hopped across the grass in
search of worms. Truth be told, riding my bike to Violet's house
wasn't just for the scenery or the exercise—as much as I enjoyed
both—but I hoped it would rid me of the residual aggravation
of dealing with Catherine this morning.

Movement in the driveway next door caught my eye. I
raised my hand to wave to my neighbor and good friend Sally
Kendall until I realized it was someone else. My hand dropped
to my side. As the figure paused to consult his phone on the
way back to his car at the curb, I recognized him.

Carl Henderson wanted Gramma's house. He'd already
made what would have been a fair offer if I'd been in the market to sell, which I wasn't. I'd told him so in person and on the
phone more than once. The two letters he'd sent had joined
the junk mail in my recycling bin unread.

I retreated a step and unlocked the door. I slipped inside
and made a beeline for the back door and my alternate trans-
portation. It may have been a perfect day to ride my bike to
Violet's house, but after my encounter with Catherine, I had
no time and less patience to try again to convince Carl Henderson I had no intention of selling my home.

Once I was safely inside the Jeep, I turned on the engine,
tuned in my favorite oldies station on the radio, and started

down the wraparound driveway. I glanced in his direction. At the sound of John Denver not wanting to leave on a jet plane, Carl pivoted and waved, no doubt signaling me to stop to chat. He cut across the front yard like an arrow to its target and called out something I couldn't hear over the radio. I just smiled and waved back, glad to be on my way.

Carl Henderson was not a man to allow his prey to escape. His run ended in a gold medal–worthy leap that landed him in the middle of the driveway, several feet away from the Jeep's front bumper. I hit the brakes. A salesman smile appeared on his face. Captured.

Carl Henderson walked to the driver's side window and tapped an index finger against the glass. Reluctantly, I pressed the button to lower the window. He spoke. Paused. Motioned for me to lower the volume on the radio. I complied. I might be caught, but I had no intention of making this easy for him. Misery loves company and all that.

"I'm so glad to find you at home," he began.

"I'm on my way to an appointment," I countered.

He continued on like he hadn't heard me. "I have something for you. It's an offer I know you're going to want to take a look at." He pulled an envelope out of the inner pocket of his jacket and held it out, its end poking inside the window.

"No, thank you," I said, all pretense of a friendly face gone.

"But you're going to be very happy with the terms." He waggled the envelope at me. "Take a look."

"I'm late," I said and reached for the shift. He took a step sideways as though he intended to plant himself in front of me as some sort of human blockade. I let out an exasperated sigh.

"I told you no. If you get in my way again, I'm going to file for a protection order against you for harassment."

That caught him off guard. I had no idea if his pushy-salesman tactics rose to the level of harassment, but the threat seemed to work.

"Of course I don't want to keep you. I'll leave it in your mailbox," he said and scurried behind the Jeep and across the lawn again.

I paused only long enough at the end of the driveway to take a quick look both ways, then headed off toward Violet's house.

I'd met Violet Bloom for the first time at Gramma's funeral. Of all those who knew Gramma well—few of whom I recalled at all, if I'd ever met them—Violet was the only one who found a place in my memory, penetrating the fog that had settled over me when Gramma died. To this day, I couldn't remember a word she'd said, but there was comfort in her words and a seed of friendship planted.

That seed sprouted days later when she'd appeared at my door with a basket of muffins and talk of her plans for a community garden—the very same garden now scheduled to open tomorrow morning due to Violet's dedication. By the end of her visit, she'd convinced me to volunteer.

So here I was, driving along the now familiar route to her house, through residential neighborhoods where the hum of lawn mowers temporarily drowned out the sweeter sounds of spring. In exchange, the scent of fresh-mown grass floated in through the Jeep's open windows.

I made the turn onto Violet's street a good ten minutes

early. I parked in the shade of one of the maples that lined both sides of the street and stepped out into the dappled sunshine.

The Blooms' tasteful white clapboard cottage stood on a quarter-acre lot in what had been a posh neighborhood 150 years ago. Now old Victorians were interspersed with a variety of other architectural styles constructed as lots were subdivided and new homes built over the years.

Like pretty much everything I'd observed where Violet was concerned, the walk leading to her front door was a tidy progression of carefully laid bricks. Well-tended beds sporting spring flowers and emerging perennials surrounded the carpet of green grass at the front of the house.

I crossed the street and followed the pansy-lined walk to Violet's front door and rang the bell. A moment later, Violet opened it.

"Oh, good," she said with a smile and motioned me in. "You're early. I was hoping you might be. I've got a bear of a day ahead of me."

Chapter Two

If anyone else had started out by saying that, I'd expect our meeting to be rushed, but I'd come to know Violet well enough to expect her to be fully present without a single let's-get-this-over-with moment. Once we were done, she'd be off to the next thing on her list.

"Let's head into the kitchen. I've got everything set up on the table there. Vic and the kids are away at his mother's, so we won't be interrupted. They were less than thrilled to be taking along their homework assignments, but so it goes," Violet said with a laugh. "I thought for sure you'd be riding your bike over today."

"Last-minute change of plans."

"Oh?"

"Carl Henderson was in the neighborhood just as I was leaving. I tried to take the coward's way out and drive off to avoid him. It didn't work."

"You shouldn't let him get to you."

"Easy for you to say. He's not trying to buy your house."

"Don't be so sure of that," she said. "He's got something going on. I hear he's been making offers on several undevel-

oped properties around town in addition to some homes." She
stopped and thought for a moment. "What did Vic say he heard
it called? Oh, right. Marlowe Estates. Sounds fancy, doesn't it?"

Violet led the way past the neat and tidy family room into
a kitchen the polar opposite of my own much-in-need-of-
updating but much-loved kitchen. Gleaming wood cabinets
lined two walls, a bank of windows another. A row of potted
herbs basked in the sunshine on the windowsill, and white
Battenberg lace valances topped the sparkling glass. A large
island filled one end of the room near the sink and appliances,
while a family-sized table anchored the other.

Violet's organizer notebook and laptop computer waited
on the tabletop, as did a plate of cookies and two mugs.

"Care for some coffee to start us off?" she asked as she
grabbed one of the mugs and headed for the ever-ready coffee
maker on the countertop.

She paused and turned, frowning. "Do you even drink
coffee? You always seem to have something else. Would you
prefer tea?"

"That'd be great," I said as I pulled out my own organizer
and located the pre-opening checklist.

Violet filled my mug with water and popped it in the microwave to heat while she pulled out a box of tea bags and set
it on the table.

"I think we're in pretty good shape for tomorrow," I said as
the microwave dinged.

"Yes, I'm happy to say we are. Everything is falling nicely
into place." Violet set the steaming mug in front of me and
took her seat.

It didn't take long to dispense with our checklists and go over the plot assignments. We'd been finalizing plans and working toward tomorrow's opening for weeks.

"Frank Wellman will be at the garden this afternoon to till the plots," Violet said. "That's about it." She closed the planner and pulled out a folder.

"Would you like me to meet him there?" I asked. "You said you've got a busy day."

"Thanks, but not necessary. I met with him yesterday afternoon to go over exactly what we need done and left a key with him so he can let himself in to get started. After my lunch date I'll stop at the copy shop to pick up the brochures and whatnot. I'll then drop them off when I meet Frank to do a last-minute check and pick up my spare key from him."

"Sounds like you've got it all under control."

"I like to think so." Violet slid a folder across the table to me. "Here's your copy of the finalized plot assignments, garden rules, and so on."

I thumbed through the pages and frowned. "I see Roy Hansen signed up for three plots."

"And you're concerned he's going to play king of the garden?"

"You read my mind."

Violet leaned forward and tapped on the sign-up list. "Don't let him bother you. Roy can be a bit of a bully, but if you don't back down and don't take the bait, you'll be fine. He'll grumble. Probably a lot. Just smile and let him. If you give in, you'll regret it."

"Whatever you say, boss."

At that she laughed. "More tea?" She got up and poured herself more coffee.

I shook my head and glanced over at the kitchen island, where a stand mixer, an assortment of measuring cups, and baking pans stood ready. "Looks like you've got some baking to do, too."

Violet nodded. "Just need to pick up a few ingredients and some groceries this afternoon. How'd you like the cookies?"

"Delicious. Did you make them?"

"Trial run for one of my entries in the baking competition at Sunday's picnic."

"Oh! And I've been a bit of a glutton. You should have just saved them."

"I'm glad you like them. Without Vic and the kids, I need someone to taste test the new recipe. I'm not always the best judge of how others will react."

"They're great. A prizewinner for sure."

"Excellent. Maybe I can add Cookie Queen to my titles."

"Well, you'll get my vote. If I get a vote."

"Sorry, judged by official judges." She laughed. "But I appreciate the support." She took another sip of coffee, wrinkled her nose, and put down her mug. "So how's it going at the house? Making any progress in your grandmother's gardens?"

"I'm just getting started, of course, but the existing beds are in fine shape. My next project is reclaiming the beds that have become overgrown around the edges of the yard and back by the woods."

"Sounds like quite the undertaking. Especially so close to the woods." She paused, then continued. "Aren't you concerned about, oh, I don't know, bears or something lurking there?"

"I've never seen a bear in the yard, though I do try to re-member to take the bird feeders in at night. And I haven't ven-tured beyond the backyard in years. I don't really think much about the wildlife except the deer who nibble on Gramma's hostas," I said. "Though I have had the occasional hiker cut through my property."

"Hikers?" She sounded skeptical.

I nodded. "You know, sometimes they get turned around back there, so they head for the nearest house to get their bearings."

"Oh, of course." Her smile didn't quite reach her eyes. "It's just good to keep an eye out, don't you think?"

I agreed in principle, and we chatted for a bit longer about the garden, involvement in the community, our plans at the upcoming picnic to promote the community garden, and whether the café or the diner was a better choice for a quick lunch in light of her jam-packed afternoon. I glanced at my watch. We'd been talking for over an hour. "I'd better let you get going. You said you had errands before lunch."

"That I do." Violet closed her laptop and gathered her pa-pers together. "And baking maybe later tonight and definitely finishing up by tomorrow afternoon, if you'll cover for me then at the garden. Shouldn't be much to do later in the day and you'll have time to work on your own plot."

"Absolutely." I grabbed my bag and headed to the door, wishing her good luck with the rest of her day.

I waved goodbye to Violet a little after eleven. The scent

of spring flowers drifted on the breeze as I crossed the quiet street to my Jeep. I stood there for a moment, drinking in the day. Unlike Violet, I had no plans and could spend the rest of the day working on any number of projects—or none at all.

When I stopped to listen closely, nature played a subtle, musical soundtrack. Birds chirped in the trees around me. The breeze rippled across the flower beds and rustled the leaves of the trees. Other sounds might intrude, but when I was in my garden, the sounds of spring surrounded me like one of Gramma's hugs.

And just like that, I knew how I'd spend the rest of my day. I checked my notebook and, satisfied my wish list was there, I pointed my Jeep toward the south end of town and my favorite plant place.

You could say Bailey's Homegrown was a Walker family tradition. I'd come here with Gramma for as long as I could remember to pick out plants in the spring, round out the garden during the summer, and shop the fall sales. Bailey's wasn't my exclusive place to plant shop, but it was by far my favorite.

I grabbed a cart and headed to the greenhouse by way of the rows of perennial plants that bordered the parking area. I passed a couple trying to choose between hanging baskets with a rainbow of petunias or those with the hummingbird favorite, fuchsia. Three coneflowers hopped in my cart, with a little help from me. I had just the spot for them in the front yard. Creeping phlox joined them, along with a few deer-resistant heuchera for the backyard.

Inside the greenhouse, I added a selection of tomato plants to the cart, some herbs, and sweet peppers. I'd come back for cucumbers and squash once I had the beds prepared.

"That's quite a cartful." Howie Tucker from the Marlowe hardware store stood at the end of the aisle I was about to exit. He motioned at my cart. "My wife loved coneflowers. Said they always made her smile."

"Me, too," I said. "I hope they share some of those smiles with my neighbors."

"I'm sure they will," he said and pulled his cart back to let me pass. "I've been trying to keep up her garden, but I'm nowhere near the gardener she was."

"If there's ever anything I can do to help, just give me a call," I offered.

"Thanks, that's really nice of you, but it's her garden. It wouldn't seem right to have someone else . . ." His voice trailed off and he looked away.

"I understand," I said, remembering what I'd heard about how devoted he was to her. He seemed no less devoted to her now, months after she'd died. If only my late husband had been half so devoted to me. I pushed the thought aside. That was my old life. My new life had no room for regrets.

I made my way to the checkout, where I arranged for delivery of five yards of mulch and most of my plant purchases. I said goodbye to Howie as the cashier rang up his purchases. The coneflowers accompanied me home, where I spent the rest of the afternoon cleaning up the front beds and putting the coneflowers in place.

As I was spreading my last bag of mulch across the newly renovated front bed, my neighbor—and best and oldest friend—Sally Kendall pulled into her driveway. I waved to her to come over.

The year I turned thirteen, my parents left me with Gramma and Grampa while they chased the footlights in summer theaters across the country. What began as a summer adventure turned into pursuit of their personal holy grail. They never looked back. My grandparents' home became my home. I felt abandoned (and nothing in the years since or my adult viewpoint has changed that feeling). I had no interest in Gramma's beloved garden. It became just another something to do when my parents didn't want me around. One afternoon, Sally came skipping down the sidewalk and asked if she could help me weed the flower bed I'd been pretending didn't really need weeding. Five minutes later, I had dirt under my fingernails and was laughing so hard I forgot how unhappy I was.

We'd been fast friends ever since. Today, she stood beside me, admiring the latest addition to my garden.

"I love them. They look like big pink daisies," she said. "All set for the big day tomorrow?"

I nodded. "We are. I met with Violet this morning before I went to the nursery."

"And this is all you bought?" Her expression said she didn't believe that for a minute.

"The only ones I brought home. I have a mulch delivery scheduled. They'll bring the rest of the plants then."

We chatted for a while about what I'd bought and where I intended to use them. When I stifled a yawn, Sally wished me luck and headed home.

After a quick shower, I grabbed a container of greens, a tomato, salad dressing, and some leftover chicken and threw together a salad for dinner. In a few months, the tomato and

other vegetable plants I'd purchased today would be produc-
ing fruit that would put this salad to shame. I could almost
taste the vine-ripened deliciousness.

I spent the evening catching up on some research and doing a little writing, though my mind kept drifting toward tomorrow's grand opening.

Tomorrow was going to be the start of a great growing season.

Chapter Three

Saturday morning dawned sunny and bright. Too bright.

I checked the time and realized I'd forgotten to set my alarm. Panic set in. I threw back the covers and headed for the shower. A short while later, I stood in the kitchen, downing a muffin and some orange juice.

A glance at the clock told me I had about a half hour to get where I needed to be. At ten o'clock I'd meet Violet at the community garden to get the season's work started. I stuffed my hat and sunglasses and some water into my backpack and headed out the front door into a perfect May morning. Birds chattered from the row of lilacs bordering my yard to the west. No time to check the feeders I'd forgotten to take in last night. I hoped a roaming bear hadn't gotten to them. I added that to my mental to-do list.

As I stepped out the front door onto the porch, a piece of paper stuck under the door knocker caught my eye. Its scrawled message was short and not so sweet.

May be late—start without me. V

Violet must have stopped by when I was in the shower. *Drat.* I glanced at my watch. If Violet wasn't going to be there, I'd better get moving. I felt in my pocket to be sure I had both sets of keys. It wouldn't be good to get to the garden and not have the key to access the tools and supplies locked in the shed—or to get back home and find myself locked out. I carried my bike down the porch steps and stepped into the spring sunshine. As I pushed my bike along the gravel path toward the sidewalk, I mentally checked off things I'd need to do in Violet's absence. Satisfied I had everything under control, I got on my bike and headed off down the tree-lined street.

I'd been away from Marlowe a little more than fifteen years, during which time I'd married and become unmarried, and long enough for Marlowe's streets to feel fresh and vaguely unfamiliar as I rode past houses my childhood friends had lived in. It's funny how much you overlook when you're in a car. On a bike or on foot, it's impossible to not say hello or wave to the neighbors, to notice the newly planted pansies lining a front walk, or even a freshly painted front door.

But I saw more than that as I rode down the street. Changes. So many changes. I wondered if anyone who'd been here all along noticed all the little details that had been lost and replaced over the years. At the corner, I paused to check traffic and gazed across at the remains of a park I'd played in as a child. I could almost hear the echo of long-ago laughter.

As I crossed Elm Street and circled the park, images from my memory overlaid what was before me. The swing sets and slides had been replaced with newer counterparts and most of the wilder areas had been tamed. What once had been a small grassy play area had expanded to cover most of the park. Gone were the apple trees and wildflowers that had once grown there. Maybe the town would consider a little less lawn and a little more nature.

But that idea would have to wait. I had no time for woolgathering, as Gramma would have called it. This year the community garden would take up most of my free time. Volunteering there would put my master gardener training to good use and allow me to do something I enjoyed more than almost anything else: share my love of gardening. I hadn't been affiliated with an extension master gardener chapter since I'd married, but I still kept the course materials with my other reference books. My late, not quite ex-husband, Bryce, never did understand my need to play in the dirt. Violet, on the other hand, had invited me to join in her project shortly after we'd met. Much to my surprise, I'd accepted on the spot and without a second thought.

At the intersection of Elm and Oak Streets, I turned left and sped off toward the center of town. It wouldn't do to arrive late my first day as assistant to the community garden's director, even if the director herself might not arrive on time. I passed the hardware store on Center Street, where Howie Tucker waved as he opened the door for his first customer of the day. Around the corner, a chain-link fence circled the once-overgrown lot behind the building.

A year or so ago, the local garden club had been offered the land to convert it to a miniature park for the town's use. But they were a small group of volunteers already involved in their share of civic beautification projects. The club contacted Violet, a community leader known for her good ideas, careful

planning, and successful completion of any project she managed. Violet had liked the idea of community green space—but
in this case, a garden that earned its keep. She suggested edible
landscaping along the perimeter and plots for individual gardeners, plus a large plot that all would work, its produce to be
donated to the local food pantry. The property owner and civic
leaders welcomed the idea. Local businesses donated supplies,
and the garden plots were now finally tilled and ready to go.

I pedaled to a stop beside the fence, leaned my bike against
it, and pulled off my backpack. From the group of a dozen or
so gathered by the gate, it appeared that more than half those
who had signed up for a plot in the garden were ready and
waiting. Some talked in small groups, others waited nearby.
Roy Hansen, middle-aged, twice divorced with yet another
wife, and easily the most vocal of the gardeners, had apparently seen me coming. He pulled himself away from the group
by the gate and jogged over to meet me.

"It's about time one of you got here," he said by way of
greeting. "We've been waiting since half past. Let's get going.
Daylight's wasting."

I smiled at my reflection in the mirrored lenses of his sunglasses, resigning myself to my fate. I stole a glance at my
watch. Roy's frown deepened. It wasn't yet ten A.M.

"I'm sure Violet will be here shortly," I said loud enough to
be heard by the others. "This is, after all, her baby, so let's give
her a chance to start things off right."

Roy tapped on the face of his watch with a suntanned finger. "Fine. We'll wait until ten." With that, he strode back to
the group he'd been speaking with when I'd ridden up.

I gave him another smile, even though it was to his back, and reached in my pocket for my phone. *Drat.* I'd left it back at the house. I began fishing in another pocket for the key that opened the matched set of padlocks on the gate and the toolshed. I could at least get ready to open things up. No doubt whatever was keeping Violet would be dispatched with her usual efficiency and she'd arrive on time. She always did.

Lisa Edwards stood a few feet away from the gate, handing out garden gloves to her two kids, six-year-old, redheaded twins. Her daughter gladly donned pink polka-dotted gloves matching those hanging out of the pocket of her mother's jeans, while her son wanted to know if the other guys were going to wear gloves. Lisa looked over at me and grinned. "Boys," she said with a shrug, but her eyes were on Roy, not her son.

At nine fifty-nine Roy looked out from the gathering of gardeners he was now animatedly chatting with, pulled off his sunglasses, and gave me a dark-eyed stare obviously meant to intimidate. I smiled sweetly in response. At least I hoped it was sweetly. What I wanted to do was tell him to take a hike. I knew he knew I wouldn't. He'd signed up for not one but three plots at the garden and had been talking the project up all around town. And he'd helped garner several contributions of tools and supplies. He was an important asset, in Violet's words. I might beg to differ—if Violet were here. But she wasn't, and a smile, sweet or otherwise, would have to do. What was the old saying? Kill 'em with kindness? The thought made me grin, genuinely this time. Maybe it was a slightly twisted way to get back at someone, but it kept my aggravation down to a reasonable level and sent all that negative energy back his way. *No thanks, Roy. You can keep all those bad vibes to yourself.*

Or maybe not. He marched over and stood in front of me, somehow managing to make his smile a threat, and said, "Well? Shall we begin?"

"In a minute, Roy, in a minute. I'm hoping Violet will be here for our opening. It's our first official day, after all, and she's put so much work into it."

He huffed, muttered a few words I couldn't quite make out, and stalked back to the group again. If he kept this up, he'd scare the creases out of his khakis.

At a few minutes after ten, Violet still had not arrived. I scanned the surrounding area. No sign of anyone approaching, no one coming or going anywhere along the narrow side street. It looked like a slow Saturday all around. I really should have brought my cell phone with me. For all I knew Violet had tried to call me and gotten nothing but voicemail.

No point in further delay. I unlocked the toolshed and grabbed the clipboard Violet kept there. The day before we'd gone over the plot assignments and the agenda for opening day. I took a deep breath. There was nothing that actually required Violet's presence. She had everything under control and ready to go. Except, apparently, her schedule this morning.

I slipped the key into the lock on the garden's gate, turned it, and removed the padlock. With a creak of protest, the metal gate swung inward. After today, the garden would be left open so the gardeners could come and go at their leisure, as would the toolshed where a log-in sheet would be kept, all on the honor system.

In front of me, the once litter-strewn, vacant lot had been

transformed. Along its edges, a ten-foot-wide border had been tilled in anticipation of planting dwarf fruit trees, berry bushes, and flowering shrubs, the first of which should arrive in the next week or so. While much of the lot remained barren ground, weeds and debris had been cleared and twenty-five plots, each four feet wide and twelve feet long, had been tilled. It had taken a lot of work to get to this day, including several work bees where many of the gardeners had volunteered to help get the area ready. I hoped Roy's sour attitude wouldn't dull any of the excited anticipation I could see on many of their faces.

"It's about time," Roy said, edging forward to slip in front of the others. "Now you're getting with the program." That garnered him a few sideways looks, but no one objected.

With one last glance across the parking lot and down the street, I clutched the clipboard and motioned Roy forward.

"Okay, everybody, the plot assignments are on the chart I have here. I'll post them on the bulletin board in a minute. Right now, I want to draw your attention to the green and white markers at the edge of each plot. Those contain the plot designation. The designation consists of a letter and a number. The plots are arranged in a grid beginning with *A*'s along the west side and ones along the north. So, the northwest plot is plot A one. If you have any questions, just give a yell. For now, I have a packet for each of you with your plot number and the general garden rules and some helpful hints Violet and I have put together for you. Any questions so far?"

"Can we just get on with it?" Roy said. "We could have already been at work if you'd just opened up when we all got here."

"Starting time is ten," I said to the group in general, then continued, addressing him directly. "Roy, you've got D one to D three. Here you go." I handed him a folded packet of papers. "They're right over there."

Roy grabbed the packet from my hand and stalked through the gate toward the rectangles of freshly tilled earth.

I welcomed the next gardener in line, a quiet older gentleman who rarely spoke but who always had a smile for everyone. Even Roy. "You've got A one and B one. Here you go."

I handed out the rest of the plot assignments and went outside to post the plot chart and schedule of upcoming work bees beside the other notices on the garden's glass-enclosed bulletin board. I was about to answer a question from Helen Goodman, a lifelong friend of Gramma's, when a commotion erupted behind me.

"I cannot believe this! This area was cleared at the work bee last week and was supposed to be freshly tilled yesterday. Is this what passes for ready to plant in your universe, Ms. Walker?" The nasally whine of Roy's voice cut through the hubbub behind me. I turned toward the sound.

Roy hurried across the distance between us in several long-legged strides, leaving a trail of footprints that cut through the overturned soil in every plot along the way.

"Is there a problem?" I asked, finding it hard to hide my growing irritation with his attitude.

"Whatever makes you think that?" he snapped.

I silently counted to five. Twice.

"If you could excuse me for a moment," I said to Mr. and Mrs. Goodman, "I'll be back in just a minute."

"Of course, dear," the older woman said, looping her

arm through her husband's. "Take your time. We've got all morning."

"And a good part of the afternoon to boot," added Mr. Goodman. He winked at me, then patted his wife's hand and they headed toward their single plot at the far end of the garden.

"Now, Roy, what can I help you with?" I said it with a smile, of course, hoping that it hid my frustration.

"For starters, you can explain why the tilling was so sloppily done. And tell me, if you can, why the garden wasn't secured after the last of the workers left last night? Take a look at this." He thrust his hand toward the nearest of his plots.

A shape stuck up above the uneven surface of the soil. I squinted. An upside-down shoe?

"Oh, dammit, woman. It's an old work boot in the dirt. Who knows what other garbage has been tossed in here. How are we supposed to grow our gardens organically—which was at your insistence, by the way—with trash mixed in the dirt?" He planted both feet firmly on the ground, placed his still clean hands on his hips, and stood there looking down at me, red-faced and ready for a fight.

"Weeellllll," I began, buying time as I moved away from him down the path between the plots. How could I explain a boot that obviously had no business being there? Roy, on the other hand, was on a roll. He marched straight back across several beds, stamping down the soil in them, much to the chagrin of their gardeners.

"Roy," I began again, but it was too late. He'd already made his way to the offending plot and was impatiently awaiting my arrival. Now would be a good time for Violet to appear. Or I could just turn and run, since the odds on her arriving in time to get me off Roy's radar seemed to be diminishing quickly. I'd never leave them in a lurch, of course, but it was always an option. I like options.

"I wonder how that got here," I said, frowning at the sole of the offending boot from the edge of the bed.

"Don't know, don't care," he sputtered. "What I *do* care about is some quality control around here. Violet would never have allowed this to happen."

I opened my mouth to speak, then snapped it shut. Until just before ten today, Violet had been the one calling the shots. She'd arranged for most of the prep work in the garden—much of it before my move back to town—and had supervised the tilling the day before. I bit my tongue. It wouldn't help to start a debate with Roy. Even with logic on my side, he'd never give in.

I bent and grabbed the boot, intending to pull it from its resting spot. It didn't move. I tugged on it. And then again. The boot was stuck on something. "What the—" I muttered under my breath.

I leaned over farther and grabbed the heel with one hand and the toe with the other. Another tug and the boot wrenched free, sending me down hard on my backside in the dirt, the boot in my hands. In its place in the garden plot was a large foot, its pale sole exposed to the daylight.

Chapter Four

Silence in the garden. I gaped at the pale foot and the ankle beneath it, then the boot in my hand and the sock hanging limply from it. I looked back at the foot. The freshly turned soil enveloped whatever was beneath it.

"Oh my God," someone gasped. A woman's voice. Somewhere behind me.

I pushed myself back to my feet. "Someone call nine-one-one." I choked out the words. Where was my phone? Home? I started to pat my pocket, then focused on the boot still clutched in my hand. "Does anyone have a cell phone handy?" My feet refused to move. My eyes locked on the foot and what I knew must be beneath it. Then a thought occurred to me: What if that's all there was? I blinked. Shook my head. I didn't want to go there even more than I wanted to not be where I was at the moment.

"Does anyone have a cell phone?" I asked again, louder this time, control returning to my voice. Of all days to forget mine. When I separated from my husband, I'd gotten out of the habit of carrying my cell phone. It was an easy way to avoid his calls. Or maybe I was channeling Greta Garbo: I just wanted to be alone. Now he was gone. That life was gone. And still, more often than not, the phone sat tethered to its charger on my desk. I'd chosen to go back to a simpler life. In the here and now, I wished the phone were tucked in my backpack. But wishes were just wishes. Just as a boot was a boot and a foot was a foot. I had to deal with them both. And whatever was beneath the soil there. I dropped the boot.

"No?" I said, my voice quavering.

"I have one," said Jacob Goodman, the first of us to recover. He waved a small flip-style phone at me. "But the reception's pretty poor here in this corner of town. No bars." A few others were shaking their heads.

"Oh." I glanced around, my gaze landing on the convenience store across the street. "Mr. Goodman, then would you and Mrs. Goodman go over to the Kwik Stop and ask to use the phone there and call nine-one-one?"

Looking relieved, he took his wife by the arm and shepherded her toward the sidewalk. The initial shock had begun to wear off and several other gardeners had pulled out their phones and were dialing, apparently without success. Lisa had moved her children over by their SUV outside the fence. No one else had moved. Even Roy had been shocked into silence by circumstances far worse than the tragic inconvenience he'd suffered with the discovery of the boot.

We stood there like that until the sound of sirens jolted us back to reality. A Marlowe police cruiser, lights strobing, skidded to a stop outside the fence. Marlowe Police Chief Sam Whitacker's SUV pulled in behind it seconds later, followed by an ambulance. He exchanged a few words with the two officers who'd emerged from the cruiser, then moved quickly toward us, taking in the scene as he walked.

"Mags." He nodded at me. "You doin' okay?" He took off his sunglasses and looked me square in the eye. The world continued to spin, now whirling me back twenty years in time. Those brown eyes used to make me weak in the knees. Now they were a lifesaver I grabbed on to for all it was worth. Around us, the officers began moving the remaining gardeners to the area outside the fence.

I swallowed hard and choked out a half laugh and stared down at the foot. "I'm not sure what I am right now."

"That's okay," Sam said quietly. He slipped an arm around my waist and led me toward the gate. I felt the warmth of his hand through the thin fabric of my tee shirt. And I began to tremble. When we reached the parking area, he took both my arms and turned me to face him. Same straw-colored hair and mustache, same deep brown eyes. And the same old caring and concern reflected there. "I'm going to have Officer Sinclair here," he said, nodding at the uniformed woman approaching us, "take you over to the café for a cup of tea. She's going to ask you a few questions. You think you can do that?" When I hesitated, he added, "I can get the paramedics to take a look at you if you need it."

I shook my head, the trembling subsiding a bit. Maybe it was Sam coming to the rescue again after all these years, or maybe it was the thought of distancing myself from the foot. Or body. Whichever it was. Whoever it was.

Officer Jan Sinclair carried on a soothing monologue as we walked along the narrow street, explaining that she understood what a shock it must have been and how a cup of tea would help me so that I could help them. We passed Howie Tucker standing in the open doorway of the hardware store.

"Maggie?" I heard him say my name, but Sinclair shook her head in response, and we kept on walking to the corner and crossed to the Marlowe Café. Once inside, Sinclair spoke briefly with one of the waitresses and we took seats at a booth to the side of the room.

"I've asked for some tea and toast for you," Sinclair said. "It's what my mother prescribed anytime I was feeling off. This has got to be about as off for you as any situation could be. But if you'd like something else . . ." She let her words trail off and sat there for a moment looking at me.

I shook my head in a belated response to her question. "No, tea will be good."

Sinclair nodded and took out a notepad and pen. "If you're up to it, I'd like to ask you a few questions about this morning's events."

My stomach clenched but I nodded. The tea arrived. Sinclair asked her questions and I did my best to get the words out.

I don't know how long I sat in that booth, alternately staring down at my tepid mug of tea and out the front window. I'd reported the morning's events to Officer Sinclair, all the while feeling as though I were passing on the details of something that had happened days before. She'd jotted down notes and encouraged me to drink the tea. I'd glanced at her over the rim of the mug. Maybe her complexion was naturally pale, but her blue eyes echoed the shock I felt. Even the no-nonsense bun keeping her frizzy red hair under control at the nape of her neck and her steady composure couldn't entirely hide that the discovery at the garden had unnerved her, too. I took some comfort in that. I tried to drink the tea as she'd suggested, but mostly I spent the time staring into the mug. At least it had warmed my hands.

Noontime customers came into the café and were seated. A pair of waitresses dressed in crisply pressed blue shirts and black skirts made the rounds of the half dozen occupied tables and orders were placed. Maybe I was being paranoid (or maybe I just looked that bad), but I could swear I was the subject of more than one conversation. The only thing I was certain of was that once the food started to be served, my stomach protested by doing a series of flip-flops and rollovers that would have made a roller coaster proud.

I couldn't see what was happening at the community garden from where I sat, but I could still picture in my mind the naked foot sticking out of the soil in Roy Hansen's plot. I lifted the mug and took a sip, and grimaced at the cold, bitter brew. I'd left the tea bag in the mug far too long. My gaze drifted to Jan Sinclair, who now stood just outside the door. Whether she was waiting for Sam or a detective from the state police or just wanted to be closer to what was going on, she hadn't said. She also hadn't answered any of my questions. Where were the gardeners? Had they been allowed to go home? Some of them were elderly and I was concerned about their reactions to what had happened. And Violet. Had she finally arrived?

My stomach rolled again. I wondered if I looked as green as I felt. As if on cue, the waitress placed a fresh mug of tea in front of me and motioned at the plate of toast I'd pushed aside. "Can I get you some fresh toast?" she asked.

I shook my head, and she took the plate and cold tea away. I picked up the mug and took a careful sip. It calmed my stomach a little and sent a fresh wave of warmth through me. I might have mustered the will to go ask Officer Sinclair when I'd be allowed to go home, but I suspected that question, too, would go unanswered. At least until whatever or whoever she was waiting for had arrived.

Strobing blue lights reflected off the café's plate glass window. Heads turned. Outside, Sinclair straightened and took a step onto the sidewalk. A state police cruiser pulled to the curb, the passenger door opened, and out stepped a man Grampa would have described as a tall drink of water. A detective, I supposed. I knew Marlowe was too small to have its own detective division, let alone those experienced in murder investigations, so the state police would have been called in.

A moment later, Sam appeared from somewhere nearby and the three of them conversed for several minutes. No fewer than three times Officer Sinclair motioned toward the café. Toward me, I supposed. Several times she referred to the notes she'd taken when we'd talked. Finally, the detective headed across the street in the direction of the garden, and Sam came inside. I looked up hopefully as he came closer.

"Hey, Mags, how you holding up?"

"Okay, I guess," I responded automatically.

Sam nodded. I suspected one look at me told him how okay I was not. He bent closer, his hands on the table in front of me.

"Officer Sinclair is going to give you a ride home. You get

some rest and we'll get back in touch later. Would you like us to call someone to meet you at your house?"

I could only shake my head in response, and he left me in the officer's care.

If I expected any grand revelation about what was happening, I was sadly disappointed. The drive to my house was silent except for the occasional coded message blurted out by the police radio. Sinclair said little, though I could tell she was still trying to be helpful even if her words weren't succeeding. Perhaps she'd exhausted her repertoire of comforting thoughts. Or maybe she knew there wasn't much point. I'd retreated inside my own head, asking myself the same questions over and over again. Who had we found in that garden plot? And a question I was almost afraid to have answered: Where was Violet?

Chapter Five

As the front door slid shut behind me, I paused and listened to the police cruiser drive away. Officer Sinclair had been kind on the way back to the house, barely saying a word beyond a bit of small talk to fill the empty air, finally commenting as we pulled to the curb in front of my house about how pretty the neighborhood was looking now that spring had finally arrived and the lilacs had bloomed.

Yes, it had been a long, hard winter that had refused to leave, particularly in ways that had nothing to do with the weather. My own personal winter continued to hang on. The haven I'd sought to find by returning home to Marlowe was falling away like sand through my outstretched hand.

I forced myself to relax. *Breath in, 2, 3, 4. Breath out, 2, 3, 4. In, out.* I looked around the room. I'd been given no instructions aside from being told to expect a call from a detective from the state police "later." Who knew when that would be? My stomach did another flip. *Inhale, exhale.*

I leaned back against the solid surface of the door. Eyes closed, I counted down the events of the past year and a half.

Discovering my husband's infidelity and the divorce proceedings. Waiting at the courthouse with my attorney with Bryce a no-show. The call telling me about the hit-and-run. My not-quite ex-husband's funeral. Putting our condo on the market. And the one bright, safe spot: retreating to the Berkshires and my grandmother's arms.

I cherished those weeks with her. If I'd known she was ill, I would have come sooner. But no one knew. Last fall, Gramma's heart gave out. Then there'd been the funeral and the probate of her estate, and finally my purchase of this house. My house. My home.

I tossed my backpack on the sofa. And realized I'd left my bike at the garden. *Great.* I'd have to go back. But not today. The police would no doubt still be there and, as images of my last view of the garden flashed through my mind, the bike lost out to the thought of having to face setting foot there again. Besides, Sam would probably see it there and arrange for its return.

I put a kettle of water on to boil. Then I dialed Violet's number on the old rotary phone on the wall by the kitchen door. The line rang once, twice, then picked up on the third ring.

"Hello!" Violet's ever-cheerful voice answered.

"Oh, Violet! How—" The voice on the other end of the phone cut me off.

"We can't come to the phone—who knows where we are, but just leave a message and we'll give you a call back pronto!"

"Nooo," I groaned. Violet's phone responded with a chipper beep and the words rushed out of me. "Violet, it's

Maggie. Please call me. If you haven't already heard, something horrible has happened. Where were you this morning? Please, call me!"

When I hung up, the handset banged onto its cradle much harder than I'd intended. The sound echoed in the quiet of the house. I sat at the table to wait for the water to boil and almost immediately was on my feet again, pacing the confines of a room I normally considered cozy and comfortable but that now felt as claustrophobic as the long-empty doghouse in the backyard. I jumped as the kettle began to whistle. A moment later, someone began pounding at the front door. I whirled around and took a step toward the door, hesitated as the kettle continued to shriek. I flicked off the heat and moved the kettle to a cool burner as the pounding continued.

I ran to the front door and pulled it open without thinking. On the doorstep stood Ron the postman.

"You okay, Ms. Walker?" he asked. "Sorry for the noise, but you didn't hear me knocking."

"Um, sure, fine," I said as I struggled to regain my composure. "Can I help you with something, Ron?"

"Got another certified letter here for you." He held out a large Tyvek envelope. "Just sign here." He handed me a pen and a green postcard which I dutifully signed and dated. I exchanged the card for the envelope. Ron nodded, turned, and strode briskly toward the sidewalk, a man with a purpose and apparently without a care in the world aside from completing his appointed rounds. I should be so lucky.

This newest letter from Cousin Simon joined its predecessor on the kitchen table. Gramma had always referred to him as "your cousin Simon," and eventually he became just Cousin Simon, like a title—or a reminder to us that he really was part of the family despite his decidedly unlovable demands and attitude of entitlement at family get-togethers.

I poured hot water over a tea bag in the oversized mug I kept on the countertop by the stove and settled into a chair at the table. *What the heck.* I grabbed a pair of scissors and sliced open the envelopes. I needed a diversion.

Inside each were several sheets of parchment-colored paper bearing a heading with Simon Gleason's name and address on each page. Apparently, Cousin Simon had never heard of second sheets.

I pulled the pages of the first letter apart. Five pages of tiny, precise script. Good grief! What could he have to say that would take five pages? For that matter, what could he have to say that would take two letters? And to send them certified? Couldn't be good. Of course, nothing involving Simon Gleason was likely to be good, considering the nasty messages he'd been leaving on the answering machine. I almost smiled. He didn't have my cell phone number, so he resorted to calling the landline. I'd kept the old rotary phone in the kitchen and the answering machine by the somewhat newer rotary phone in the living room like so many other things in the house, because they reflected Gramma's life here.

I glanced back toward the desk in the living room. Sure enough, the light on the answering machine was blinking. How could I have missed it? Had Violet called? I dropped the unread pages on the tabletop and headed into the living room to confront the message, whatever it might be.

One message. I pressed a finger against the playback button on the answering machine.

"Maggie?" A whispered voice. *Who?* A pause. I leaned closer. "Maggie? Are you there?" Then nothing.

I frowned at the machine. The whisper was too soft, just a harsh, indistinct blur of words. The message told me nothing. Worse, it raised more questions. Was someone playing tricks on me now? If only I'd subscribed to caller ID, but Gramma never had; and when I'd had the landline switched to my name, it had seemed an unnecessary expense at the time. And I really didn't feel like taking the time to buy the new phone needed to make use of the service. I sighed. Wishing and regrets never changed a thing.

On the kitchen table the letters from Cousin Simon waited patiently. Unlike Simon himself.

With another sigh—it had wound down to become a day of sighs—I settled back in the chair at the kitchen table. Once again, I picked up the letters from my cousin. The first was postmarked a week ago and contained nothing more than a demand to return his phone calls and a recap, in excruciating detail, of what had transpired concerning Gramma's estate. I set it aside. The second letter was dated a few days later. I began to read his fountain pen–scripted words.

Margaret,

You have refused to return my calls.

    You have left me with no choice but to pursue legal means to obtain what is rightfully mine. I have decided that, in the interest of family peace and unity, I will give you

the opportunity to do the right thing—and to save yourself
the ultimate consequence of having to pay my legal bills as
well as your own when all this is said and done.

I intend to make a personal inspection of the property,
though I have been assured by good authority that its value
far exceeds that which formed the basis for your purchase
of the house and grounds. Your actions and those of the estate's executor have denied me my Constitutional Right to
due process. If I have to sue you, it will all become public,
and everyone will know what you have done. Why do you
need to be so greedy? That house is mine as much as it is
yours. Pay me the fair value of my share of the property and I
will deed my ownership interest in it to you. Refuse to do so
at your own risk.

Simon Edison Gleason III

The following pages contained lists of questions about
what had happened to certain "family heirlooms of great
value." I stared at the pages, willing some epiphany of logic to
make sense of what he'd written. Cousin Simon had certainly
slipped a cog this time.

Even as a child Simon had always demanded what he considered to be his fair share, whether it was apple pie or time on
the tire swing that had once hung from the oak tree in Gramma's
backyard. Somehow his fair share had always been just a bit
fairer than anyone else's. Back then, there'd always been another pie to eat or another sunny afternoon to play, and to
keep the peace we'd all given in to him. Now things were
different. We were adults, and Simon's games could have far

more serious consequences. I had no intention of giving in one bit.

The truth was that Cousin Simon hadn't shown any interest in the house before or after Gramma's death. Oh, on a regular basis he'd called the attorney who had served as the estate's executor and inquired when his check would be in the mail. Patient he had not been. Through it all Simon never expressed one iota of interest in any of it, just the money the sale would bring. Now it seemed Simon was intent on making me pay again, one way or another.

I reached for the phone, intending to dial the number of Sally Kendall, the one person in town I knew without a doubt I could count on. It rang. I grabbed the receiver and brought it to my ear.

"Hello?" No response. "Hello? Violet? Is that you?" Nothing. "Who's there?" A click and the line went dead.

I stared at the phone. Someone needed a new hobby. And I needed to do something productive—and that didn't include Cousin Simon's foolishness or the mysterious prankster.

I dialed Sally's number and clutched the old phone's handset to my ear, willing Sally to answer. But it just kept ringing. And ringing. Finally, her voicemail picked up. I disconnected the call. This wasn't something I wanted to leave on voicemail.

My next thought was to try calling Violet again. Why hadn't she called? Family emergency? Nothing less than that would have kept her from the garden this morning. Surely not an accident of some kind. Wouldn't Sam or Officer Sinclair have told me if something had happened to Violet?

I dialed each of her numbers with as little luck as before.

As dreadful as finding a body at the community garden was, it wasn't a personal attack on me. I rubbed my hands together in an attempt to stop their trembling. I turned and walked back across the room. I just needed to think clearly. Logic had gotten me through all the trials of the past year and a half. All the emotional turmoil could be put in its proper place if I simply thought about it logically. But I also realized I couldn't do it alone.

I wrapped my arms around myself, quieting the tremors. Outside the window, the sun shone down on a curiously normal-looking world. When Sally's decades-old Beetle pulled up to the curb, I nearly cried out loud. I was at the door, pulling it open when Sally started running up the walk, losing the newsboy cap she'd been wearing. Blond curls tumbled out, bouncing behind her shoulders, her vintage Dr. Scholl's sandals clacking on the stone walkway. Tears burned at my eyes as she drew me into a huge hug.

"I heard what happened. Are you okay?" She pulled back, studying my face, then pushed me inside. "Stupid question. Of course you're not okay. You've seen a dead body. Horrible thing, especially in a place of such good karma. Geez. How are you holding up?"

"I'm fine," I said when Sally stopped for a breath. Seeing the doubt on her face—and before she could begin again, I explained. "I'm horrible, but now that you're here, it's so much better. I've been feeling like I'm adrift in the middle of the ocean and don't know which way to paddle even if I had an oar to paddle with, which I don't."

"You need a cup of tea," she said, steering me toward the

kitchen. I almost smiled. Tea. A universal cure-all if ever there was one.

"Already got one. Can I make you one? Maybe coffee?"

"Tea will be good. Do you have any of that mint tea? I've already had way more than my quota of caffeine for the day. Besides, I'm starting to like those herbal teas of yours." Sally took a seat at the table, motioning me toward the cupboard with a sweep of her hand. "Go ahead, do your stuff."

Ordinarily, Sally would go into mother-hen mode and sit me down and feed me tea and cookies—homemade if we happened to be at her house. This time, she let me do the prep work, keeping my hands busy as a sort of occupational therapy, I supposed.

I grabbed the mason jar containing dried peppermint leaves from the shelf by the fridge. It felt good to go through the incredibly mundane task of refilling the kettle with water and filling the tea ball with the dried herbs. Sally sat behind me in companionable silence as I set out fresh china cups and saucers on a bamboo tray and a matching dessert plate for something to accompany the tea. We both preferred our tea plain, so I didn't bother with milk or sweetener. I added a package of biscotti I'd picked up while running errands the day before. I paused. Had it just been yesterday morning I'd run into Catherine Whitacker at the Grocery Mart? Time had stretched out in *Twilight Zone* proportions.

"So, do you want to talk about it?" Sally asked softly.

"Huh?" I said, tripping over a thought.

Sally reached over and grabbed a sweet as I settled onto a chair. "I don't know why I enjoy these things so much." She took a small bite, thought, and said, "Maybe because I don't make them."

I laughed, temporarily distracted. "You're the one who wants to be Martha the Second."

"Hey, I like Martha. She got a bad rap. But that's history," she said, suddenly serious. "I'm more interested in what's happening in the here and now. Tell me what happened this morning."

"How the heck do you even know something happened? Is the Marlowe grapevine really that fast?"

"Yup. Small town. And my second cousin is one of Marlowe's finest," she said.

"And he already filled you in on what we found at the community garden?"

"Actually, he called to tell me I ought to check in on you. Jan Sinclair told him you looked pretty green—and I don't mean your thumb."

"Yeah, they had me wait at the café while they did whatever it is they do when a body is found. I just sat there. It was like my brain was full of sludge. Officer Sinclair ordered tea and toast for me. Judging by the look on the waitress's face, I must have looked pretty awful. The tea did help, but even one bite of the toast was too much. My stomach still doesn't feel right." I poked at one of the biscotti but thought better of it. Maybe once I'd had some of the peppermint tea.

"You actually saw the body? That must have been awful. Maybe you were in shock."

I shook my head. "I didn't see who it was. There was this boot in the soil. When I pulled it, it came off in my hands." I stared into my empty hands, repeating a story it felt like I'd told dozens of times before. "There was a foot. It was so pale." A vision of the foot filled my mind. "It looked huge, I don't know. Maybe my memory is playing tricks on me." I looked up at Sally. Her eyes were full of concern. "I have no idea who it was. I didn't even ask. How could I not have asked?" My hands had started trembling again. I clasped them together until my knuckles turned white.

The kettle began to shriek. I nearly jumped out of my skin.

Sally got up to prepare the tea, warming the teapot with hot water, then emptying it before adding the tea ball and more hot water.

"It's not surprising that you didn't ask. You were probably having enough trouble just wrapping your mind around the fact that you'd discovered a dead body. Don't beat yourself up by asking why you didn't think to ask who it was." Sally brought the teapot to the table and covered it with a tea cozy to steep.

"So, who was it?" I finally asked.

She shook her head. "Apparently, Chief Whitacker and the state police had them herd everyone who wasn't a cop out of there. So even if you'd asked, you wouldn't have gotten an answer."

"But they must know who it was," I began.

"Probably. It's hard to imagine some stranger ending up buried in the community garden." She furrowed her brow. "How the heck did they get in there anyway? Didn't you have a tiff with Violet about the key to the garden?"

"I wouldn't call it a tiff," I said. "When we first started

talking about the garden, she wanted it kept locked. I didn't see any reason to treat it like Fort Knox."

"And she won."

"I deferred to her," I said. "She's the garden's director, after all. I'm just her assistant. Honestly, I don't know why people insist on acting like there's some sort of competition between us. It's not like we're constantly at odds."

"Hey, don't count me among the gossipmongers. I know you and Violet are friends. Nothing says friends can't disagree." Sally pulled the cozy off the teapot and began to pour. It smelled heavenly.

"I just wish she'd call me back. I left a message on her voicemail." I took a sip of the steaming brew. "She left a note on my door this morning, saying she was going to be late, but as far as I know she never did show up and now I can't reach her."

"Maybe she got delayed somewhere. You know how it is. Sometimes she overbooks herself. And that's not even taking into account her kids' activities. For all you know, she did eventually arrive there and has been busy talking to the police."

"That's true," I agreed as Sally pushed the plate of biscotti toward me. "It's just not like her to abandon anything, let alone this. She really loved the idea of getting people together to garden."

Sally nodded as she reached for another biscotti. She looked up and met my eyes, a thought forming visibly on her face. I gasped at what I was sure was the same thought.

"The picnic," we said in unison.

"Are you going to be able to do your garden talk tomorrow?"

My mind raced. Weeks ago, I'd committed to doing a talk on composting at the town's annual spring picnic—an event that had grown over the years from blankets and baskets of food on the common to a full day of activities and entertainment at the town fairgrounds. Gossip was bound to be on the menu as sure as hot dogs and barbecued chicken. I wasn't sure I could face all the questions. Or the speculation.

"I don't suppose I have much choice." I half laughed. "And Violet will be there. I heard she hasn't missed the town picnic in twenty years."

"At least. She's been a fixture since she entered the apple pie contest at nine and won." Sally leaned forward conspiratorially. "There are still those who question whether a child that young could have made a pie that good all on her own."

"Knowing Violet, even for such a short time, I can't imagine her cheating. Not even as a kid."

"Yeah, she's a straight shooter all right. Not many people really believe that she cheated. Sour grapes on the part of the others, if you ask me. What adult wants to be bested by a kid? Especially the pie ladies."

We both laughed at that, a welcome relief to the tension that had built through the day. I took a long drink of tea and sat back in my chair.

"I already have the talk prepared. Violet made some suggestions, so I'm sure she'll approve. Besides, if I'm a no-show or try to cancel, she'll probably show up on my doorstep and escort me to the fairgrounds. I just don't want to hang around at the picnic. I know I won't be able to enjoy myself. People are bound to be curious, and frankly I'm just not up to answering their questions—not that I have any answers anyway."

"I hear you. You could stay just long enough to give the talk and hand out your information packets. How about I pick you up fifteen minutes before showtime and whisk you away afterward? You appear just in time to give your talk and disappear right afterward," Sally suggested.

I blew out a long breath. "Sounds good actually." I found myself nodding. "As long as the Q and A is limited to composting or gardening in general, it should work out okay." I smiled. Like *The A-Team*'s Hannibal Smith, I love a plan, especially when it comes together. Which this one might not. I gave her a sideways look. "Just one flaw in your plan."

"And what might that be?"

"Once you leave the fairgrounds, you'll never get another parking space. My talk is scheduled for eleven. By then all the parking will have been grabbed up by hungry picnickers."

"Ah, but you forget one thing."

"And that would be?"

"I'm on the organizing committee. Chairman of the food committee, to be precise, the grand high magician of good eats. As such, I reserved myself a prime parking spot with easy access coming and going, just in case something comes up that requires my attention briefly elsewhere. So, shall I pick you up at ten forty-five?"

"Sure," I said. It sounded like a good plan, but inwardly I feared that even such a simple plan could go awry in ways I couldn't even imagine.

"Good. I'll see you then," Sally said, downing the last of her tea. "Right now, I've got a few things to do to make sure everything is in place."

As I walked her to the door, I asked, "Will you let me know if you hear anything?"

"Of course I will," Sally said as she wrapped me in her best bear hug. "Now don't you worry. Just lock the door behind me, let the answering machine and voicemail take any calls, and get yourself some rest. That's all that's on your agenda for the rest of the day."

I watched Sally start down the front walk, but instead of going to her car, she turned right and cut across the grass to the gap in the lilac hedge dividing my front yard from her driveway. She turned once and waved before disappearing from view.

Outside sunshine and shadows danced across the yard and garden. A light breeze ruffled the fresh foliage. I grabbed my garden gloves and went outside.

After a few hours of tugging at weeds, filling the garden cart a half dozen times and adding its contents to the expanding compost pile at the back of the garden, dark shadows had begun to creep across the yard and the darkness enveloped the area beyond the edge of the trees.

I headed back inside for a hot shower and something to eat. The hours of physical labor had not only exhausted me, they'd grounded me. I found myself able to focus on my obligations at the town picnic the following day. But my labors hadn't entirely erased the unease that gripped me after that morning's events.

I locked the door behind me and, for good measure, I checked the downstairs windows to be sure they were closed and locked, too. *Snug as a bug in a rug*, a memory whispered in my ear.

Satisfied that the house was secure and as safe as I could make it, I refilled the teapot and placed it along with my cup, the bag of biscotti, and a piece of fruit on the tray and started up the stairs to the small bedroom on the north side of the house that I'd begun converting into a home office. There I went about the task of reviewing my notes, organizing the handouts, and reading through the talk I'd prepared for my presentation at the picnic.

I packed it all in an oversized canvas tote bag along with information on the community garden. There were still several plots available—actually fewer than we'd anticipated—and Violet had intended my talk to be a good promotional tool to try to use every square foot of soil available for planting. I hoped it wouldn't be long before we could get back on track.

And that brought my thoughts squarely back around to Violet. Where the heck was she and why hadn't she returned my calls? If she'd given a statement to the police, surely she was home by now. I reached for the phone on the desk and dialed Violet's number. This time the call didn't go to voicemail. An automated voice informed me her voicemail box was full; I let out an exasperated huff. I disconnected the call and dialed her home number. This time the answering machine picked up. Less frustrating, but no more helpful than my first call.

"Come on, Violet, where are you? It's Maggie. I need to talk to you. Call me, will you?" I hung up and turned to the window.

It was getting late. The evening shadows merged across the backyard. The darkness in the woods was impenetrable, though the last of sun's rays still danced off the leaves as they shuffled in the light breeze. Satisfied I'd done all I could to prepare for the next day, I grabbed a bite to eat, took a long, hot shower, and headed for bed.

A few minutes later I was pulling a patchwork quilt over myself and closing my eyes against the memories of the day.

Chapter Six

On Sunday morning I woke to sun streaming in through the windows. The white cotton priscillas that crisscrossed them moved vaguely in the air drifting in where I'd left one window open a crack. I had a full minute and a half of early morning bliss before my half-wakeful state dissipated and the memory of Saturday's events flooded in.

A glance at the clock told me I'd slept right through the alarm, not a surprise all things considered. But I still had plenty of time before Sally and I were due to leave for the picnic. Downstairs, I checked the answering machine on the chance that Violet had called. The machine sat silent, its red-light zero a solemn testament to its lack of messages. I swore under my breath (sorry, Gramma). Maybe Violet had gotten my message but decided to forgo calling back in favor of talking at the picnic. I hoped. It seemed like something she would do, and I like nice, logical explanations.

Right on time at a quarter to eleven, I heard Sally's Beetle cheerfully honk hello.

I grabbed my tote bag and walked down the sidewalk to meet her. A few minutes later, we pulled up to the entrance to the fairgrounds where the annual town picnic was held. It looked like a good turnout—not surprising on a warm, sunny day. Pedestrians passed us carrying chairs and coolers, preferring to park along the side streets and avoid gridlock later in the day.

True to her word, Sally parked in a prime spot reserved just for her marked with multicolored balloons bearing a sign reading FOOD COORDINATOR and another, more ominous sign that read:

DON'T EVEN THINK OF PARKING HERE.
VIOLATORS WILL BE EATEN.

"Wow," I said as we got out of the car, "and I was wondering what would keep someone from parking here."

"You think I'm not serious? What do you think would happen if I came back from a supply run and couldn't find a parking spot?"

When I didn't answer, she said, "Well, it wouldn't be pretty, I can tell you that. Deny some of these people their after-dinner cuppa coffee and all hell could break loose."

We maneuvered around a family of five, complete with a rolling cooler, a stroller, and a golden retriever tugging on its leash. The green was filling fast. Perhaps I could get lost in the crowd and avoid what was sure to be a banner day for the Marlowe grapevine.

"I was talking to Joyce Bellows from the garden club the other day," Sally said. "She told me she doesn't think you can grow lavender around here. She tried a couple of times but it never made it through the winter. I'd love to include some lavender in my herb garden, but I'd really prefer to not have to keep replacing it."

I shifted my tote to the other shoulder as we passed Officer Jan Sinclair in civilian clothes, shaking her head at the broken wheel on the cart she'd been pulling. It tilted precariously, threatening to spill its overpacked contents. The man with her laughed and handed her the toddler he'd been carrying and picked up the cart. So, Officer Sinclair had a family. Funny, I'd never pictured her as anything but a police officer. But of course Jan was much more than that. Perhaps that explained her motherly ways during her questions yesterday.

"What do you think?" Sally asked, stopping and turning to me. "Earth to Maggie Walker."

"Oh, the lavender?" I asked.

Sally nodded. "We're almost there," she said and began to lead the way again.

"Um, yes, you should be able to grow lavender just fine. Maybe Joyce was trying a variety that wasn't cold hardy."

"Excellent. We can continue these green thumb lessons real soon. Oh, turn left there." Sally pointed to a space running between two food booths. "The dining tent is right through here."

I followed obediently, silently going over the details of my talk for the fifth time since I'd gotten up that morning. I never could figure out why I got so nervous every time I spoke to a group. It wasn't that I didn't know my subject matter or that I hadn't thoroughly prepared. Maybe, I decided, it was because the more I learned, the more I realized how little I really knew.

Compost, for instance, the subject of my talk today. It was a subject that could be addressed on many levels. It was a perfect recycler: plant waste decomposed into compost, which amended the soil in which new plants grew, the waste from which would make more compost.

"Here we are," Sally announced.

The dining tent was large, no sides needed today, just the top to offer some shade for those needing a table for their picnicking. Outside, picnickers had already laid down blankets and patterned cloths. Young children scampered about under the watchful eyes of family and friends while their teenaged counterparts tried to look cool scattered about in small groups.

As we entered the tent, I recognized Howie Tucker, owner of the hardware store located next to the community garden. Howie was widowed like me, though the end of his marriage was less drama and more sorrowful loss. His wife had succumbed to a long illness around the time Gramma had died.

When he found out about my avid love of plants and that I was a master gardener, he'd suggested that I give a talk at the community picnic. He'd sold Violet and me on the prospect of using the picnic as a forum to entice more members to the community garden.

"Maggie!" Howie turned off the portable radio on the bench beside him and stashed his cell phone in his pocket. He crossed the room in half the steps it would have taken my shorter legs and grasped my hands in his. "I wondered if you'd come. I've been checking my voicemail for a message from you canceling."

"I wouldn't think of it," I said, though truth be told the thought had crossed my mind far more than once.

"Well, if you had, I could understand entirely. It must have been awful for you. I just hope we can leave yesterday's unpleasantness outside the gates today."

I breathed a sigh of relief. Perhaps those I encountered today would be equally sensitive to my desire to talk about anything but the body we found at the community garden.

He glanced at his watch. "It looks like it's just about time to get started."

"Hey," Sally said, "I see you're in good hands, so I'm going to head back to my station."

"You go ahead, Sal," Howie said. "I'll keep an eye on things here."

With a wave Sally headed back the way we'd come, and Howie made his way through the maze of tables toward the announcer's mike.

By the time I'd reached the makeshift plywood stage and podium, he'd begun his spiel to entice more picnickers into the tent. I unpacked my bag and arranged handouts about composting and the community garden on one of the front tables. People drifted in and joined those already seated inside. Others paused outside the tent. Violet was not among them.

"Good morning," I began. I recognized a couple of gardeners in the audience and a few faces of people whose names I couldn't place. "I don't know about you, but this is the kind of spring day that gets me to thinking about ways to make my garden bigger and better this year." A couple of heads nodded in response. "One of the simplest, easiest, and in my opinion best ways to do that is to make and use your own compost. Now, I'm sure you've seen compost at the garden center, bagged for sale alongside various types of mulch and other soil amendments. While it would be a bargain in terms of what it can do for your garden at twice the price, what if I told you that you could get it for free?"

At the back of the tent, Howie smiled and shook a finger at me in mock reproach. We both knew his profits were safe. Most people would prefer to purchase bags of compost rather than make their own. I returned his smile and turned my attention to my audience.

"How many of you have made your own compost?" A scattering of hands rose throughout the crowd. "You, sir," I said and pointed to a twentysomething man standing beside one of the support posts. "Would you recommend compost making to others?"

"Heck, yes," he said. "My neighbor doesn't believe I'm not using fertilizer. I think he thinks I'm sneaking out in the middle of the night to douse my tomatoes."

"Nature's been growing everything from weeds to trees organically since the first seed sprouted. Today I'm going to talk about compost—making it and using it. In its simplest form, composting can be nothing more than a pile of plant waste gathered from your yard and allowed to do what nature's been doing since the dawn of time: decompose."

Thirty minutes later I'd finished sharing the joys of compost and handed out all my informational brochures, including a couple of plans for simple compost bins, with latecomers asking for more. "These are all available in the handout box at the entry gate to the community garden. Just stop by—Oh!" I'd gotten so involved in my talk that I'd forgotten that the community garden was currently off-limits. "I'm sorry, I— I—" I sputtered.

"You can pick them up at the checkout at Tucker's Hardware Store," Howie said as he joined me at the front of the tent. "Just stop by anytime after Monday and I'll make sure we have some on hand."

After the last of the line had disbursed, I turned to him. "Thank you so much. I can't believe I did that. I—"

"Don't give it a second thought."

"I'll have more of these run off and drop them at the store tomorrow morning if that's okay."

"Sounds like a plan."

I spied Sally heading in my direction. My escape was at hand. I thanked Howie for all his help. He smiled and ambled away.

Before I could take more than a step, a hand touched my arm. Relief flooded through me at the sight of Gramma's old friend Helen Goodman. She stood beside me, a warm smile on her wrinkled face and no apparent aftereffect from what she'd seen at the community garden the day before. "I won't keep you but a minute, dear. I just had to tell you how much I enjoyed your talk."

"I'm so glad you liked it," I said. "Have you tried composting?"

"Oh, no, I always thought it was like having an open garbage pile around—a sure way to attract vermin. I know you said a proper compost pile shouldn't smell, but it just seems that if you throw your spoiled fruit and vegetables out there, it's bound to smell and attract flies and all sorts of things."

"I know that seems like how it would be, but it isn't so if the compost pile is properly maintained. Did you get one of my handouts?"

"Yes, I did," she said and reached into her oversized purse and pulled out what appeared to be all three informational packets I'd prepared.

"So, are you thinking of starting a compost pile now? If you are, I'd be happy to lend a hand setting it up."

"My granddaughter is helping me this year with the garden chores and has suggested putting in a compost pile, but I've been resisting the idea. After what you've said about how good all that compost will be for my plants, I think I may just say yes."

"I'm so glad to hear you're willing to give it a try. I don't think you'll regret it."

I glanced at Sally, who'd been sidetracked by the red-faced vendor at a baked potato booth. I could almost see the steam escaping from his ears. She glanced in my direction and shrugged.

"Will you be staying for the picnic?" Mrs. Goodman asked.

"No, I'm afraid I'm feeling a bit under the weather, so I'm going to call it a day."

The old woman patted my arm. "I understand. Terrible business that poor man who died at the garden, whoever he was."

And there it was. Helen Goodman was the last person I would have expected to bring up the subject.

"Man?" I asked before I could catch myself. Even I couldn't contain the demon that was curiosity.

"Yes, I heard it was a man you uncovered at the garden. No one seems to know who he is or how he died, though. Thank goodness this will put an end to people saying it was Violet Bloom. Have you heard anything?"

"No, nothing," I said. "I didn't even know it was a man." I looked for Sally, hoping my means of escape was near. No such luck. It appeared Sally was doing her best to mollify the upset vendor.

Mrs. Goodman gave my arm a squeeze. "It's going to be fine, dear. Why don't you come with me? I've brought some peach pie for dessert. We can be a little wicked and have a slice before lunch."

"Well, I can't believe she showed her face here," a voice I all too easily recognized as Catherine Whitacker's said from around the corner. "Poor Violet Bloom has worked tirelessly for this community—on so much more than that little garden. In comes Margaret Walker, swooping in to save the day. Master gardener indeed."

"I heard she tried to push Violet right out of the community garden project," another voice said.

"Really? I didn't know that," a third woman added. "Do you think that's why Violet isn't here today? She must be very upset at what happened yesterday. All her hard work and this is what comes of it."

As if what happened was my fault.

What had I done to deserve this? And where was Violet? If she was here, she would have come to my talk, I was sure of that. And now my concern was confirmed. Apparently, Violet was a no-show for the first time in decades.

"Well, I for one think Ms. Margaret Walker has some explaining to do. Don't you, Catherine?" The snooty voice I recognized as that of Rita Merchant, queen mother of the local garden club. The one reason I hadn't become a member.

Violet had warned me about her, unfortunately only after our first encounter. I'd been unprepared for the loud, negative rebuff of my brief comments when asked to introduce myself at that first (and only) garden club meeting I'd attended. Apparently, Rita was a big fan of chemical enhancement of nature and scoffed at all things organic as hippie trends. Hippie? After I'd calmed down at home that evening, the phrase made me chuckle. Since that day I'd avoided Rita Merchant whenever possible, which had really been quite simple since she seldom frequented anywhere I favored. Local greenhouses and garden shops were my shopping jaunts of choice, while Rita preferred the expediency of presenting a list of requirements to her hired help and left the mundane details to the professionals.

The voices drew closer. Helen squeezed my hand and said softly, "I'll let you be on your way. Get some rest, dear. Trust in the authorities. Everything will work out just fine. You'll see."

And with that she tactfully withdrew before the opinionated quintet rounded the corner. I wasn't quite so quick.

A perfectly coiffed, white-haired matron was the first to come into view. She wore her Sunday finest—right down to the sensibly heeled pumps and matching handbag. That would be Joyce Bellows, Rita's second-in-command at the garden club and all social functions of any significance in Marlowe. Color rose in her cheeks and an expression of surprise danced across her face as she recognized me. Next came Rita Merchant and my old nemesis Catherine Whitacker, followed closely by two other women I didn't recognize. A barracuda smile pasted itself on Catherine's face while icebergs danced in her blue eyes. Whether Rita and the others realized they'd been overheard and whether or not they cared in the least I couldn't tell.

"Why, Maggie Walker, it's nice to know you live up to your commitments even when confronted with the sort of situation you find yourself in," Catherine said as she put a pair of sunglasses into place.

Situation? That was an odd way to phrase it. "Catherine, what on earth are you talking about?" I asked, realizing I'd just chomped down hard on the bait.

Four pair of eyes darted between Catherine and me.

Catherine let out a heavy sigh. "Of course, being the chief of police, my husband has instructed the department to keep all of this quiet. Sam doesn't like to let details of the investigation out, but it's really quite obvious to anyone familiar with police investigations." She paused dramatically, perhaps trying to elicit a confession. To what I had no idea.

"Oh, Catherine, please go on," Rita said.

"Of course. We know Frank Wellman was preparing the plots at the garden late on Friday afternoon. His truck was there when I drove past on my way to the precinct to remind Sam of our plans to join the mayor and her husband for dinner. Frank Wellman would have locked the gate when he left that evening, no matter how late it might have been."

"How do you know?" one of the women dared to ask. "Maybe he forgot."

"Absolutely not," Rita interjected in a tone and with a

look meant to put the woman in her place. "He's always been quite responsible whenever we've had the need for his services. He's incredibly reliable and trustworthy. I wouldn't employ him otherwise. If he was told to lock the gate, he locked the gate."

"And we know Violet insisted on the gate being locked," Catherine added.

Gray and white heads nodded in unified agreement.

"And who had a key?" Catherine directed the question at me, then answered it herself. "Violet, of course, since this was her pet project. And Margaret as her assistant." Again the barracuda stare and the bobbing heads.

I was about to defend myself when I felt a tug on the strap of the tote bag slung over my shoulder.

"Hi, gals," Sally said with a burst of enthusiasm. "What a morning it's been." Turning her attention to the other women, she said, "I do hope you ladies have a spot staked out for lunch. The tables inside the main tent are pretty well taken and blanket space is going fast."

Catherine turned her head and looked at Sally through opaque lenses but didn't speak. Sally seemed to be one of the few people in Marlowe who could openly challenge Catherine in public, and for some reason I couldn't comprehend, Catherine let it go.

Rita took her cue. "We're well taken care of. I've had a small tent set up near the brook. Very pleasant under the maple trees. Our luncheon should be ready by the time we get there." With that she turned and headed off past the vendors toward whatever private dining experience awaited them. As the others followed, Joyce flickered what I took to be an apologetic smile in my direction.

Catherine lagged behind a moment as if deciding whether or not to pursue the conversation with Sally present. As she turned to follow the others, her phone buzzed. I could just make out what she said as she stalked away. "I'm at the picnic, of course. . . . Sorry, I've been busy. I thought whatever it is could wait until I see you later."

"What do you say we get out of here?" Sally suggested and motioned in the direction of her special reserved parking space. She took my arm and started walking. "Denny just called. They announced whose body it was on the radio."

I stopped and spun around to face her.

"Carl Henderson."

Carl Henderson? Two days ago I'd refused his latest attempt to purchase my property. Now he was dead. And I'd found him.

"What on earth was he doing at the community garden?" Sally asked.

"Certainly not helping. As I recall he did everything he could to keep us out of there. I know he spoke to Howie Tucker about it. I walked into the hardware store and saw them having quite the conversation just before we signed the lease. Howie said Henderson told him that if he ever wanted to develop that lot, he could run into trouble—if nothing more than bad press—if he let us use it, then kicked us out. Prince of a guy."

"Yeah, tell me about it. How many times has he been by to make you an offer on your property?"

"Too many. Offered to make it well worth my while. Cash on the barrelhead for a tidy profit, in his words. Of course, that tidy profit was a few cents on the dollar more than I paid."

"I think they call that negotiating room."

"Well, if that's what he had in mind, he was doubly disappointed. I hate playing games like that in the first place, so even if I was inclined to sell, I probably wouldn't want to deal with him. But I'd never sell."

"Is that what you told him?"

"More than once. Okay, actually, at first, I said I'd just moved in and wasn't interested in going through the whole thing again. He said he'd give me some time to think it over and be in touch. Since then, he's been back twice; I've gotten a half dozen mailings from him and twice that many phone calls. The last time I told him no way, no how. I was hoping he'd just forget me. But then he showed up again on Friday morning."

"Well, he's not going to be remembering you now," Sally said dryly.

"No, I suppose not," I said. Then a light went on. "Oh, no." I stole a look over my shoulder in the direction Catherine had gone.

"What's the matter?"

"He was Catherine's older brother, right? I never knew him back when I was living with Gramma and hadn't made the connection, but now I remember some mention of that."

"From her father's first marriage. Catherine is actually from his third marriage, though no one really talks about the first one. Her father left town after the divorce and started his second family, came back here after that marriage fell apart. By then Carl and his mother had moved to Pittsfield, I think. Carl came back here to work for his father's real estate firm, just after you moved away and got married," Sally said. "I don't suppose your paths ever really crossed."

I thought about that for a moment. "No, I don't remember him before he stopped by that first time to talk about the house. Never did say why he was so interested in buying it."

"Probably another one of his development schemes."

"Violet mentioned something about a new project he was supposed to be working on."

Sally nodded. "He always had something going on. Got to be pretty good at getting what he wanted much of the time, though I know a few people who won't be sad to see him done with what they considered messing up the town."

"Like what?"

"Oh, he'd buy up historic houses and break 'em up into apartments, rent 'em cheap and do zero maintenance or use his own people who wouldn't know a chimney from a fire hydrant. He was not known as a good neighbor."

"Enough for someone to want him dead?" I found that hard to believe, but then again, if someone had told me I'd stumble upon a dead body on Saturday, I never would have believed that either.

Sally shrugged. "Anything's possible. He did get under some people's skins."

"Yeah, I seem to remember Gramma saying something negative but can't remember exactly what or why. Maybe that's why I wasn't keen on talking to him in the first place. Of course, then I ran into Catherine on Friday before all this started—or at least before we knew it all started—and she said she was going to send her brother over to see me. I didn't make the connection at the time."

I glanced around. It felt like the world had been upended again. The relief I felt that Violet wasn't the body I'd found in Roy Hansen's plot was short-lived. I still hadn't heard back from her in response to the messages I'd left. Where was she?

"You look like you're ready to make your escape," Sally said.

"Nothing would please me more," I agreed. But there'd been a murder. Now it looked like Violet was missing. Both were tied to the community garden. "I want to find out if Violet is here somewhere. I was sure she'd show up for my talk, but there's been no sign of her."

"I haven't seen her today, but, of course, that doesn't mean anything in particular. Things have been pretty hectic."

"So, where do you think she'd be if she was here?"

"Her family usually sets out their blankets on the north side," Sally said. "Let's go see if we can find them and get to the bottom of our shrinking Violet."

Clusters of people enjoying their meal in the sunshine filled the picnic areas. Many engaged in lively conversations, only bits and pieces of which I could make out. More than once, I heard Carl Henderson's name mentioned and speculation about Violet's whereabouts and the reason for her absence. Too often the conversation stopped when we drew close.

Along the way, I spotted a number of community garden members. I greeted them and inquired if any of them had seen Violet. No one had. And no one mentioned the events of the previous day. That is, until Sally pointed out Roy Hansen and his new wife, Betty, at a portable picnic table set up under one of the old oak trees along the riverside.

Roy busied himself, reclining in a lounge chair with a glass of something in his hand. His wife stood at the table with another woman, setting out the contents of a couple of coolers.

"Oh, come on," the other woman was saying, "your coleslaw is always great."

"Thanks, but not as good as what we had at the café."

"I hardly noticed. For me it's the company," Betty said. When she spotted Sally and me headed in their direction she said, "Oh, Maggie. We were just talking about the garden. My sister and I had dinner at the café on Friday and we took a walk over to look at the garden on our way. It looked so good. It's terrible what happened yesterday."

"Thank you. It was. You didn't happen to see Violet there, did you?"

Betty shook her head. Before I could ask her anything more, she called over to Roy. "Honey, Maggie from the community garden is here."

Roy set down his drink next to a bowl of chips and a portable radio and headed toward us. Sally stepped back and chatted with the two women.

"Didn't think I'd see you here today," he said.

"I had a talk on compost to give."

"Oh, that." He didn't look impressed. "I suppose you heard the news." He nodded toward the radio.

"Yes, we have. We're checking to see if anyone's seen Violet today."

"Nope. Haven't seen her today. I expect the police want to ask her a question or two, though. Maybe you, too." His lips curled into an anything but friendly grin. "Anything else?"

When I confirmed that was all I wanted, he turned his back on me and returned to his chair. I'd been dismissed.

Sally and I moved along. When we reached the north side of the fairgrounds, we were out of luck. No one we spoke with had seen Violet or her family. And no one we'd spoken with had mentioned Carl Henderson. Not to our faces at least. But they were all sorts of curious about where Violet might have gotten to, with nearly as many speculating about her being on the run.

We started back toward the entrance to the fairgrounds, keeping an eye out for the Bloom family and inquiring about them with anyone we knew. No one had seen Violet but many had plenty of questions of their own or—worse—theories about what had taken place at the community garden. *No, thank you.*

"Well, that's darned peculiar," Sally said. "I can't imagine what's going on. First, she's a no-show yesterday without so much as a 'what happened there' to you—or anyone else it seems. Now her family's a no-show at the picnic, which she hasn't missed in as long as I can remember. You don't suppose—"

"You, too?"

"No, not really, but it doesn't make sense." Sally pulled out her cell phone and waggled it at me. "Since I know you probably forgot yours again. Do you know her phone number offhand? I want to try her at home before poking around here anymore."

"Sure," I said and recited Violet's home phone number. "I know her cell number, too, if you want to try that one as well. I have them memorized after the number of times I've called her over the past month. But you'll probably just get the answering machine. I tried last night and got no answer. Her cell went to voicemail. Still nothing again this morning."

"Yeah, well, that's what it seems to be doing now. No answer. No machine. It just keeps on ringing." Sally dialed again and disconnected a moment later only to dial again.

"That's not going to make any difference."

"Not calling Violet," she said by way of explanation. "Hi. It's Sally Kendall. Who was the big winner this morning? . . . Really? She must be dancing on cloud nine after coming in second to Violet Bloom for so many years. . . . Oh, really? Kind of takes some of the fun out of it for her, doesn't it? Tell her congratulations for me and I'll stop by for a piece of that apple pie later, so she better save me some. . . . Well, I've got an errand to run, but I'll be there in a half hour or so. See you then."

"So?" I prompted.

"So, Violet was supposed to enter her prize-winning apple pie, but she didn't drop it off at the judging table this morning and no one has heard a word from her."

"This is too bizarre. I'm really worried about her. If she had some kind of family emergency, I think she would've let someone know."

"You'd think. Frankly, this doesn't sound like Violet at all. Not at all." Her voice drifted off as she stared into the crowd making its way to and from the parking area.

I followed Sally's line of sight. Catherine was headed back in our direction at full speed, her makeup smudged, her face red and splotchy.

"You don't think she's just heard?" I asked.

"I don't know, but what do you say we get out of here?" Sally suggested.

"Sounds very good to me." Sometimes a tactical retreat is the only way to go.

It didn't take us long to make our way to the car and, thanks to the special reserved parking spot, we were on our way back to my house without delay, narrowly making our escape. I stared out at the passing yards as we drove by, at the spring flowers in bloom. Everything seemed so normal. Until we pulled onto my street.

Out in front of my house a Massachusetts state police cruiser waited. Parked behind it was Marlowe Chief of Police Sam Whitacker's SUV. Sam and another man I recognized as the detective I'd seen from my vantage point at the café stood on the sidewalk talking. When they spotted Sally's car, both men turned in our direction.

Sally pulled to a stop at the end of my driveway.

"You want me to stick around?" she asked.

I did, but I said, "You've got work to do. I'll be fine."

Sally didn't look convinced. As I opened the door, she tried to reassure me.

"Maybe he's got some news about what happened yesterday."

I slid out of the car and closed the door with what I hoped was a convincing smile.

"Okay," she relented. "I'll take you at your word. Just promise me you'll call if you need me. There are more important things than the picnic. I don't want to hear you've packed and left town when the day is over."

"Don't worry. I have no intention of doing anything so drastic."

Sally nodded. As the Beetle pulled away from the curb, she called out, "Call me tonight."

Chapter Seven

"**M**s. Walker," the detective said, extending a hand. "Matt Quinn." His handshake felt warm and firm. His hazel eyes were sincere, inspiring confidence and trust. Beside him, Sam wore his professional meant-to-be-reassuring smile. But for no reason I could put my finger on, I felt at a disadvantage, a bit apprehensive, definitely outnumbered. Maybe it was some subconscious association connecting the two of them to Saturday's events. I needed to focus.

"I thought I was going to be disappointed," Sam was saying, "though it surprised me to think you'd gone to the picnic. You doin' okay?"

"To tell the truth, the picnic was the last place I wanted to be, but I had a talk to give and didn't want to bow out at the last minute."

"That so?" Sam said.

I nodded. "What did you two want to see me about?"

"I have a few questions," the detective answered for the two of them.

"I told Officer Sinclair all I know yesterday."

"Well, I like to ask my own questions. Do you mind if we go inside?" He motioned toward my front door.

"Oh." I glanced from the detective to the front door. Thoughts scurried through my head. Had I tidied up after myself this morning? I'd been operating on automatic pilot before Sally picked me up. All things considered, what did it matter? Someone was dead. While I doubted I could add anything to help the investigation, if Detective Quinn had questions, the least I could do was answer them. "Sure," I said, still silently hoping good habits had prevailed over stress and distraction. Maybe he'd answer a few of my questions before we were through.

"We'll talk later," Sam said, giving us both a nod as he turned toward his vehicle.

"What kind of talk?" Quinn said.

"Excuse me?" I asked, puzzled by the question. I slipped my key in the lock and opened the door. He followed me inside.

"What kind of talk did you give this morning?"

"Oh, sorry. Compost."

It was the detective's turn to look puzzled.

"Compost," I explained. "When you recycle yard and kitchen waste into nature's fertilizer. You put together grass clippings and fallen leaves, weeds that haven't gone to seed, and kitchen scraps, and basically let them rot."

"Right," he said as if he understood, though the crease between his eyebrows said otherwise. Pushing compost as small talk aside, he continued. "Okay. As I said, I have a few questions."

I motioned to the seating area, and we settled in.

"I really can't tell you much. We saw the boot in one of the garden beds. I pulled on it, thinking someone had just tossed an old boot on the soil. When it came off in my hands, we realized there was a body there. Well, a foot." I stumbled over the words. "I don't know what else I can tell you."

"You could let me ask a few questions for starters." A smile twitched at the corners of his lips as he pulled out a pen and notebook. He jotted a few lines in it, then focused on me.

"Oh, of course. I'm sorry," I said, one hand waving aimlessly. "I just don't know what else I can say. I really don't know that much."

"As I understand it, Violet Bloom is in charge at the community garden."

"Yes, she is the project's director."

"Then, wouldn't she have wanted to be there for the opening day?"

"Of course she would have wanted to be there." I leaned forward, trying to make him understand how very un-Violet–like this was. "She was *supposed* to be but—"

"But?" he prompted.

I let out an exasperated breath. "But something happened. She left a note on my door saying she'd be late and to start without her. Everyone was anxious to get started. I waited as long as I could, but when it got to be ten o'clock and Violet hadn't arrived, I opened the gate and we got started." I paused, catching my breath, recounting events that seemed to have happened months before.

"May I see the note?"

I frowned. "I'm not sure what I did with it." I tried to think through sludge-clogged brain cells. Had I stuck it in my pocket? In my backpack? Did I even still have it? "Is it important? All it said was that she was going to be late and to start without her. No reason for her being late. Just asking me to cover for her."

"Uh-huh," he said as he jotted something more in his notebook. "So where exactly did you find this note?"

"It was stuck under the door knocker on the front door."

"And did you try to call her when you got the note?"

"No."

"Why not?"

"I was already outside and didn't want to be late, especially if Violet was going to be late. Anyway, there wasn't much point in calling."

"Why not?"

"Why? Because she left the note. Why would I question it? It was pretty straightforward."

"But you don't have it?"

"I don't know. I can't remember what I did with it." I could hear my voice rising.

"I could help you look for it," the detective said evenly. He looked me straight in the eye as though the offer, which sounded innocent enough, was a challenge. A challenge for what? Had he heard Catherine's accusations? Did he suspect me of something? Did he want to search my house? That was ridiculous. Why would he want to do that?

"I'm not sure what I might have done with it. I can check after we're done here and let you know if I find it."

"Okay." More jotting in the notebook. What was going on here? He glanced back at me before consulting his notes. "Did you try to call her when she didn't arrive at the community garden by the time you were supposed to open the gate?"

I shook my head. "No."

"Why not? Weren't you concerned? Didn't the note say she'd be there?"

"It said she'd be late and to start without her. It didn't say how late. Besides, I don't always carry a cell phone. I don't really see the need."

He smiled. The first one I'd seen, and it was rather nice. Of course, that didn't mean he was being nice. "That makes you a bit of an anachronism, you know. Most people these days won't make a move without their phone."

"It's not such a bad thing. How many people truly need to be in contact all the time? Certainly not me."

He nodded again and made another note. What the heck was he writing down? I couldn't think of anything I'd said that would be particularly helpful. He flipped back several pages, apparently checking previous notes.

"So, when Mrs. Bloom didn't arrive, you went ahead and started without her."

"That's correct. I would have waited longer, but some of the gardeners were getting antsy."

"And you needed to unlock the gate to gain access to the garden plots, correct?"

I nodded.

"You're sure the gate was locked."

"Yes, I'm sure."

"Do you know who else besides yourself and Mrs. Bloom would have had a key?"

I thought about it for a moment. "I really have no idea. Violet gave me a key so I could get access when I needed to and to let anyone in who needed access if Violet wasn't able to be there."

"Like yesterday morning."

I nodded.

"So there were two keys that you're aware of."

"Four, actually. Violet kept a spare and she gave me a spare in case I needed to provide it to someone for temporary access. Both locks use the same key."

"And did you provide a key to anyone?"

"A couple of times over the past month someone needed access, but it was only for a day and they gave the key back."

"Do you have both of your keys now?"

"I do," I said. "Do you want to see them?"

"That won't be necessary," he said. "But I would like the names of those you lent a key to."

"Just one. Howard Tucker from the hardware store next door to the garden. A few times he offered to drop off supplies we'd purchased. He's been a big help. He always did what he said he was going to do and returned my key."

The detective made another note in his book. "And Mrs. Bloom's keys?"

"I know she let Howard Tucker use her key once, and Roy Hansen. He's one of the gardeners and has helped get support from the community—supplies, that sort of thing."

"So to the best of your knowledge, only you and Mrs. Bloom had keys to the gate."

I nodded. The detective made another note. I clenched my hands in my lap. My fingers felt like shards of ice. This didn't feel right. Would I have been the only one she gave their own key to? That would mean with the gate locked Saturday morning and the body inside, either Violet's or my key was used to put the body there. "She could have given out keys to others, but I have no idea," I said. Then a thought occurred to me. "I know she had her spare because she was lending it to the man who tilled the garden plots on Friday. I'm sorry. I can never remember his name." The detective looked up at me, his pen paused mid-scribble. "But I've got it here. Just give me a sec." I retrieved my planner and flipped through the pages for the contact information I'd written there. "His name is Frank Wellman. Would you like his phone number?" When he nodded, I read off the number and placed the planner on the coffee table in front of me before continuing. "When I talked to Violet Friday morning, she said he was supposed to start that afternoon, so he should have been done by mid- or late afternoon. I know she had a full afternoon planned, lots of last-minute things to do for the garden and other things. She told me she'd left a key with him. There could have been others. As I said, I don't know. We didn't always discuss if we'd loaned someone a key."

"Have you been in contact with Mrs. Bloom since you spoke to her Friday morning?"

"No, that's the strangest thing. I haven't been able to reach her. I keep trying but there's no response." *And she didn't show up at the community picnic*, I added silently to myself. Was this why he was here? "Has something happened to Violet?" I asked.

He looked at me for a moment, his face wearing an expressionless mask that revealed nothing to me. It was a handsome face but maddeningly uninformative.

"Do you think something happened to her?" he asked.

"I—I don't know. But I'm certainly concerned at this point." I leaned forward. Violet's whereabouts were as important as his investigation. "In the time I've known her, she's always been very committed to anything I've worked on with her. This past winter, before I moved here, she asked me to help her with some revamping of Downtown Park. That's a project of the garden club. She'd read about invasive plants, and burning bush is a real problem as far as invasives go. It was and still is sold as an ornamental and the park had four or five bushes. Anyway." I was babbling. I drew in a ragged breath and curbed my wordy explanation. "She wanted my help in suggesting alternatives, so we worked together on it. She was very involved in researching availability and finding plants that would satisfy the garden club members as far as aesthetics were concerned while getting rid of invasive plants such as the burning bush."

"And you didn't speak with her yesterday." This time it wasn't a question. "What about the night before?"

"Friday?"

"Yes, Friday night."

"No, not Friday night."

"And you didn't have any problems working with her?"

"Problems? No, of course not. Violet is a wonderful person to work with." Why would he ask that? Something told me his investigation had tapped into the local gossip mill. I was beginning to feel that there was a lot of information Detective Quinn knew that he wasn't about to share with me.

"And she didn't stop by here on Friday night?"

"What? No. I told you I didn't see her. I haven't spoken with her since our meeting on Friday morning." I was growing increasingly concerned at the direction his questions were going. Had something happened to Violet that was being kept a secret? And, if so, did he think I knew something about whatever it was?

"Perhaps she stopped by and you weren't home," he suggested.

I shook my head. "I was home all evening."

"Alone?"

"I was doing some research, did a little writing, prepped for Saturday's opening."

He checked his notes again.

"I don't understand," I continued. "Has something happened to Violet?"

"Why do you say that?" He didn't look at me, just jotted a few more words in that notebook of his.

What if the thing he wasn't telling me was that he knew exactly where Violet was, and it wasn't good news? I tried to read his expression and failed miserably.

"Please. She's a good friend. I need to know if she's okay and I can't reach her. With what happened at the garden, I'm worried about her. Have you been able to speak with her? Has something happened to her?"

"I'm afraid I can't tell you that," he said simply.

"You mean you won't," I said, standing up, ready now to show him the door. He didn't move, so I asked the other question nagging at me. "How on earth did Carl Henderson's body end up buried in the community garden? Do you know who put it there? Was Violet there?" I could swear a look of surprise flashed across his face. The mask slipped back in place.

"Did you know Mr. Henderson?" he asked.

I hesitated. Any way I phrased my answer, it would come out badly. "I've met him," I hedged.

"Met?"

"He's been trying to buy my house. I have no interest in selling. But he's very persistent."

He jotted something in his notebook, then flipped back a few pages, checking his notes. "And when was the last time you saw him?"

"Friday morning," I said, realizing how close to being the last person to see him alive I might be. "He tried to make another offer."

"And?"

"And I told him I didn't want to hear from him again."

"That's it?"

When I told him that was all, Quinn didn't look convinced. Surely he couldn't think I had anything to do with Carl Henderson's death. No matter how annoying his attempts were, that was no reason to harm anyone, let alone kill him. I decided a good offense would serve me better than becoming defensive, so I circled around to my earlier question. "What about Violet? Do you have any idea why she's disappeared?"

He countered with another question. "Do you know what Mrs. Bloom's relationship was with Mr. Henderson?"

"Relationship?" He waited while I fumbled for an answer. "You'd have to ask her. You don't know where she is, do you."

He shook his head. "We're looking into where Mrs. Bloom might be. There's really nothing else I can tell you," he repeated.

"Why?"

He let out a deep breath and closed his notebook. Had he guessed what my next words would be?

As he stood, he gave me an unconvincing smile and said, "Because we're in the middle of an investigation and I don't have that information to share with you. But we'll talk again. If you should hear from Mrs. Bloom, please let us know. Thank you for your time."

"That's it?" I followed him to the door.

"For now." He opened the door.

"Wait a minute. You come in here and ask me all sorts of questions about Violet and what I was doing on Friday night and then you just leave without any explanation?" I could feel my voice rising again. *Calm down, Maggie.*

"It's what I do. Again, thank you for your time and your assistance. We'll be in touch."

Don't bother, I wanted to say and slam the door behind him. Instead, I said nothing but watched him walk down the sidewalk to his cruiser. Any other time I would have appreciated the view. Today the thought was merely an observation. The man had irritated the heck out of me.

I closed the door gently and looked at the clock. Nearly two. It felt much later. Again, I found myself wondering what I should do. Carl Henderson was dead. The police were looking for Violet. It sounded like they suspected her of killing him. The detective wasn't saying. I desperately wanted to talk to Sally about this, but she'd be at the picnic for a few more hours.

As was my usual habit when at a loss for direction, I made myself a cup of tea and fixed something to eat. I brought my cup and plate upstairs and settled in at the desk in the spare room that was morphing into my office. I powered on my laptop and opened the article I'd been working on on Friday. That seemed such a long time ago. Had it really only been two days?

My thoughts circled back to the events of Saturday morning and Violet. Where could she be? I stared at the screen. There was nothing more I could do to figure out what was going on with Violet or what happened to Carl Henderson, and whether or not his death was related to Violet's disappearance. I could stew about both until Sally got home, or I could do something productive. I opted to write. I could, after all, be patient for a little while. Writing would keep my mind busy and maybe save a bit of my sanity.

The piece was due to be submitted by the end of the week. It was the third of what I hoped would be a long-running column for the local newspaper. Writing about my garden relaxed me as much as working in the garden did, just with fewer calories burned.

It didn't take long to proof and polish the piece. By the time I hit send, I was ready for some real time in the garden, but I had one more thing I wanted to do first. I'd learned a little about Carl Henderson, although for the most part he and his business dealings were in the realm of the great unknown. Perhaps my friend Mr. Google could help me with that.

I tried a search on his name alone. Over twenty-two million hits. Adding *Marlowe* reduced the number but not enough. I added *obituary* but it hadn't been published yet. I clicked back and scanned the list of search results. I selected one that looked promising: an article in the local newspaper about his appearance before Marlowe's zoning board of appeals two years ago. He'd met some opposition and had withdrawn his request. I opened a new window and searched the newspaper's online archives for follow-up articles, but there were none. Apparently he'd dropped the project.

That didn't mean Carl Henderson's name didn't make the paper. On the contrary, there was a number of articles about run-ins with the board of health concerning rental properties owned by CLHN Properties, LLC, a company further research told me he controlled. There was also a couple of letters to the editor concerning his treatment of tenants. Farther down the list I found a brief article on the settlement of a lawsuit a former business partner had brought against him. On a hunch, I added Violet's name to the search. Bingo. She'd been at the zoning board hearing on another of Carl Henderson's projects and had spoken at length about it. Others had, too, but Violet's comments had been most quoted. So there was a history between them. I wondered if he was the kind of person to hold a grudge. Could he have tried to

hurt Violet and she fought back? Or maybe she witnessed someone else fighting with him and ran out of fear?

I leaned back in my chair. Given where his body was found,
I didn't doubt Carl Henderson had been murdered. He didn't
simply fall face-first in the garden and shovel dirt over himself.
Someone had made a poor attempt to hide his body there. But
who? And why?

I had plenty of questions, lots of speculation, and absolutely
no answers. It seemed Carl Henderson didn't play nice with
others. Not tenants, not people he did business with, and not
those whose property he wanted to own. The police wouldn't
lack for suspects. I just wished Violet wasn't on that list.

That turned my thoughts to my last encounter with him on
Friday morning, and my meeting with Violet after that. Violet
would have been at the community garden sometime on Friday
afternoon. Carl Henderson's body was placed there on Friday
or overnight before its discovery on Saturday morning. How
could her disappearance not be connected in some way to his
murder? The coincidence would be far too improbable for it
not to be.

I tried Violet's phones once more. This time the answering
machine at her house came on, but I didn't bother to leave a
message. And her cell phone's voicemail box was still full.

While I was changing into jeans and a tee shirt that wouldn't
mind dirt and grass stains, I heard the phone ring. I paused to
listen, ready to run, as my answering machine picked up the
call. At the sound of Cousin Simon's voice, I finished dressing.
Whatever he had to say could wait. Until doomsday if I had my
druthers. I'd had just about enough of Simon for one lifetime.

Without another thought, I headed out the back door. My haven awaited. I stood on the back stairs, surveying the acre of cleared land and the edge of the woods beyond. Grampa had carved out a large lawn, with flower beds running along the sides. I decided to start with deadheading the spring flowering bulbs and then spreading some mulch where it had become thin.

I finished turning over the soil in what would be a new butterfly bed featuring native milkweed when I decided to call it a day. My back had begun to protest and the last couple of days had caught up with me.

The phone rang again as I closed the back door behind me. I paused to listen to the audio from the answering machine. As soon as I heard Sally's voice, I picked up the kitchen extension.

Chapter Eight

We sat at my kitchen table sharing the remains of an apple pie Sally's husband had won at the picnic's silent auction. He was still there with their kids enjoying the afternoon festivities. Sally had come home early. She'd given me just enough time for a quick shower before appearing at my back door.

Word had spread quickly about Carl Henderson's demise, but it hadn't put a damper on the day. On the contrary, the fairgrounds were abuzz with speculation by the time she left. We'd listened to the full announcement—such as it was—on the news broadcast when Sally had arrived. I'd filled her in on my online research. Now we sat, digesting the meager information available to us.

What I'd found online was interesting and spoke to Carl Henderson's character, but it didn't answer any of our questions. I glanced at my watch, then got up and turned on the radio on the kitchen counter. Maybe they'd have new information.

"To reiterate our top story this hour, tragedy has struck a local family. Real estate developer Carl Henderson was found dead in the Marlowe Community Garden on South Street on

Saturday morning. Sources tell us that an attempt to conceal his body had been made by burying it in one of the garden plots. Efforts to reach local community leader Violet Bloom, who had spearheaded the garden project, have been unsuccessful. Calls placed to her residence have gone unanswered. Authorities continue to respond with 'no comment' to any and all inquiries. We hope to have more for you later today."

"Well, that didn't help," I said as I switched off the radio. "What about your cousin? He works at the police department, right? Couldn't he tell you something? I can't believe they don't know more."

Sally shook her head. "I saw Robby this afternoon. Either he's out of the loop or he's not saying." She shrugged. "He did tell me they've been instructed to keep everything inside the department. Apparently, the mayor has been all over the chief to get this over and done with pronto. She's not at all happy about a murder in our little town, especially when she hears the latest gossip over breakfast at the café."

"Puts Sam in a tough spot," I observed as she sliced off another sliver of pie.

"That's true," Sally said. "It's really in the hands of the state police."

"I can't stand this anymore," I said, pacing the kitchen floor. "From what was on the news, they're more concerned about Violet not being available to comment than about her safety. What if she saw something and is in hiding?" I let out a ragged breath and settled back into the chair across from Sally. "What if something's happened to her, too?" I said softly.

Sally tried on a reassuring smile. "I know you're worried. I am, too. But unless you have an idea of where she might have gone, assuming she's in hiding, then I don't know what we could possibly do. Any suggestions?"

I shook my head, trying to clear the cobwebs. "I really have no idea."

I stared out the kitchen window at what was shaping up to be a beautiful evening. How could the world look so normal when everything around me was anything but?

A pair of cardinals were taking turns at the bird feeder. "I don't know whether to be relieved it's not Violet or afraid of what might have happened to her." I turned back to Sally. "Where the heck is she?"

Sally shook her head and pushed her plate away.

"You know what I want to do?" I asked.

"I can think of all sorts of possibilities, so why don't you give me a clue."

"I want to find out where Violet is." I got up and grabbed my car keys from the basket on the counter. "If she's not at home, maybe her husband is. Someone's got to know where she is. Something's very wrong with this whole picture."

"On that I'll agree." Sally downed the last of her tea and set down the mug, a look of regret on her face. "I don't suppose I could convince you to just stay here for some idle speculation."

"Not a chance. If I'm going to figure any of this out, I need information. Something strange is going on and I want to know what."

"You could try asking that cute cop again."

"Ha!" I pointed my keys at her. "You should have heard the questions he asked. Who else had a key? Was I sure I didn't see Violet on Friday night? And a bunch of questions I couldn't answer—and those I could, he didn't seem to believe. From the sound of things, he thinks I'm involved."

"Hon, they haven't even said it wasn't an accident."

"Really? Who hides a body if they're not responsible for the person's death?" I knew I had her there. Whether or not we knew how Carl Henderson had died, something was seriously up where Violet was concerned. And I needed to find out what.

"So, who had a key?" Sally asked.

"Violet and me."

"There had to be someone else."

"She bought the locks for the gate and the shed at the hardware store. Both locks use the same key. There were four keys altogether. She kept one, she gave me one, with a spare for each of us. As far as I know, she didn't have any other copies made. But then, maybe she did."

"And did you tell the cute cop this?"

"Yes. And I think that was one of the questions Officer Sinclair asked me at the diner. Though, to tell the truth, it's all pretty fuzzy when I try to remember. I was spending a lot of my time trying not to throw up."

"I hear you." Sally stood, collected our dishes, and brought them to the sink. "So, do you really want to go over to Violet's house?" she said over her shoulder.

I jiggled the keys at her in response. "Come on. I have to do something and all roads lead to Violet at this point. Phone calls aren't working. That leaves the direct approach."

"I suppose so," Sally said reluctantly.

"Hey, if you'd rather not come, that's fine. I'm all grown up and can do this on my own."

Sally turned around and leaned back against the sink. "Not a chance. Maybe we'll be pleasantly surprised and she's just lying low and avoiding the phone, considering what's happened. Maybe she feels responsible since she was supposed to be there on Saturday morning and wasn't. You know, embarrassed about letting everyone down."

"Maybe," I hedged, "but I've got one heck of a bad feeling about this."

"For once, my friend, I hope you're wrong."

The thought of poking our noses into something that might have resulted in Violet going into hiding made me uneasy, but not nearly so uncomfortable as sitting back and waiting for someone else to find out what had happened to my friend and if that was tied into Carl Henderson's murder.

The drive to Violet's place took a little under ten minutes. I eased the Jeep in next to the curb in front of Violet's house. There wasn't a sign of life to be seen. The kids' bikes lay abandoned on the lawn—odd since I'd witnessed on more than one occasion Violet's near obsession with putting things in their proper place. The bikes each had their own designated spots in the family's two-car garage. Yet there they were. The drapes in the front windows were drawn. Violet had commented just the other day how much she loved the sun shining in through the huge bay window. The knot in my stomach did a flip and clenched tighter.

"It doesn't look like anyone's home," Sally said.

"No, it doesn't. But I want to try. When we drove up, I saw

a car in the driveway where it wraps around to the back of the house. Maybe they're just lying low."

"Maybe." She didn't sound convinced.

Neither was I, to tell the truth. As we moved along the path leading toward the house, it looked for all the world as though Violet's family had come home then left again.

I pressed the brass doorbell button. We waited. No response. I pressed it again. Then I knocked so hard my knuckles hurt. I was about to give up when the door was thrust open.

Victor Bloom stood there, the anxious expression on his face quickly replaced by one of disappointment. His complexion was as gray as his closely cropped hair. Lack of sleep had painted dark circles beneath his eyes. A day's growth of unshaven stubble covered his cheeks.

"Vic, are you okay?" I gasped.

"I was hoping—" he began, then stopped. I could almost see the shift in his thoughts. "Come in, please." He opened the door and motioned us inside.

The entry was dark. He hadn't bothered to turn on the sconces flanking the doorway. We followed him into the cavernous parlor. Etched by a single lighted lamp, shadows crept across the cream-colored walls. A landline phone sat on the coffee table in front of the sofa, its cord trailing off toward the wall. An uneaten sandwich and empty coffee mug sat beside it. Vic motioned us toward twin wingback chairs. He sat down heavily on the sofa.

"Daddy?" The child's voice came from the foot of the stairway in the entry hall.

"What is it, sweetheart?" Vic responded but didn't move, his voice heavy with exhaustion.

"Johnny won't get out of bed."

"It's okay. Let him go to sleep early if he wants to."

"When's Mom getting home?"

"Soon, baby. Go check on your sister, will you?"

When the girl had disappeared back up the stairs, I said, "Violet's not here?"

"No." He shook his head, dejected. "I'd hoped, I—I—" His eyes darted around the room. "No one seems to know where she is. She's not answering her cell phone. Her car has vanished." His eyes met mine. He let out a jagged breath. "I filed a missing person report. The police don't seem to have a clue."

"And let me guess," I said. "They're not telling you anything."

He shook his head, got to his feet. "Can I get you something? Coffee, maybe?"

"We're fine," Sally said. "Why don't you sit? Try to relax."

"I don't know if I'll ever relax again." He sat on the edge of the sofa, his knees touching the coffee table, hands in his lap, just inches from the phone. "That detective from the state police was here, left just a few minutes before you got here. I thought you might be him coming back with some news. Or maybe Violet. God, I wish she'd call."

"I'm sorry" was all I could think to say.

"Maggie, Violet said she was going to see you on Friday night after dinner. I told the police to check with you. That maybe you could tell them where she went."

I shook my head. "I have no idea. We met here on Friday morning. That was the last time I spoke to her." My stomach clenched. There was no reason for Violet to come to my house on Friday night. Was there? What if something happened that she needed to deal with before Saturday morning? Why hadn't she made it to my house? Where had she gone instead?

Vic put his head in his hands. Their three kids were upstairs. All of them were in the dark as to Violet's whereabouts. One way or another, this would be sorted out and Vic would find a way to deal with it, just as I had dealt with Bryce's accident, his death, and his infidelity before that. But first we needed to find Violet.

"Do you mind telling us what Violet said about going to see Maggie on Friday night?" Sally asked.

"Said?" He looked momentarily nonplussed. "She didn't say anything. She wasn't here when we got home yesterday afternoon. The children and I have been visiting my mother for her birthday. We left here on Wednesday, started back Saturday morning."

"Then how—?" My question hung in the air between us.

"She sent me a text Friday night while we were at dinner," he said. He glanced at the silent cell phone he held in his hand. "It said she was leaving to meet you"—his eyes met mine— "and not to wait up for her to call."

"Did she do that a lot? Send text messages instead of calling, I mean."

"Usually she called. Sometimes she'd send a text. I just wish I'd had a chance to talk to her. I might have had something to tell the police." His voice broke.

Sally and I exchanged glances. I couldn't help but wonder at the coincidence: Violet had left a note for me and sent her husband a text when a call would have made more sense in both instances. No opportunity to speak with her meant no opportunity to ask her what was going on.

For that matter, no proof that either was from Violet. I sidestepped that train of thought. I was starting to sound paranoid. But why was she being deliberately evasive? Or was someone else playing at misdirection? The knot in my stomach bounced around like a billiard ball.

"I know this might seem unimportant, but do you know if Violet made the pies she intended to enter in the baking contest at the picnic?"

He didn't answer, just looked at me. Then he stood. "Come on," he said simply.

Victor Bloom led us down the hallway I'd walked on Friday morning when I'd met with Violet for our last planning session before opening day at the community garden. Just two days ago. Just two days.

When we entered the kitchen, the table Violet and I had worked at was cluttered with dishes. The kitchen island, however, was as meticulous as it had been on Friday morning; the mixer, measuring cups, and baking pans stood untouched.

"As you can see, the pies weren't made. When we got home, I expected to be overcome with the smell of her apple pie as soon as I opened the door. Nothing. No pies. No Violet. Nothing since then. Why hasn't anyone seen her?"

"I don't know, Vic," I said. "I wish I could tell you something." Should I tell him what I was doing, what I planned on continuing to do? I decided to go the easy route and offered a few words of attempted comfort. "I'm sure the police are doing everything they can to locate her. I'm so sorry to bother you. But could you tell me something else?"

He mumbled something I took to be an affirmative response.

"What about the things she needed to make the pies? I know she planned to buy groceries on Friday. I'm just not sure if she had everything she needed. Can you check to see if—"

"No." He waved a hand. "No groceries. The list she keeps inside the cupboard door is gone. I'd added chocolate milk for the kids the morning before we left. No chocolate milk in the fridge. No cereal for breakfast this morning. No sign she'd been shopping at all."

"Then she didn't go home after her errands on Friday," I said, more to myself than to the others.

"And she never made it to your house that night," he said.

"No, she didn't."

He shook his head. "Good God, that means she's been missing since Friday. You don't think she was at the garden when—" He stopped midsentence.

"I don't know what to think," I said. That was not entirely the truth. I wasn't sure which of the many thoughts swirling through my head I should settle on. The only thing I was sure of was what a bad idea it would be to float my various theories to Violet's husband.

"I'm sorry," Vic said. "It's the not knowing. The children are asking about her and I don't know what to say."

That always was the worst part, I knew. Not knowing. Even as difficult as knowing Bryce had cheated on me was, it was better than the uncertainty, the wild swings between suspicion and hope.

"I'm sure the police are doing everything they can." I tried to sound reassuring. Even to my own ears the words sounded trite.

"Daddy?" The little voice from upstairs had returned.

"I'll be right there, sweetie."

"I guess we'd better be going," Sally said.

"Thank you for stopping by. If you should hear anything. Anything," he said.

"We'll call," I said.

"Please, try to get some rest," Sally added, laying her hand on his arm. "If you need some help with the children, I'm part of a family support group. We try to help in times of family emergencies with making sure they're taken care of and distracted as necessary." She pulled a pad from her purse and jotted something down. "This is my home number. My husband, Dennis, is at the house now, so feel free to call even if it's as soon as we walk out the door. Call anytime. Denny works from home, so he's usually there if I'm not. He'll be just as glad to lend a hand as I am, and he knows who in the group to call."

"Thank you. You're very kind." He stuffed the folded paper in his shirt pocket. "I don't think I'll need this, but I'll keep it handy, just in case."

We stepped outside into the fading daylight. Sunset-fueled shadows reached from the tree-lined street toward the house.

When we got in the car, we fastened our seat belts, I slipped the key in the ignition, and we were ready to go. But I made no move to start the car.

"Yes?" Sally raised her eyebrows at me.

"It's so strange."

"Darn straight this is strange," she said "A dead body in the community garden. And now it's confirmed that Violet is missing and who knows what's happened to her. It's so far from normal that *strange* doesn't begin to cover it."

"No, that's not what I meant. I mean, I agree with you, but that's not what I meant when I said it was strange." I chewed on my lower lip while Sally waited impatiently.

"Well? Are you gonna share?" she prompted.

My fingers tapped in frustration against the steering wheel. "It's just that I can't help but wonder, why would Violet send her husband a text message saying she was coming to see me rather than call him? And then she went out of her way on Saturday morning to stop by my house and leave a note on the door. Why didn't she just call both times?"

"Well, you do have a habit of forgetting to take your phone with you," Sally said.

"And she knows that. But she could have called my home phone and left a message if I didn't answer. Why stop at the house and leave a note on the door? It's like she was deliberately avoiding speaking to anyone. And where the heck was she between the time she left home on Friday night supposedly to see me and when she left the note on my door early on Saturday morning? It just doesn't make any sense. Especially when it would have been just as easy—easier in my case—for her to use her cell to call."

"No, it doesn't track at all," Sally said. "And that's assuming Violet sent the text message to her husband and left the note for you."

I stared at her through the shadows. So, my idea wasn't so far-fetched. "Maybe she didn't. Maybe it wasn't Saturday morning that she disappeared when she didn't show up at the garden. Maybe it wasn't even Friday night when she supposedly left here to meet me at my house." My mind raced. "What if something happened to her earlier in the day? Or what if—"

Sally finished my thought. "What if she crossed paths with whoever left that body at the garden?"

I nodded mutely.

I'd met with Violet from around ten to a little after eleven on Friday morning, going over details for Saturday's opening day at the community garden. I closed my eyes, trying to remember what Violet had said. "On Friday she told me she had a bunch of errands to run that afternoon—a ton of things to do to get ready for the weekend."

"If she was planning on entering the baking competition at the picnic, she certainly had a lot to do once she got home from the garden on Saturday," Sally added.

I nodded in agreement. "I asked her if she needed help, but she just said it was mostly other things but thanks anyway. Later while we were chatting, she even made a joke about remembering to bring her sunbonnet on Saturday and not get mixed up and show up wearing the wrong hat."

"What's that supposed to mean?"

"You know—she was involved in so many projects she was wearing all those hats and trying to keep everything straight."

"Oh, well, that's not very helpful." She thought for a moment. "So did she give you any idea at all about where she was headed on this plethora of errands she was about to run?"

"Let me think." I turned the key, flicked on the headlights, then stopped, my hand resting on the shift. "She said she was going by the garden at some point to post the notice about plots still being available and anyone interested in participating should come by the garden the next morning. And to leave the brochures we had made up there. She was going to meet with the guy who did the tilling. I wasn't really paying attention to most of what she said. The garden part I remember, though."

"I wonder if she did that."

"I don't think she got that far. Now that I think about it, I don't recall seeing the notice posted there. But I don't know. I wasn't looking for it, you know?"

"Okay, so let's say something happened to her before she got to the garden. Where else was she going?"

"I wish I knew," I said. We sat in silence while I tried to remember what else Violet had mentioned.

"She was going to the copy shop to pick up the brochures," I said finally, "and, um, groceries—baking supplies and things she needed for the picnic. Ah, what else?" I chewed on my lip, concentrating. "Lunch. She was meeting someone for lunch."

"That's great," Sally said, "but where does any of this get us?"

"Home for tonight," I said, shifting into drive. "Tomorrow I'll start asking questions, find out where she went."

"We, you mean," Sally said. I smiled at her in the gathering darkness. I knew I could count on her. "I don't for a minute believe Violet is involved in what happened at the garden. She's definitely driven, but I don't think she'd harm anyone." On that I couldn't agree more. "But she might have seen something," Sally added.

Assuming we were right, that made me all the more concerned for Violet. As I steered the Jeep away from the curb and started down the street, I glanced back at the Bloom house. It looked more forlorn than it had when we drove up a short while earlier, only now I knew just how uncertain life had become for those inside. Violet Bloom was indeed among the missing. And I meant to find her.

Chapter Nine

I bolted upright in bed. The room was pitch-dark around me. Out in the hallway strobing blue light reflected off the walls. What was happening? My feet hit the cold floor. I ran from the bedroom into the hall. The crackle of a police radio seeped in through the closed window. With a shaking hand I pulled aside the curtains. Something had gone horribly wrong.

A police SUV bearing a designation from the K-9 unit sat in front of Sally's house, a German shepherd and its handler stood nearby. The rear of a cruiser in Sally's driveway was partially obscured by the lilac hedge between our houses. A third cruiser sat at the curb. I couldn't see any movement from my vantage point, but this didn't look good. I put a hand to my throat. Something had happened at Sally's house.

I slid the window open and listened. The night was eerily quiet, even the peepers had paused, listening to the night. The cold seeping in through the open window sent a shiver through me. Muffed sounds. Voices. I strained to hear but could make out nothing. I didn't want to confront whatever was happening outside, but I had to know.

I slipped into jeans and a sweatshirt, grabbed sneakers, and pulled them on. I ran down the stairs, trusting instinct and familiarity to keep me from falling in the dark.

I twisted the dead bolt on the front door but forgot the security chain in my haste, sending a jolt through my arm as I yanked the door. Well, at least it worked. *Take a deep breath.* Panic wasn't going to help anyone. I detached the chain and opened the door more slowly. But my enforced calm didn't last long. By the time I reached the bottom porch step, I was running again, headed toward the opening in the hedge.

"Hey!" a voice called from the direction of the cruisers parked at the curb.

I ignored the voice and plunged forward, through the opening and right into the bulk of Detective Quinn as he turned toward the commotion behind him. I nearly toppled over, but he grabbed me and held me upright.

"You can't be here," he said simply.

"What's going on? And don't give me any of that 'I can't' or 'I won't tell you' crap. Where's Sally? Is anyone hurt? Why are you here?" I demanded.

"Take a breath," he said. "Your friend is fine."

"Maggie, we're okay," Sally's trembling voice said from a few feet away. She emerged from the shadows.

I ran toward her and threw my arms around my friend as though I'd never let go.

"Are you sure? Denny? The kids? Dreyfus?"

"We're all okay—husband, kids, even the dog," Sally said, giving me a last squeeze, then wrapping her arm through mine and pulling me aside to where her husband stood. "Thank goodness we kept Dreyfus inside today."

"I don't understand. What happened?" It had to be something serious judging from the police response.

"We're not sure. They're not saying anything. Denny got home late from the picnic—well after nine—and I put the kids right to bed. Den and I followed right after. Nothing seemed unusual. Dreyfus was a little fidgety, but he gets that way sometimes when we've been gone all day. A little while ago, there's this pounding on the door. It's the police. Say they want to check to be sure we're home and okay. Weird, right? Then I see it's the K-9 officer with his dog and more of them are prowling around the yard. Then the state troopers are here, too. None of them will say boo, but when I asked them to go next door to make sure you're okay, they said they'll get to it soon. I was just arguing with this one when I heard your front door open." She nodded toward the detective.

I glanced back at Quinn, who was now standing an arm's length away.

"Mrs. Kendall, why don't you head back inside with your family? As you can see, Ms. Walker is just fine," he said. "And, Ms. Walker, if you'll go back to your house, we'll be with you shortly."

"So, what's happened?" I asked again. "Why are you all here?"

"That's none of your concern," he said calmly.

"None of my—" I sputtered.

"Well, it certainly is *my* concern," Sally said, inching closer to the detective, who towered nearly a foot taller than her. "You all invade my property and won't say what's going on? I think we have a right to know." Denny walked up behind her and put a hand on Sally's shoulder.

"You're obviously looking for something or someone," Denny said. "Are we in any danger?"

"We're following up on a report. I'm sorry, but I can't say more at this time. Right now, we need you inside your respective houses. That would be a tremendous help to us." When they didn't move, he added, "Please. Let us do our jobs."

"Oh, for crying out loud!" I said and turned toward the hedge. "I'll talk to you later," I said to Sally.

"You've got that right," Sally called as they headed toward the house with Denny leading the way.

The detective said nothing but, as I reached the hedge and turned back for one last look, I saw that he'd joined the K-9 officer and was speaking with him. He had his notebook out and was flipping through its pages and consulting something he'd written there. Quinn was nothing if not consistent. I wondered what was in that notebook and wished there was a way I could find out.

I spent what seemed like hours alternately pacing, staring out various windows facing next door, scared and frustrated and generally sputtering my frustration in the empty house.

No one stirred at the house across the street—not a surprise since the retired couple who lived there hadn't returned from Florida yet for the summer. Lights went on in the other houses nearby, but most residents stayed put, probably staring out their own windows at the scene being played out on our usually quiet street. Perhaps they'd witnessed Detective Quinn banish us to our own homes.

Sometime before the light broke across the hilltops, I settled in a chair facing the front door and felt every bit of the energy holding me together drain away. My eyes closed and I slept. For how long I didn't know. I was jarred awake by the near simultaneous ringing of the phone sitting near my right hand and knocking at the front door.

"Just a minute," I called toward the door. Light streamed in through the windows where I'd pulled the curtains aside. What time was it? I glanced at my naked wrist. No watch. No time to check the time. I grabbed the phone.

"Hello?"

"He's on his way over," Sally's voice whispered from the landline.

"I don't think he can hear you," I said. No need to ask who *he* was. "Besides, it sounds like he's at the door already. I'll give you a call when he's gone, okay?"

"I'll be waiting."

I walked slowly toward the door. Let him wait. I rubbed a hand across my eyes and opened the door. Sure enough, Detective Quinn stood there.

"I'm sorry if I woke you," he said.

"It's that obvious, huh?" I leaned on the half-open door and ran my hand through my hair. I may have slept but it certainly didn't feel like it. "Are you coming in or just stopping by to tell me to stay in my house again?" The tone of my voice surprised me, but the realization didn't bother me like it normally would. Gramma always said I was grumpy without my seven hours' sleep a night. What little sleep I'd gotten, having been slouched in a wingback chair since being awakened by the hubbub outside, made me all the more so. I was tired—physically, mentally, and emotionally—and if he had any intention of questioning me again without giving any kind of answers in return, he would surely stomp on my last raw nerve. Being civil at this point was hardly my biggest concern.

"If you don't mind, I'll come in," he said. "It's a little chilly out here this morning."

And likely to be a little chilly inside, too. Maybe a whole lot, I thought as I stepped aside and waved him through the door. I bypassed the chair I'd fallen asleep in earlier and settled in on the sofa, a far more comfortable alternative. The detective took a seat across from me. And, of course, he pulled out his ever-present notebook.

"So," I began, "to what do I owe this pleasure." I crossed my arms over my chest and leaned back into the overstuffed cushions.

Before he responded, Detective Quinn bowed his head as though he were reviewing notes on what I could see was obviously a blank page. Buying time? I tried to gauge his expression. I could swear he'd suppressed a smile, which of course only annoyed me all the more.

"What I'd like to do is go over with you the events of yesterday afternoon and evening."

"What *I'd* like to do is get a bit of information about what the heck is going on here," I said as I leaned forward, bumping my knees on the coffee table. "What happened at Sally's house last night? Was someone hurt?"

"I'm afraid I can't go into details right now," he said. My expression must have shown exactly what I thought of that comment because he added, "I know this is difficult, but we need your assistance. We were there to follow up on a lead."

"What sort of lead?" The words popped out of my mouth. "Never mind. I know: you can't go into it right now." This time he didn't bother to stop himself. A smile broke across his face. *Dazzling* would pretty much sum it up. If he wasn't so annoying, that is. I sighed, leaned on my knees. "I don't know what I can tell you. I haven't seen or heard anything and have no idea what's going on over there."

"Let's start with yesterday afternoon."

"You were here."

"Yes, I know that. After I left, did you go out?" And just like that, the professional mask descended.

Uh-oh. "Why?" I asked. Inwardly, I cringed. I had a feeling the detective wouldn't have a favorable reaction to any snooping around I might do.

He raised an eyebrow. And made a note. I was beginning to think he was doing that just to bug me.

"It would help us in our investigation."

Of course it would.

"What was the question again?"

"Did you go anywhere yesterday afternoon or evening?"

"I was at a loss for what to do, so I hung around here after you left."

"Okay. Did you go next door?"

"No. I told you, I was home after you left here."

"You're sure."

"Absolutely."

"And did anyone come to visit you during that time?"

"Right after you left? Not that I'm aware of."

"Is there a reason you wouldn't know if someone stopped by?"

"I was upstairs."

"Doing what?"

"Finishing an article I was writing. It's what I do when I'm not gardening. Did some online research. Later I did some work in the garden." I paused the replay of my afternoon at that point. Sally stopping by and our visit with Victor Bloom wouldn't make a difference in his investigation, but something told me he wouldn't approve.

A nod. A note.

"Perhaps you spoke to someone on the phone? Sent an email? Online chat?"

"Hey, what is this? Do I need an alibi or something? I sent off an email with the article attached when I finished it. And I did have several messages on the answering machine, but I didn't return any calls."

"Did you notice what time your neighbors returned home last night?"

"I'm not sure of the time. Sally came home early and we—" Well, that let the cat out of the bag. I might as well confess. "Sally came home, and we decided to go to Violet's house to see if she was home."

"And?" he prompted. He didn't look the least bit surprised.

"And we spoke to her husband. Did you know he hasn't

seen her since he got back on Saturday and the last time he heard from her was on Friday? And then it was just a stupid text message." I let out a huff.

"Yes," he said. "I am aware of that. Please rest assured, we are looking for Mrs. Bloom. Do you have any idea where she might be?"

"No! I'm afraid that something has happened to her." My voice continued to rise. I got up and began to pace, flailing my arms to punctuate my words. "You can't think she had anything to do with what happened at the garden, do you?"

He sat back and waited for me to catch my breath. When I spoke again, I'd gotten the rising emotions churning in me under control, at least for the moment. I stood there, facing him.

"Don't you think it would be fair to tell me what's going on?" I asked, trying to sound as calm and rational as I could. "First, someone is killed and buried in the community garden and now someone's been hurt—maybe worse—right next door to me. Please, can't you tell me what's going on?"

He closed the notebook. "I'm sorry," he said. "I really can't discuss an ongoing investigation." He paused, put the notebook in his pocket. "But I can tell you that everyone is fine next door. No one was hurt there, but we did recover a piece of evidence related to Saturday's incident. As for Mrs. Bloom, we're doing all we can to find her. We're following up on a number of leads." He stood and started to the door. "Thank you for your assistance. We'll be in touch."

A moment later he was gone. A minute after that, before I heard the engine of his cruiser roar to life, the phone rang. I was half tempted to let the answering machine pick up while

I ran upstairs to bury myself in bed. But I didn't want to miss a call that might shed a little light on things. It was probably Sally, and she just might have learned something from the closemouthed detective. I was right, on both counts.

"Hi, Sally. I thought I was supposed to call you."

"I couldn't wait. How'd you know it was me?"

"Who else would be calling me at this hour? Besides, I know how patient you are not."

"True. So, what happened? What did he have to say?"

I started to answer her, then thought better of it. "Can you come over here?"

"Sure, I think the dome of isolation has been lifted. I'll be right there. Back door."

I walked back to the kitchen and unlocked the inside and exterior porch doors. A moment later, Sally came jogging across the lawn.

"Coffee?" she asked, rubbing her hands together.

"Yes, but it's really not that cold, you know."

"I know, but I could use some caffeine right now."

I stepped into the pantry and came out with Gramma's coffee maker that I'd banished there when I moved in. "Will this be enough?" I asked as I retrieved the container of coffee I kept stashed in the refrigerator.

Sally nodded. "If not, we can go to the café where there is always fresh coffee."

"If you don't mind, I'd rather not."

"Why not? You love Marie's tea selection—not to mention her killer scones."

I flinched.

"Yikes! I'm so sorry, Mags. I didn't mean it like that. I know it's close to the community garden, but then so is half the town."

"That's not it. I just don't want to relive the time I spent at the café while they did whatever they were doing at the garden and, if I went back this soon, that's exactly what would happen."

"Geez, I'm so sorry. We'll find someplace else next time we're looking for refreshments."

"Agreed." I inserted a filter and spooned coffee from the jar into the coffee maker's basket. "So, what the heck happened last night?" I asked as I filled the reservoir with cold water and pressed the start button.

Sally shook her head. "I'm really not sure. Denny got home around nine thirty. I put the kids to bed and fell into the sack myself. I felt Denny come to bed a few minutes later and must have fallen asleep right away because I don't remember anything else until the police were banging at my door. Once they figured out we were all there and okay, they told us to stay inside and wait. When the detective got here about fifteen minutes later, we went outside. He asked us where we'd been and what time we'd gotten home, if we'd seen anything. He even asked about the piles of mulch and manure we'd had delivered for the garden and if the garage was kept locked. Denny answered. I was so upset about what was going on and trying to keep the kids out of the way, I forgot to mention our little trip to the Blooms'. I don't think he was very happy with our answers. He just frowned and wrote things in that notebook of his. Of course, what could we tell him? We didn't see or hear a thing."

"Same here, though I did tell him about going to Violet's house and talking with Vic. He wasn't impressed with our sleuthing. And, of course, he didn't have much to say, except that you were all fine over there. And they found something."

"That's us. Just fine. Unnerved, but fine," Sally echoed. "Hey, wait a minute. What do you mean they found something?"

"No idea. You know how tight-lipped he is. All he said was it was something related to Saturday's incident."

I pulled a mug from the cupboard and poured it full of the fresh brew. Sally took the mug and breathed deeply. "Ah, liquid caffeine." She took a long drink, then put the mug down.

"So, what are we supposed to do?" I asked. I had a few ideas but wanted to see if she was on the same track.

"Well, if we listen to the powers that be, we act like good little girls and stay home waiting for them to call."

"Can't say I like that," I said. "I can't say I like it at all. Especially the questions he's asking. I feel like he's about to say he wants me to come downtown for further questioning or read me my rights."

"What?" Sally set down her mug. "He accused you of something?"

"Oh, no, nothing so direct. If he did that, he'd actually have to tell me something, which so far he hasn't. He's just so darned mysterious."

"I think that falls under the protect part of the protect-and-serve directive. You know, ignorance being bliss and all."

"Crap."

"True." Sally took another sip of coffee.

"Some days it just doesn't pay to get out of bed."

"True enough," Sally said. "But since we *are* out of bed, what do you suggest we do with this bushel basket of questions you've collected?"

"Well, if you're fully caffeinated, I say we take a little drive and try to see what we can find out."

Chapter Ten

"Here," I said as I pulled the Jeep into a parking place at Just Food, the local organic market.

"Okay, I give up," Sally said. "Do you suddenly have a craving for kale?"

"Nope. I want to talk to Libby Sheridan. If we're lucky—and I think I'm due for some luck right about now—she's working today."

"So?"

"So, I think maybe that's who Violet was having lunch with on Friday. They did so pretty regularly. If that's the case, maybe she said something that will help to figure out where she is." Sally didn't look convinced, and I had to admit it was a jump conclusions-wise, but it felt like a good place to start. With a huge grin on my face for the first time in days, I headed for the store.

Inside, the fresh produce section greeted us with a riot of color from the display of apples, oranges, and lemons, and more greens than most people could name if quizzed. The fragrance of baking bread drifted toward us from the back of the store. Employees restocked shelves, and, even at this hour on a Monday morning, customers browsed the aisles.

"Maggie?" Libby Sheridan, the owner of Just Food, called my name from the customer service counter near the checkouts. I'd met Libby after I first moved back to Marlowe and came here in search of organic greens while snow still clung to the ground. We got to talking about the prospect of a community garden and she'd suggested a supplier for organic seeds and another for organic seedlings, saying that this was a real opportunity to promote all the best in gardening practices. I'd agreed with that one hundred percent and had passed the information along to Violet. Violet had been receptive to the idea but had cautioned that she didn't want to restrict the growers to particular suppliers, especially considering the limited means of some of the gardeners. Libby had sweetened the pot by offering to donate enough to provide materials for those in need. A woman of principle.

Libby wrapped her arms around me in a quick hug. "I hear you've had a rough couple of days."

"News spreads fast."

"Small town. Gossip is a major-league sport, you know."

"So, what do you hear?" I asked.

"Come on in back and have a seat. Another batch of scones is about to come out of the oven. Date, cranberry, walnut."

"Add a cup of coffee to that and you've got a deal," Sally said.

"What can I do for you?" Libby asked once we'd filled our mugs—mine with Just Food's special herbal blend tea and Sally with an organic coffee—and taken seats at a small table in the corner of the store's kitchen. A plate of oven-fresh scones and muffins sat in the center of the table. "I'm guessing it has something to do with the fact that you seem to be standing in the eye of a whirlwind."

Sally grinned as she reached for one of the promised scones. "That's an understatement."

I agreed. "That pretty much sums up my weekend."

"So, it's true," Libby said. "I thought the rumor mill had just gone crazy. You really found Carl Henderson's body at the community garden?"

"Unfortunately, yes."

"It must have been horrible for you."

"You have no idea. Look, there's another problem. I'm hoping you can help. Violet Bloom is missing."

Libby didn't blink. "So I heard. I was hoping it isn't true. Some say she might have had something to do with what happened to Carl Henderson. I also heard you were the last person to see her."

"I may have been, but that was Friday morning, so it's not likely. Frankly not only am I concerned about Violet but I'm not feeling very comfortable with the way the police have been asking me questions about it. It's as though they're more concerned with questioning her than finding out if something's happened to her." I took a deep breath. "When I talked to Violet on Friday morning, she said she had a lunch date. I'm hoping it was with you. She also said she had a bunch of errands to run, one of which was picking up baking supplies and food for the picnic. I know that she likes to shop here, and I wondered if you'd seen her."

"Sure, I saw her on Friday," Libby said. "I had to cancel lunch at the last minute. One of my cashiers went home sick so we had to shuffle things up a bit. But I saw her back here later. Let's see, it was about four or four thirty, I think. We were getting ready for the after-work rush. She had a cartful. Usually, she zips through with a handbasket, but this time she had a cart, and it was packed. She even had some of that maple syrup from Tom's Temptations in Shaftsbury that her kids love. Have you met Tom? In a few years he's turned a hobby into a mission. He's one of our bestsellers. Anyway, I commented on the sugary stuff and asked how she liked it. She laughed and said she loved it but wished she could just bottle all the energy in it because she had so much to do, she might just need that sugar high to get through it all. Then she got serious and said she had a big weekend ahead and would love to chat but had to fly."

"Did she say where she was going next?"

"Not to me. But Rose was working the register." She walked over to the door and looked out into the store. "Rose?"

We followed her to a woman restocking canned peaches on the endcap a couple of aisles away. Packaged in old-fashioned mason jars, they looked like they belonged on Gramma's pantry shelf.

"Rose, did Violet Bloom mention where she was going on Friday afternoon?"

Rose set a jar into place and pursed her lips. "I think she said she was going to the post office and the bank. Or maybe she said she'd already been there. I really don't recall. She was real concerned about wasting time in line and was happy she didn't have to wait here."

"Did she mention anyplace else?" I asked.

"Nope." She thought a moment. "Oh wait, she said she

wanted to pick up some spare garden gloves for any last-minute sign-ups the next morning. Not a clue what she meant, and she rushed off before I could ask."

"You haven't heard about the community garden?"

"Oh, that," Rose said. "Gotcha. I forgot about that." She lifted another jar into place. "I prefer my veggies grown and picked for me, thank you very much."

"Thanks, Rose," Libby said and turned back to us. "I hope we've managed to help at least a little."

"I think so. Thank you so much."

"So did this get us anywhere?" Sally asked me as we got back in the Jeep.

"It gives us someplace to go. Are you game?"

"Game for what?"

I grinned at her. "To find the answers no one wants to give us."

"Absolutely," she said. "Next stop?"

"Gossip central. The good old USPO."

Sue Rivers had been Marlowe's postmaster—or postmistress, if you prefer—for over twenty years. I remembered the Saturday morning my grandmother brought me to the post office to collect a package that Sue had called to say looked a bit delicate to be left on the porch by the mail carrier. The box was marked FRAGILE on all six sides in red magic marker. It was oversized but lightweight. When I shook it as I walked away from the window, Sue had said, "Are you sure you want to do that?" Gramma had smiled back at her, and I'd managed to contain my curiosity until we got home to unwrap the package. It contained a china doll wrapped in layers of tissue and shredded newspaper and in pristine condition, for an antique. It was a gift from Cousin Simon's mother. Since she'd had three sons, none of which had shown an appreciation for dolls of any sort, even if they were family heirlooms, she'd given it to the only female child in their generation: her sister's daughter, me. The doll had remained my companion until her face had been shattered during the move to my first apartment in Boston as a newlywed. I'd cried for days over the loss, something Bryce had scoffed at. His lack of empathy should have told me something right then and there.

As I climbed the steps to the post office, I hoped Sue Rivers was there. I hadn't seen her since I'd applied for a passport here years ago. Unless things had changed drastically, she would know everything that went on inside these four walls, and likely most of what went on in town to boot.

Stepping inside the lobby was like a visit to my past. The interior wall contained rows of brass-fronted post office boxes, their tiny windows evidencing the letters waiting inside. To my right, the marble floor passed through a set of double doors to the oak counter, worn smooth by who knew how many hands rubbing against it. Perhaps my luck had changed. Only one customer waited in line.

The clerk behind the counter nodded at us as he passed a book of stamps to the white-haired matron. When she turned to walk away, he asked if he could help us.

"I was wondering if we could speak to the postmaster if she's here."

"Sure, she's here. I think she sleeps in one of the sorting bins," he said conspiratorially, then chuckled at his own joke.

"I heard that," said a voice from out of sight around the corner behind the counter. A moment later Sue Rivers came into view. Her stark black hair was pulled back in a tight ponytail and an oversized pair of glasses sat atop her freckled nose. She hadn't changed much since the last time I'd seen her. That had been years ago and at first I wondered how she could still look virtually the same. Maybe she was channeling Dorian Gray with a portrait she'd retrieved from the dead letter department. Of course, I was much younger then and that might have skewed my memory of Sue's age at the time. And then again, I thought as she stepped closer, maybe a little color assist from Miss Clairol was responsible for the illusion.

Sue disappeared again. A moment later, a door opened to the side of the counter. Sue scowled at me. "Something wrong with your mail delivery?" The corners of her eyes crinkled despite her attempt to keep a straight face.

"No. Everything with that is fine." I smiled and she gave up on the pretense. "Of course, if you could manage to misplace the mail, I don't want to get—"

"Can't do that."

"I know, but it never hurts to ask."

Her eyes grew serious. "Those certified letters giving you trouble?"

"Nothing I can't handle. But there is something I do hope you can help me with."

The smile returned. "Always happy to assist a customer in distress."

"You know Violet Bloom?"

"Course. Everyone in town knows Violet." The smile remained in place but the look in her eyes changed ever so subtly.

"I'm kind of following her footsteps, trying to find her."

"Wouldn't it just be easier to call her?"

Sally rolled her eyes and occupied herself examining the collectable stamps in the display case.

"She's missing. No one has seen her since Friday afternoon. She was running errands and we think she planned on stopping here. If you could tell us if she did stop here and whether she might have mentioned anything about where she was headed next—"

"Do the police know this?"

"That she's missing? Yes, they do."

"Then perhaps you should let them handle it. I'm sure she'll turn up." She started to walk away. I reached out and touched her arm.

"But we're very concerned about her, and the police aren't telling any of us anything. I need to find her."

Sue leaned close to my ear and spoke so softly I could barely hear her. "From what I hear, I would think you have enough of your own troubles to deal with."

My mouth dropped open. I had absolutely no idea how to respond to that. Of course I had problems: Violet's disappearance and the appearance of Carl's corpse in the community garden ranked right up there at the top. The community grapevine must be having a grand old time speculating about both. But what if she meant something else? No one knew about Cousin Simon's threats, and those were more annoying than anything. At least I hoped so. Had she heard something about the police investigation? I was tempted to ask. I snapped my mouth shut instead.

Sue leaned back and said in a louder voice, "Have a good day. We have work to do here." With that she turned and headed off past the post office boxes toward the door marked POSTMASTER at the far end of the lobby. It clicked shut behind her.

"Neither rain nor sleet nor doors slammed in our faces," Sally said as she opened the door to the great outdoors.

"Yeah," I replied as I followed her. "That was darned strange. What's with that sudden about-face in attitude?" I was on my way through the door when a hand on my arm stopped me. I turned to see one of the maintenance workers. He looked vaguely familiar, but I couldn't place him. Still, I stepped back and let the door close. Sally watched from the steps outside.

"Glad to see you back home again," he said. "Your gram was always such a nice lady. She used to say how she hoped you'd come back home one day."

"Thank you. Did you know her well?"

"Just from when she came in to mail off packages once or twice a month. She was real nice. Never a mean word for anyone. Like I told you at the cemetery, she's gonna be missed by a lot of people."

So that's where I'd seen him. There had been so many people at the service, all the faces had blurred. "Thank you," I said. "That's very nice of you to say."

"That's not why I stopped you." He looked over his shoulder at the closed door at the end of the lobby. "Don't let her bother you," he said quietly, leaning on his broom. "I think she might be embarrassed to say but she was hiding in her office when Mrs. Bloom was here last week. Ms. Rivers never did care for her much, but lately she don't want anything to do with her. Didn't even like us talking about that garden you're doing behind the hardware store. So, when you came in to ask about her being here, she couldn't very well admit she was hiding out and avoiding her. She thinks we don't know, but, well, we do. Can't hardly miss it. Don't mention it, though."

"Why doesn't she like Violet?" I asked. *Everyone likes Violet*, I thought. *Absolutely everyone. But maybe not.*

He just shrugged. "Beats me. Started making a point to avoid her around the holidays."

"But you saw Violet when she was here on Friday, right?"

"Sure," he said. "I was sweeping up like today. Emptying the recyclables bin. Cleaning off the tables in the lobby. Straightening the displays. I think I did the inside of the windows, too. It looked like it might rain, so I skipped the outside."

"Do you remember what time that was?" I asked, trying to get back on track.

He thought about that for a minute. "Probably 'bout nine thirty or so," he said. "Just gettin' ready to take my morning break."

"Did Violet say anything?" I asked, mentally crossing my fingers. "Did you hear her mention where she might be going?"

"She wasn't here long. Only a few people in here at the time and only one of them in line ahead of her. She came in, checked her box. Looked like she had a pickup card and headed to the window. Came out with one of those yellowish envelopes."

"Did she say anything?"

"Not to me. I said hello, but I don't think she heard me. She was too distracted looking at 'em."

"At what?"

"The pictures. That envelope she picked up had a piece of paper and a bunch of pictures in it."

"Pictures of what?"

"Don't know. Wasn't close enough to see and she left right after that. Not my business anyway."

"Well, thanks for your help," I said.

As we got in the car, I relayed the conversation to Sally.

Her response pretty much summed up my own thoughts. "This just gets weirder. Now she's got a bunch of pictures."

"Might have nothing to do with anything."

"Maybe Violet was being blackmailed," Sally speculated as she adjusted her seat belt. "Maybe the postmaster wasn't the only one who was not a fan of Violet Bloom."

"Maybe," I agreed as I turned the key. While it was possible there was a whole different side to Violet from the one she'd shown me, it just didn't ring true. "But does any of that have anything to do with where Violet has gone and who killed Carl Henderson?"

As I pulled out into traffic, Sally asked, "You're not going to do it, are you?"

"Do what?"

"Do what she said—let the police handle it."

I glanced sideways at her. "You want me to?"

She shrugged. "Up to you. I for one would like to know what was going on in my own yard last night."

"Did you see anything?"

"No. Not really. It's hard to see where they were poking around in that corner of the yard from the house or the road. That's why we set up the compost bins and the mulch pile there. Handy but generally out of sight. I couldn't really get a look this morning either. They'd strung that yellow tape around the area. Said not to go beyond it until they came and took it down."

"Who said that?"

"Your friend the detective. He seems like a nice enough person—except when he's bossing someone around in their own home, of course."

"You can say that again. I will be very glad when I don't have to see him and his stupid notebook again."

"You know," Sally said as she grinned at me, "maybe you could make real nice and he'd let you have a look at it."

I rolled my eyes as I maneuvered around a turning car. "I highly doubt that would convince him to share anything and it just might make him more suspicious of me."

"Oh, come on now, Mags," Sally said. "You can't seriously think he thinks you had anything to do with Carl Henderson's death."

"All I know is how uncomfortable I felt when he was questioning me. I kept thinking his next question was going to be 'Why'd ya do it?'"

"You know, Sue Rivers may be right. He will probably figure out the truth without our help."

"Forgive me if I don't quite believe it's all going to work out for the best on its own."

"So where are we going?"

"Let's stop for a bite at the Center Street Diner."

"I thought you didn't like the service there."

"I don't, but today I don't need speedy or even friendly service for that matter. The gray-haired brigade should be there and I'm betting if we eavesdrop a bit, we can pick up on some of the talk around town, maybe come across someone who saw Violet on Friday afternoon." Never underestimate the power of a small-town grapevine.

Chapter Eleven

We pulled into the last parking place in front of the diner. Despite the crowd, luck was with us. The group of four ahead of us needed a full-sized booth, but the lone space remaining was a small table for two near the rear exit. Not the best spot to observe and listen, but it would have to do.

"Looks like that one's yours," one of the waitresses said as she waved us toward the table. "Go ahead and take a seat. I'll be with you in just a bit."

We walked down the narrow aisle between tables, passing by a booth where Mr. and Mrs. Goodman sat. Their plates were empty and Mrs. Goodman was saying something to her husband as he studied the dessert menu.

On the opposite side four older men were having a not quite quiet discussion about today's gossip special. "First time in a decade Violet hasn't won."

"No one knows where she is."

"Do you think she had something to do with that body they found?"

"I bet that Walker woman knows something she's not sayin'."

"Quiet. That's her just walked past."

I kept on walking, my eyes straight ahead, until I reached our table. As I pulled out my chair, I spotted Howie Tucker at a table near the entrance. The diner's blue plate special of meat loaf and fries sat untouched in front of him. He picked up his fork and stared at the plate as though reminding himself what to do next. He looked so lost. When this was over I'd see about helping him with his wife's garden. Maybe feeling more comfortable tending her garden would help him recapture some happy memories.

I took the seat facing away from the diners, leaving Sally to sit facing them.

"Is it that you don't want to look at them or you don't want them to see you?" she asked, unrolling her utensils and putting the paper napkin in her lap.

I leaned closer. "I'd really rather not be the one being watched. I just want to listen. I'm sure there's plenty of talk about what happened on Saturday at the garden. Pretty much all of it is going to be speculation. I'm hoping for something a little more fact based. Maybe something useful someone saw or heard."

The waitress came over and dropped two menus on the table, took our drink orders, and left. Sally picked up her menu as she studied our fellow diners, who were no doubt studying us. I pretended to peruse the menu and leaned back in my chair, all the better to eavesdrop.

I recognized the voices of Rita Merchant and Joyce Bellows from the garden club. According to them, Carl Henderson had optioned several properties bordering the woods behind my house, extending into the undeveloped wooded area as well. Popular opinion said his plans were now as dead as he was. When they moved on to Violet and began speculating on whether she was involved somehow in his demise, I'd had enough.

"So, who else is here?" I asked Sally. "We came in pretty quickly, so I didn't get a good look at everyone."

Sally held the menu up and made a pretense of reading it as she glanced around the small dining room. "Howard Tucker is here." I nodded. She craned her neck. "Looks like he got the special—looks pretty good, too."

"I get it," I said. "You're hungry. You didn't get to finish your scone earlier. Though you do have that bag of them in the Jeep." She started to protest so I said, "I'll buy you dessert. Happy? So, who else is here?"

"The minister and his wife from the Congregational Church. One of the clerks at the Grocery Mart. Looks like she's here with her mother. Or maybe it's her aunt. I don't know. They look enough alike to be twins. A group from the senior center, who haven't taken their eyes off us since we walked past. Oh, and that cute old couple who came to see you last week."

"Mr. and Mrs. Goodman." I turned around hoping to catch Mrs. Goodman's eye. Mrs. Goodman looked up and our eyes met. She glanced around at the other diners, then smiled at me and nodded. She reminded me so much of Gramma. I could almost hear her say, "It's okay. Don't let them get the better of you."

The door opened and in walked Catherine Whitacker. I twisted back around in my chair.

"I think maybe this wasn't such a good idea after all," I said, glancing at the rear exit. Why did the sight of Catherine always make me want to beat a hasty retreat?

"Why?" Sally echoed my thoughts.

The waitress arrived and put down our iced teas. "What can we get you today?"

I glanced at the menu, still sitting unread on the tabletop. The waitress tapped her pencil on the order pad. *Hurry, hurry*, it signaled in code.

"What do you say, Sally—a couple of BLTs?" I suggested.

"Sure, can't go wrong with that."

"Coming right up," the waitress said.

As soon as she had moved out of earshot, Sally said, "Okay, so tell me what the heck was that all about?"

"Catherine Whitacker just walked in. How could you miss her? The last thing I want to do is see her. If I have to tell her how sorry I am about her brother, I'm bound to say the wrong thing and she'll go for the jugular."

The bell at the door jingled again. Without thinking, I turned around to look. My eyes locked with Catherine's just as she was taking her seat. "Damn," I muttered under my breath.

"Damn, indeed," Sally said. "That cute detective just walked in."

"Huh?"

"I said—"

"I know what you said. Catherine saw me."

"Oh, shoot, and here she comes," Sally warned.

I didn't move a muscle. I watched the expression on Sally's face melt into a blank mask as Catherine drew closer. Finally,

I felt a presence at my back. Catherine came into view as she eased past the table and turned to face me, her back to the exit, blocking any retreat I might plan. She pulled off dark glasses and glared at me.

"I must say, Margaret, I'm more than a little surprised to find you here."

"Why's that, Catherine?" I said with a tentative smile.

"I would think that's obvious."

"I'm sure I don't know what you mean."

If looks really could kill, I'd be sprawled on the floor, riddled with stab wounds.

"Maybe you could enlighten me," Sally interrupted. If her intention had been to break the rising tension at the table, it backfired. Again, the daggers look. This time to both of us, but Sally stared her down. It was like watching a Ping-Pong match.

"Excuse me," the waitress broke in, edging past Catherine and putting two plates with BLTs, potato salad, and pickles on the table in front of us.

"If you'll excuse us," Sally said.

"But I haven't explained myself," Catherine said with gritted teeth. "Have I, Margaret?"

"What is it you want, Catherine?" I didn't have to worry anymore about saying or doing something to offend Catherine. Apparently, my presence was more than enough. All I wanted now was for her to leave so I could take just one peaceful bite of my sandwich.

"I would think you'd want to stay at home, considering all that's gone on. Somehow you managed to find my brother's body in that so-called garden of yours. They tell me someone smashed his skull in with a shovel. A shovel!" Her voice rose in intensity and pitch.

Heads turned in our direction. Conversations stopped. I wasn't the only one anticipating what would come next.

Catherine pulled in a ragged breath, obviously attempting to compose herself. When she spoke again, it was in a much softer but no gentler voice. Her words were deliberate and clipped. "Don't you think it's an amazing coincidence that a bloody shovel was found in your neighbor's yard, Margaret?" The last words came out as a hiss. Catherine bent closer. "I know what happened to your husband. A hit-and-run was so very convenient. What did you have against Carl, Margaret? You can't call it an accident this time."

"Excuse me." Detective Quinn's voice intruded from close behind us. "Is everything okay here?"

Catherine was so close, I couldn't turn to look at him. She straightened, turning her head to look over her shoulder. "Everything's fine," she said.

"I'm very sorry for your loss, Mrs. Whitacker," he said. "Do you need a lift home? Or perhaps to the police station. I just left a meeting with the chief. Your husband is quite concerned about you."

"I said everything is fine." She turned her attention back to me. "Why didn't you tell me you'd already spoken with my brother when I suggested he stop by to discuss your property? Don't look so surprised. Did you think I wouldn't find out? The police know all your dirty little secrets. I think the detective here might want to ask what else you're trying to hide."

The detective placed his hand on her shoulder, but Catherine was wound too tight to notice anything but me. I bit back my initial response and opted for my best attempt at calm and rational.

"Actually, I didn't make the connection when you mentioned that," I said, trying to ignore the rest of what she'd said and to keep my voice from shaking. "He's been trying to buy my house for a while. I didn't realize he was your brother. I told him I have no intention of selling my home and asked him to leave. That's the extent of it."

"Really, Margaret," she said, "it's just an old house. Not any historical or architectural significance attached to it. But still he would have tried to get you a fair deal. He always made a good deal. He was a wonderful businessman. Now he's gone. And someone is going to pay."

I just stared at her, my mouth open but no words coming out. Catherine was actually tearing up. Even more surprising, I found myself feeling sympathy for the woman. Until the next words she spoke.

"If you had anything to do with this, anything, you won't get away with it."

Detective Quinn stepped closer and wrapped his hand around her upper arm. "Mrs. Whitacker." Catherine continued to ignore him.

"Catherine," I said, "I just want you to know how sorry I am for your loss. Truly sorry. I didn't know your brother well. But I had no interest in selling my property and I told him so."

"No? Then what did you have against him?" She pushed at the detective's hand.

"Absolutely nothing," I said, amazed at how calm I sounded. "I think you should go back to your own table now. Or leave."

Catherine's mouth opened and closed wordlessly. Detective Quinn pulled her by the arm. "Mrs. Whitacker, that's enough. Consider carefully before you say anything further. It's time for you to go." He leaned close to her ear and said something I couldn't hear.

Catherine shook off his hand and started back down the aisle. Every head turned in her direction, every eye followed her movements as she grabbed her purse from her table and stalked out the door. The detective followed close behind.

The low hum of simultaneous comments from the other diners filled the air.

"Wow," Sally said. "Can you believe that?"

Truth be told, I'd believe almost anything where Catherine Whitacker was concerned, though I had to admit, this was one for the books as the most unexpected performance by a difficult personality.

Sally leaned closer. "Did you hear that?" she said, barely above a whisper.

"It sounded like she thinks I'm responsible for her brother's death."

"Not that! She said he was bludgeoned to death with a shovel. His head beaten in. Do you think that's what they found in my yard? How could she know that?"

I shook my head. "Sam must have told her. Or she overheard him talking to someone about the investigation. Either way, he's not going to be happy when he finds out his wife is sharing information about the investigation with everyone in town."

Sally stared open-mouthed at me. "How can you be so calm?"

Calm? No. In the aftermath of Catherine's tirade, I wasn't sure I could stand—my legs were so shaky.

"Maggie, they found a bloody shovel near your house. That must be what they found at *my* house! The police dog must have led them to my mulch pile. Oh my God, Carl Henderson's killer must have been in my yard. Near my family." Sally's eyes grew wide. She stared at me. "I know this sounds silly, but I want to go home to be sure everything's all right."

I nodded and pushed my plate aside, my lunch as appetizing as the plastic-coated menu. A killer. At Sally's house. No one was home there for the better part of that day. But I'd been home alone until Sally got back. Maybe with a killer just a stone's throw away. Bloody shovel in hand.

Chapter Twelve

I watched Sally run up the sidewalk and in through her front door. Goose bumps danced along my spine and down to my fingertips. Trying to warm myself in a way the sunshine couldn't, I ran my hands up and down my arms, then gave myself a hug before putting the Jeep in gear. I followed the driveway around my house and parked on the grass a few feet from the back porch door.

Stepping out of the Jeep, I looked first at the house. Nothing appeared out of place. The pots of basil I'd been acclimating to the outdoors sat contentedly on the stairs in the diffused sunlight beside the larger pot containing a rosemary plant Gramma had overwintered for the past three years. But as I glanced around the yard something was off. Was it just the knowledge that a killer had been so close by me the night before or was it something else? Was there some sign that he'd been here, too?

I looked back at the woods at the rear of the yard where the shadows solidified in the thickening undergrowth. I'd spent long hours in those woods as a girl, following the winding paths along the hillside, looking for elusive wildflowers and animal signs. Those paths ended in backyards in neighborhoods much like mine. That didn't interest me then. Today the woods didn't look so welcoming. For all I knew, someone stood just out of sight. Watching.

I closed the kitchen door behind me and threw the dead bolt, locking out the world. My stomach growled. I'd barely nibbled on the scone at Just Food and the BLT at the diner had been left untouched. Catherine could kill my appetite on the best of days. I grabbed an oatmeal chocolate chip cookie from the jar on the counter. Maybe it would help me think.

The pie and whatever else Violet was planning to enter would have been delicious. So why hadn't she? It was obvious, especially when I considered the detective's line of questioning, that Violet's disappearance was somehow linked to Carl Henderson's death. And if that were so, then it was most likely whatever happened to Violet happened on Friday, not Saturday. That meant the note left for me on Saturday morning was left by someone else, presumably the person responsible for her disappearance and Carl Henderson's death. And that brought me right back to the thing that concerned me most: a murderer had been at my house and Sally's. I had no doubt he—or she— left the shovel in Sally's mulch pile. But why?

I grabbed another cookie and double-checked the lock on the kitchen door.

At the desk in the parlor, a red three flashed on the answering machine's message indicator. I took a deep breath and another bite of cookie, then pushed the playback button. The first message began.

"Ms. Walker?" a female voice said. "This is Officer Jan Sinclair. We met Saturday morning. I'm just calling to see if you're all right. Would you please give me a call back?" She proceeded to leave her cell phone number.

My first thought was how nice of her to call. My second thought was more skeptical. Why would the officer bother to call? Had I been that big a wreck after what happened? Or was she going to try to question me to see if I'd say something more—or perhaps different from what I'd told Detective Quinn?

"You're being paranoid," I said out loud, startling myself with the sound of my own voice. I jotted down Jan Sinclair's name and number, then hit the playback button to listen to the second message.

Cousin Simon's voice came through loud and clear with yet another demand for his "proper cut" of the estate proceeds. He went on for several minutes, reiterating things already covered at too-great length in his letters. I had no kind thoughts concerning his message and, before he'd finished, I pushed the delete button. There was no third message, just the click of the caller hanging up. The nonmessage was annoying but compared to Cousin Simon's, not so much. I picked up the phone and returned Jan Sinclair's call. Her voicemail kicked in and I left a message, assuring her I was much better and thanking her for her concern. I hung up the phone very happy I'd avoided further questions, even from someone as nice as she'd been to me.

As I sat there, my mind began to drift into the world of what-ifs, second-guessing, and wondering. What if I had sold the house and returned to Boston after Gramma's death? I'd never have found that body. What if I'd forgiven Bryce one more time?

He wouldn't have been crossing the street, not looking because he was in a hurry for court. That car wouldn't have hit him. Would I still have been sharing the condo with him? Would he have changed for me this time? Would he still have died in some senseless hit-and-run? I got up and headed into the kitchen. My stomach growled. Better to think about the here and now and finding something more substantial than a cookie to eat.

Inside the fridge I pulled out the ricotta I'd purchased on Saturday morning and brought it to the table. I grabbed flour, a bowl, and a cookie sheet from the pantry. After emptying the container of ricotta into the bowl I filled the empty container with flour and added that to the ricotta. I mixed them together until a dough formed, then proceeded to roll and cut gnocchi for dinner. Gramma's recipe box included her gnocchi recipe—from scratch, of course—starting with boiling potatoes. This recipe, one I'd been given by a friend who declared it the easiest gnocchi recipe ever, was my go-to since I tend toward quick, easy, and tasty recipes.

While I was rolling and cutting the gnocchi, I tried to focus my thoughts, but Catherine's accusations had messed with my mind more than I wanted to admit. What if Violet had gone into hiding because she'd seen something at the garden that day? What if she was in hiding because she'd killed Carl Henderson? No. Someone else had to be responsible for that. The police might think so, but I couldn't imagine a situation where Violet would physically harm anyone.

When I'd finished laying out the gnocchi on the cookie sheet, I put a pot of water on the stove to boil. That done, I went back to the pantry and gathered garlic, walnuts, and a bottle of extra-virgin olive oil. I grabbed spinach and Parmesan from the fridge and a handful of basil from a pot on the windowsill. A few minutes later, my food processor had done its work and I had a lovely batch of pesto. I dropped the gnocchi into the boiling water, set the table, and poured myself a glass of iced tea.

As I satisfied my appetite, my thoughts ran around in circles. I still had no idea where Violet might be or how her disappearance was related to Carl Henderson's murder. And worse, I was now wondering how safe I was in my own home. Could someone get into the house?

I rinsed the dishes and grabbed the large Maglite I kept in the entry closet and, after checking the dead bolt on the front door, began an inspection of the house. I listened carefully for sounds that didn't belong, all the while wishing I had the can of pepper spray I used to keep in my purse. I'd gotten rid of it when I moved back here; still, I wished I had something more dangerous than a big metal flashlight to keep an intruder at bay. Note to self: look into replacing that pepper spray. Even safe havens aren't always safe.

In each room, I checked windows to be sure they were securely locked, made sure the boogeyman wasn't hiding in closets or under beds. Finally, I finished in the kitchen, checking the dead bolt on the back door. Again. Satisfied that the house was secure, I put the kettle on to make a cup of tea and decide on my next move.

But before the water had a chance to boil, pounding erupted at the front door.

"Now what?" I said to the empty room. "Now you see who's at the door," I answered myself out loud.

I put my eye to the peephole. No one was there. Something moved to the left near the front windows—a shadow flickering in the afternoon light. I pressed my eye closer but of course I couldn't see beyond the peephole's range. I held my breath. Nothing. Whoever had been pounding on the door had stopped. How foolish would I feel if I called the police and it turned out no one was found prowling around the house—in broad daylight no less. It could be someone's idea of a joke. Maybe. One thing was certain, unlike a character in a bad horror movie, I had no intention of opening the door to see who or what was out there. I could just stay here, locked safely inside the house.

As I started to walk back toward the kitchen, the pounding at the front door erupted again.

I stalked back to the door and put my eye to the peephole again. If someone was playing tricks—

But the only trick was the face I saw staring at the door before he thrust his fist at it again. I jumped back and the pounding resumed. Cousin Simon had come to call.

Could I pretend I wasn't home with my Jeep parked in plain sight out back? While it was true that I often went out on foot or used my bike, Cousin Simon had no way of knowing that. He'd assume I was at home whether I actually was or not. Besides, if I didn't answer now, he'd likely be back.

I took a deep breath to steel myself for the inevitable and opened the door.

"Well, it's about time," Simon huffed. "I've probably bruised my hand trying to get your attention. What took you so long?" And there he stood, pressed blue jeans with a razor-sharp crease down the front of each leg, sweater vest, and button-down shirt in a shade of blue that just matched his eyes.

"Hello to you, too," was all I could manage to say in response.

"You are going to let me in, aren't you?"

"Oh, sure." I stepped back to open the door wider, though I would much rather have shut the door in his face and sent him on his way.

"To what do I owe this pleasure?" I asked when he'd stepped inside and I'd closed the door behind hm. He gave me a curious look when I locked the door, but I wasn't taking any chances. With Simon for backup, there was no safety in numbers.

"Since you haven't returned my calls or answered my letters, I really didn't have much choice but to come to see you in person, now, did I?"

"I'm sorry about that, Simon," I said, though in fact I was anything but sorry. "It's been a bit busy here the last couple days. The world has pretty much gone to hell in a handbasket. Quite frankly I don't understand what you're going on about. The estate is settled. I assume you received your share when the rest of the heirs did when the estate assets were distributed. All according to Gramma's will," I added.

"Oh, I got a check, all right." He took several steps into the living room and looked around. "This is really quite a nice house. Larger than I remembered."

"Well, you didn't really spend a lot of time here once you got older. When was the last time you visited? I think we were twelve or thirteen at the time, weren't we?"

He stopped his perusal of the view of the side yard from the parlor window and turned to face me. "That has nothing to do with anything. I'm as much our grandmother's heir as you are. I saw the will, you know, so I'm well aware that the bulk of her estate was to be divided among her grandchildren. There are six of us cousins. While the others may be satisfied with the pittance we received, I for one am not."

"It's not like she was wealthy, Simon." I walked to the center of the room, stopping several feet away from him. "She had the house and a small amount in the bank that she kept for emergencies. No stocks or bonds. What little jewelry she had, she willed to specific people."

"Yes, I know," he said.

"Most of the cash went to pay the bills she left, and the rest was split between the cousins. I don't know what more you're looking for."

"The house."

"This house? This house is mine. I bought it. The money went into the estate and was distributed. End of story." I'd reached the end of my rope where Cousin Simon was concerned. His demand for what he imagined was his fair share of the estate was ludicrous. Unfortunately, Simon wasn't finished, not by a long shot.

"The house is part of the estate," he insisted.

"The house *was* part of the estate. In accordance with the instructions in Gramma's will, it was sold, and the proceeds of that sale were disbursed among us."

"Sold to you."

"Oh, for crying out loud, Simon, what is your problem? The will specified family had the right of first refusal. I was the only one who put in an offer on the house. If you were interested in it, you should have made an offer then. It's—too—late—now."

"My problem is that the price it was sold to you for was obviously far under its true value."

I drew in a lungful of air and let it out slowly. This was going to take every ounce of patience I had in me. "Simon, the house was appraised. It was offered to the heirs if any of us were interested in buying it. I was the only one who made an offer on the house. The offer was for the appraised value. Case closed."

"Hardly." He began a slow stroll around the living room. "It's a beautiful house. Nicely maintained. Lots of period details. A good bit of land with it, too."

"Not that much land. Five acres, and you know it. Most of that is woods. The rest was sold off years ago. As for the house, I have put a lot of work into it since I bought it. It did not look like this when I moved in. Gramma wasn't able to maintain it like she and Grampa used to. Things got put off. A lot of things over many years. I had to deal with that. There were repairs to be made and cosmetic fixes, too. I'm still working on those. This house looks the way it does because I invested in it. You'd know that if you'd bothered to visit her."

"That's got nothing to do with my rights here."

It pained me to realize a member of my family could be dumb as dirt.

"You have no rights here anymore. You've seen the

accounting for the estate. You signed the papers needed to settle the estate. I don't know what else to say or do to convince you."

"You can see that I get my fair share. Especially since you've gotten more than yours."

"What's that supposed to mean?"

"It means that I'm not stupid. You got the house for a price that was obviously under its value, and you got part of that purchase price returned to you."

"I what? That's ridiculous."

"It's in black and white on the final accounting for the estate. You received a check that included a portion of what you paid for the house."

The last of my patience evaporated. "Let me explain it one more time for you. The check I received from the estate was for my share as an heir. You received a check in the same amount. It has nothing to do with what I paid for the house. It has nothing to do with the fact that I bought the house. If someone else had bought it for the price I paid, I still would have gotten the same check, as would you. Understand?"

"I want what's rightfully mine!" he shouted.

"You've already gotten it!" I yelled back. "How many times do I have to say it? Look, just talk to Attorney Maxwell. Maybe he can explain it to you so you'll understand."

"I've already spoken to him. He's not returning my calls either."

Big surprise there. If Simon was making ridiculous demands of Gramma's lawyer like he was of me, no wonder the man had stopped responding.

"And did he explain the figures to you before he stopped returning your calls?"

"Oh, he tried to snow me with a lot of that legal double-talk like lawyers usually do. I told him if he didn't make good, I'd be making a complaint to the state ethics board and hiring a lawyer of my own."

"And what did he say to that?" I asked, knowing I was only egging him on but unable to stop myself.

At first, I thought he wasn't going to respond. Finally, he said, "He told me to do what I felt necessary but that I should realize I'd be paying an attorney for nothing since everything he did was perfectly aboveboard."

Of that I had no doubt. The estate's lawyer had represented my grandmother for many years. While I hadn't dealt with him personally before Gramma died, I knew he was an attorney who not only made sure all the i's were dotted and all the t's crossed, but he also knew how many paper clips were used to keep the various documents together. Gramma would have made sure the person looking after her interests knew what he was doing and knew it well. My dealings with him had confirmed that. Unfortunately, all that didn't change the hardheadedness of the man standing three feet away from me.

"Look, Simon, I'm not giving you money to make you go away," I said. "So just forget it. If I have to hire a lawyer to defend some crazy lawsuit from you, then I'd rather spend the money stopping you than give that money to you. And when I win in court, I will sue you right back to get the money I paid my attorney to fight your frivolous suit. You'll have to pay my lawyer and your lawyer, and you will still not get anything more from me of Gramma's estate." I turned my back on him, stalked to the door, and opened it. "Go home, Simon. I don't want you in my house."

For the second time in the same day, for no reason I could fathom, I'd been accused and found guilty in a fantasy only real in someone's mind.

I thought for a moment he was going to stay put and I'd end up calling the police after all to get him out of here. Happily, he thought better of it and walked out on his own, turning to glare at me.

"I know what you can get for this house. And that an offer was made. If you're smart, you'll agree to sell," he said from the porch. "This isn't the last you've heard from me."

"Great," I said as I slammed the door behind him.

I watched him stalk to his car, get in, and sit there for a few moments, no doubt engaging in a little multitasking by stewing and plotting. Maybe it wouldn't be a bad idea to get some legal advice of my own. I let out a sigh of relief when he drove away. I'd had enough of Cousin Simon for today.

No sooner had his car pulled away from the curb than I spotted Sally heading in my direction.

I opened the door. Before she made it all the way across the threshold, she asked, "Who was that?"

"That would be my infamous Cousin Simon."

"Really? Well, that's weird."

"Yes, he is." I motioned toward the seating area. "Come on in and explain why the interest."

Sally settled onto the sofa and I the chair across from her.

"Denny noticed his car drive up and mentioned that he was here Friday morning after you'd driven off."

"I'm sure he was scoping out the place. He thinks he has a claim on the house as part of his 'rightful inheritance.'"

"Yikes," Sally said. "But you haven't heard the weirdest part."

I leaned forward, now very interested in what Simon might have done while I wasn't at home to show him the door, or the property line, as the case may be.

"Denny says Carl Henderson was leaving when your cousin pulled up. Seems they had a little talk before going their separate ways."

That definitely qualified as odd and, considering Carl was now dead and Simon had his beady little eyes on my property, set off all sorts of alarms. "Did Denny mention seeing them to Sam or Detective Quinn?" I asked.

"I don't think so. He had no idea who it was, so it didn't seem particularly important, but now?" She shrugged.

"Do me a favor? Will you ask Denny to give Sam a call? If I do, he's still going to want to hear it straight from Denny."

"No problem," Sally said. "Who knows? Maybe it will lead to a break in the investigation." She thought for a moment. "Maybe the two of them were in cahoots and had a falling-out. If your cousin killed Carl, he'd be out of your hair for good."

I grimaced at the thought. Cousin Simon a cold-blooded killer? Even if he somehow managed to get into the garden, I had a hard time picturing him digging a hole and burying Carl Henderson there.

At the sound of the ringing phone, I nearly jumped out of my skin. "Hold that thought," I said, as I crossed the room and picked up the phone.

"Hello?"

"Maggie?" A hoarse whisper. "Maggie, go before it's too late." The call ended abruptly with a loud click.

I stood there with the phone to my ear for a moment longer, listening, then lowered the handset slowly onto its cradle.

"Who was it?" Sally asked. "Is something wrong?"

"I don't know. The last time I chalked it up to being a silly prank. Now I'm not so sure."

"What do you mean, a prank? What did they say?"

"Last time it was a message on my answering machine on Saturday. Sounded like the same voice, though who knows. One whisper is pretty much the same as another. The message just asked if I was here and hung up. This time the voice asked if it was me and told me to get out, then hung up."

"Creepy." Sally stared at the phone as if willing it to respond. "I think you should tell the police."

"Tell them what? That I got a creepy phone message and a second call? They'd chalk it up to a prank if they even gave it that much consideration. Which is probably all it is. Stupid thing, whoever's doing it, and really bad timing. The police don't want to hear about prank phone calls, especially not with all that's happened in the last few days."

"I still think you should tell someone. Call Sam, he'll listen."

"That's the last thing I want to do."

"Then call the cute detective."

"No."

"Why not?"

"I told you why not. Besides, I don't want to give him another excuse to ask me more questions."

Chapter Thirteen

Where had I put that lawyer's phone number? As soon as Sally had gone, I decided to make the call. I rifled through the desk without success, but finally found it tacked to the bulletin board in the kitchen. I called, hoping Attorney Maxwell would be in. He wasn't, but would be back. His assistant told me he'd left instructions: if I called and he wasn't there, she was to set up an appointment. Apparently, he'd anticipated Simon's next move and my reaction to it. I'd be his last appointment of the day.

I made the thirty-minute drive to the lawyer's office without any delays and arrived an hour early. I decided to stop for a cold drink at a sub shop a short walk from his office and relaxed for a few minutes reading the newspaper.

Carl Henderson's face sat above the fold on the front page. The article offered less information than I already knew, just a rehash of what had been on the radio and the basics of Saturday's discovery. Fortunately, the gardeners hadn't been publicly identified, so they wouldn't be dealing with the extra stress of questions from the media and curiosity seekers. I hoped.

The paper contained the usual selection of local news along

with a community calendar of upcoming events and reviews of two plays that had opened in the past week: one at the local college and the other put on by the community theater. And on page seven I found my byline and the article I'd submitted the week before.

A month ago, I'd met the paper's editor at a dinner at Sally's house. We'd chatted over salad about growing greens and other veggies. Talk had drifted to the paper and how he'd be interested in a gardening column. A star was born. Well, at least a fledgling columnist.

I ran my finger across the page, smiling. For the first time in days, I felt really good. I hoped the feeling would last through my meeting with Gramma's attorney. I checked my watch. Time to go.

Richard Maxwell's office was on the third and top floor of a building that had managed to maintain the charm of having been built early in the last century. Marble from a nearby quarry framed the entry. Dark wood–paneled walls and doors lined the first-floor hallway. I opted to take the stairs to burn off some of the nervous energy building up inside me.

Framed period photos of old street scenes filled the walls of the reception area inside the office. His secretary sat behind a desk that looked as old and well-preserved as the building. She smiled as I walked in.

"It's been a while," she said. "How's life at the old homestead?"

"Overall, all that I'd hoped. The last few days have been a bit dicey, though."

She nodded as she picked up the phone and announced my

arrival. "You can go right in," she said after placing the phone back in its cradle.

Gramma's attorney sat behind a mahogany desk strategically placed in front of a floor-to-ceiling bookcase situated between the two windows. He looked to be a couple of decades younger than she had been, and I found myself wondering how well she'd known him outside their professional relationship. She must have trusted him in many ways to have named him executor of her estate over anyone in the family or her friends.

The afternoon sun streamed in. I caught a glimpse of the buildings across the street and the rolling hills beyond them. Dick rose and shook my hand, then motioned for me to take a seat in one of the twin chairs facing his desk.

"Thanks for seeing me on such short notice."

"I think I have a pretty good idea of what you're dealing with." He tapped a manila folder lying on the desk's blotter. "Simon has been in touch. I should have suspected he would try something, considering he almost balked at the final accounting when asked to assent. When it was explained to him that without his signature the disbursement would be delayed, that there'd be further legal costs, and there'd be no distributions until after it was all settled, he decided to sign. So, I suppose it's not a big surprise he's trying for a second bite of the apple."

"But can he really cause trouble for me?" I asked, hoping the answer would be no but knowing legal questions were rarely so simple. "He doesn't have anything to sue about, right? Everything that was supposed to be done was done, wasn't it?"

"That's right. We followed probate procedure to the letter. Everything was done that should have been done."

"I thought so." I hoped I hadn't insulted him. "But he's just got me so rattled I had to talk to you. He's called and been leaving messages on my answering machine. He's sent letters. Now they're coming by certified mail. He even came to my house this afternoon, threatening to get an attorney involved if I didn't give him what he kept calling his rightful share."

"What did you say to him?"

"I told him we all got our rightful shares and that I wasn't about to pay him anything more." I gripped the arms of the chair and leaned forward. "He just wouldn't listen. I had to ask him to leave."

"For what it's worth, I'd say you did and said the right things."

"But do you think he's going to pursue this?"

Dick shrugged. "He certainly seems inclined to try. He may decide to drop it after the reception he got at your house. Or he might keep on with what he's been doing so far to try to wear you down. Or he might up the ante and consult an attorney. There are those out there who would write a letter to try to get something for him. The case has no merit, but the truth is, anyone can sue about pretty much anything. It might not stand up long in court, but there would still be the need to respond to any suit he filed. Of course, that would be the point of filing suit—to encourage you to settle for some sum and cut your losses."

"You mean it would cost less to pay him money he doesn't deserve than to defend myself against an unfair lawsuit."

"That's the gist of it. But it likely wouldn't be just you named in any suit. He'd name the estate and likely me as its executor as well."

"And you'd settle."

"It's often more about the costs of litigation than the merits of the suit."

"That's not fair."

"No, it's not. But the law isn't always about what's right. Sometimes it has to be about compromise."

"So, what should I do about him?"

"You could do nothing at this point. Wait and see what he does next. Maybe we'll get lucky."

"I hope so. I'd feel better if we did something. Maybe you could send a letter warning him off?" I kneaded the shoulder strap of my purse.

"I could do that if you like. I'm not sure how much good it will do, but you never know."

"I'd feel much better doing something. This whole thing with Cousin Simon has left my nerves raw and now with Carl Henderson being killed and my friend missing, I'm at my wit's end."

He raised his eyebrows. "Carl Henderson is dead?"

I nodded. "Did you know him?"

"Only by reputation. But I take it you did."

"Not really. But I found his body."

For the first time the professional mask slipped. "Found? What happened?"

I drew in a ragged breath and told him the short version of what was becoming an increasingly lengthy story.

"Good Lord," was all he said at first. "So that's who it was.

The one day I skip the morning paper. Been tied up in meetings all day. Mondays." He shook his head and added softly, "Why on earth would someone bury him there? They had to know he wouldn't stay hidden for long."

"I have no idea. The further this goes along, the more questions I have. And so do the police. A detective has paid me a visit twice. And with Violet missing—"

"Someone is missing?"

And so I told him about Violet. Most of it, anyway. I left out much of what had happened over the last couple of days. As soon as I mentioned looking for answers on my own, his disapproval of the idea became clear.

"Maybe you should leave it to the professionals."

"That seems to be the popular logic," I replied. "But I don't know. I just can't sit back and wait for whatever is going to happen. Maybe I'm paranoid, but I get the feeling I'm a suspect."

"I think the term they use now is *person of interest*." He smiled, obviously trying to put me at ease. "But I don't expect it's just you. They're probably questioning anyone with anything to do with the community garden project or Carl Henderson, which is probably quite a long list. But if you feel you need to retain counsel, this isn't my area. I can recommend someone." He consulted his computer and jotted down a name and number, then handed me the piece of paper. "I've known him for years. He knows his stuff and should be able to answer any questions you have."

I took the slip of paper and stared at the name. Had it really come to this? Would I need a criminal lawyer?

"I hope I don't need to call him," I said and thanked him.

"As do I. But if you feel the need, call him. He'll either tell you not to worry at this point or advise you what to do. I'll let him know he might be hearing from you."

I nodded and tucked the paper into my purse, then thanked him again and headed for the door.

During the drive back home, I debated calling the attorney he'd recommended when I arrived home or saving the number as a "just in case." By the time I'd run a few last-minute errands, I'd decided I didn't need a lawyer and that I was definitely being paranoid. That was, until I turned onto my street and spotted the police cruiser parked in front of my house.

Marlowe's finest was at my front door. Well, in front of my front door. At the sight of the cruiser, I considered turning around, turning the corner, or just plain speeding past the house and continuing down the road. I didn't pursue the thought far enough to consider just where I'd go, but the idea of avoiding the police—local or otherwise—greatly appealed to me at the moment, paranoid thought or not. Moments after I spotted the patrol car, its door opened and Police Chief Sam Whitacker himself stepped out. I groaned out loud.

There'd be no slipping around the corner, no avoiding the inevitable. Goodbye, quiet cup of tea. Hello, adulting. I just hoped my old friend came bearing news and was not on a mission to do an impression of Detective Quinn and his annoying notepad.

Sam had spotted my car. He paused, waved, and shut the door of the cruiser. I eased the Jeep into my driveway, putting my best smile on my face as I stepped out of the car and walked toward him.

There was a time, once upon a time long, long ago, when seeing him would have sent a thrilling shiver down my spine. That was before I'd married Bryce. Those days were long gone. In the here and now, the shiver was more one of dread that his wife, Catherine, might be nearby. It wasn't just that Catherine resented my prior relationship with Sam. Catherine had disliked me since the first day we met back in seventh grade, years before either one of us knew Sam. I'd tried to figure it out from time to time over the years without success. Eventually I just gave up and accepted the fact that Catherine would be a thorn in my side whenever our paths crossed. Like Friday morning at the market or at the town picnic on Sunday or earlier today at the diner. The woman was relentless in her animosity. And now with her brother's body being found by me—*why me?*—things would only get worse.

"Hey, Sam," I said. "What brings you here today?" *Please, no more questions,* I added silently.

"I've been tied up at a meeting all afternoon and thought on the way back to the station I'd check on you. Can't an old friend stop by to see how you're doing?" he asked.

I felt myself relax a bit. A genuine smile replaced the artificial one. Maybe this was a social call, not a professional one. After all, he'd shown his concern on Saturday, and I had no doubt it was genuine then. "Sure," I said, "come on inside." As he followed me to the kitchen, I asked, "Did Dennis Kendall call you? He saw Carl Henderson and my cousin, Simon Gleason, talking on Friday morning."

"He did. Don't give it another thought. We'll look into it."

I was sure he would. I was just as certain I'd never be told whatever they learned about that conversation.

"So, how are you doing?" he asked as I grabbed a pitcher of unsweetened iced tea from the refrigerator.

I shrugged. "It's all surreal. I came back here thinking I could settle down and live a nice, peaceful life. Garden a little. Write a little. Truth is, it's turning out to be anything but peaceful."

"The best-made plans," he said.

"True enough," I agreed. I put glasses of ice on the table for both of us and filled them with the cold tea.

"I wish I could make this easier for you," he said.

"I know. You're a good friend, Sam." I thought for a moment as I put the sugar bowl on the table beside his glass. "There is something you can do for me."

"Oh?"

I took a seat across from him. "It's just that, well, that detective, he's been here twice asking me questions. First about the body at the community garden and then about Violet."

"He's just doing his job." He stirred three overflowing spoons of sugar into the tea.

"I know that, but he won't tell me anything. And the way he asks the questions, it makes me feel like I'm the prime suspect."

Sam laughed out loud. "Prime suspect? I think you've been watching too much true-crime TV."

"I'm serious," I said.

"So am I. Look, he's not about to give you information

about an ongoing investigation. Likewise, he needs to ask all those questions to help figure out what happened."

I nodded. "I know, but—"

"You're curious."

It was my turn to laugh. "Yes." I became serious again. "But it's more than that. I'm not just curious in the usual sense. I need to know what's going on. I feel like all eyes are on me. Violet's missing and things are being said about her. Things have been said about me. I need to, I don't know, clear her name and mine, I guess."

"Mags, you were in the wrong place at the wrong time. Let the professionals do our jobs. Sit back and let it work itself out."

I stood up and began to pace the kitchen floor. At this rate, I was going to need to replace that old linoleum sooner rather than later.

"There were police in my front yard yesterday morning. I heard they found a bloody shovel in the Kendalls' mulch pile. That means whoever killed Carl Henderson was right outside my door."

Suddenly Sam was all business. "Who told you that?"

"What?"

"Don't give me that, Mags. Who told you they found a bloody shovel that was used to kill Henderson?"

"I heard it somewhere," I hedged.

"Where?"

I could hear my younger self chiding Cousin Simon at some long-ago holiday gathering. "No one likes a snitch!" I'd chanted.

"I overheard it at the diner," I said. Why was I trying to cover for Catherine?

"If someone's leaking information, I need to know. Was Sally Kendall's cousin there by any chance? Did your good friend get him to discuss this case with her? And you?"

I never did condone tattletales, but there was no way I was letting anyone else take the blame.

"Catherine."

"What?"

"Catherine Whitacker. You know, your wife. She was talking about it at the diner. She also implied that I was responsible somehow for what happened to her brother."

"Mags, I know you and Catherine don't get along, but this is crazy."

"I agree. This whole thing is crazy. But it's true. If you're looking for a leak in your department, look no further than your wife."

I sat back in the chair and took a long drink of my iced tea.

"Maggie Walker, so help me, if I find out this is some attempt to get even with Catherine for some of the things she's said to you—" he began.

"Or about me. Let's not forget the really nasty stuff she's said behind my back."

Color spread up from his collar and across his cheeks. "So, she hasn't been very nice to you. That's no reason to say something like this about her."

"Unless it's true. And it is," I said simply. "Go ahead. Check it out. I wasn't the only one who heard her spreading her insider information. Ask Detective Quinn. He was there. He put a stop to what she was saying."

His face colored a deeper red. "I'll deal with it," he said. I believed he would. That was one wall I wouldn't want to be a fly on.

After a minute he added, "And I don't want you running all over town poking your nose into this."

"What's that supposed to mean?"

"It means we know that you've been asking questions and it needs to stop. You're impeding a police investigation."

"Oh, come on—how am I impeding your investigation in any way, shape, or form? I've talked to a few people. Big deal. Half the town is talking. Probably the whole town. I haven't done anything that's gotten in between the police and their investigation."

"It's not just that," he said, rubbing a hand across his face. "You could be putting yourself in danger."

"More danger than having a killer hiding evidence in the yard next door?"

"Look, Mags—"

"No, don't you dare 'Mags' me. You look, Sam. If someone is watching me or wants to hurt me, ignorance is definitely not going to protect me. The more I know, the safer I'll be."

He reluctantly shook his head, silently conceding that I was going to do what I was going to do regardless of what he said about it.

We sat there in silence for a few minutes while I refilled his glass. Sam stirred in several spoons of sugar before taking a long drink that half emptied the glass.

"So," I said finally, "now we both know that I can keep a secret. Tell me something. I know you can't tell me details about what happened to Carl Henderson and where that investigation is leading, but there's something I'm really worried about. Please, Sam, can you tell me what you know about what happened to Violet? Do you think whoever killed Carl did something to her as well?"

"Violet Bloom," he said simply.

I waited but he didn't go on. He sat there for a while, swirling the rest of his tea around in the bottom of the glass. Finally, he drank it down and set the glass on the table.

"There's really not much to say."

"She's missing."

"Yes." He nodded.

I got up and took the pitcher from the refrigerator, but he put his hand over the glass. After I poured myself a bit more iced tea and put the pitcher away, I sat down, hoping I'd given him enough time.

"From what we've been able to ascertain," he began slowly, "she left home sometime on Friday. She ran several errands, including a stop for lunch, alone. At some point during the late afternoon or early evening her errands took her out of town. She hasn't been seen or heard from since. No reports of anyone seeing or hearing anything strange. Nothing out of place at her home or office. It's as though she just drove off into the sunset."

"Then her car hasn't been found."

Sam shook his head.

"And what has *your* investigation uncovered?" he asked.

"My investigation?" I smiled. "My investigation has consisted of chasing my tail. I've asked a few people if they spoke to her on Friday, but no one who did remembered anything out of the ordinary. It wasn't unusual for her to run a long list of errands at a time, which is pretty much what she was doing on Friday. She had a lunch date that got canceled and shopped for groceries later in the afternoon. They weren't at the house, by the way. And she apparently said she was heading over to see me on Friday night, but she never showed up here. She never mentioned stopping by when we talked earlier in the day. As far as I knew, we were going to meet at the community garden on Saturday morning; but when I was heading out early Saturday, I found a note on my front door saying she'd been delayed and to start without her. But you already know all that. I didn't think anything of it other than to be a bit surprised she wouldn't make sure she was there to launch a project she'd put so much hard work into."

"Maybe she didn't."

"Didn't put all that work into the garden? No way. Believe me, she worked her tail off getting that garden organized. It's been amazing working with her. That's why I couldn't understand why she wouldn't be there."

"Unless she couldn't be."

I sat back in my chair. "You mean unless something happened to her." My heart sank. Of course I'd considered that Carl Henderson's death and Violet's disappearance were related. Still, I'd hoped there was some other explanation no matter how precarious that hope might have been. Sam's words cut that thread.

"We don't know if Violet Bloom is missing of her own accord or if something happened to her. You don't have the note, so we can't check it to see if it might have been left by someone else."

"But what if Violet didn't leave that note on my door on Saturday morning?" I asked.

"You mean was she already out of the picture on Friday night?"

"Right. What if the note was just a distraction? Something to make people think Violet was still running around town on Saturday morning when nothing was further from the truth. I think maybe whatever happened to Violet happened on Friday night."

He nodded. "It's one of the scenarios we're looking at. She told her husband that she was coming over here to go over last-minute details with you. We've checked his phone and verified the text message. The state police have the family's answering machine, but a summary of the messages indicates that she wasn't answering the phone from late Friday morning. We've traced her movements through the afternoon until the time she told her husband she was going to meet you. Maybe she stopped somewhere else before her intended stop at your house."

"Or maybe the text her husband received wasn't from her any more than the note to me was." From his expression, I could see I wasn't the first to question who sent that text to Victor Bloom. "Sam, what do you think happened to Violet?" I asked.

Sam shrugged and got up from the table. "Hard to say."

"Come on," I urged him. I stood, palms flat on the table-top, staring him down. "I know you have an opinion about this. What do you think happened to Violet?"

Again, the shrug. "I don't know anything for sure. But the possibilities are these." He counted off on his fingers. "She had something to do with Carl Henderson's death and made herself disappear to avoid the consequences." He raised a second finger and pointed to it. "She saw something either where Henderson was killed or when he was being transported or when his body was being buried in the community garden and ran out of fear and now she's afraid to come out of hiding for fear his killer will go after her or her family." He raised a third finger and pointed to it. "Same as the last possibility except the killer caught her and we just haven't found her body yet."

We stood there in silence for a moment. I closed my eyes. There it was. The undeniable elephant in the room and he'd just given it life. I raised my eyes to his. He was staring, studying me.

"And the only person who knows for sure is the one who killed Henderson," he added.

"And Violet, if she's still alive."

"Yes." He reached out and took my hand. "I'm telling you this because I want you to understand how dangerous this could be. If whoever killed Henderson thinks you've found out something"—he gripped my hand tighter—"it could be very dangerous for you. I want to be sure you understand that."

"I know: he could decide I'm a threat and come after me." I said the words, as much as I hated to give them that power.

"Exactly. He's already left his calling card in your neighbor's yard. You need to be smart about this. So, are you going to leave the investigating up to those of us who get paid to do it?" he asked.

I squeezed his hand, then let it go. "I wish I could promise that I will."

"But." I knew he knew there had to be a but.

"But I don't think I can do that."

"Mags," he began. Then his cell phone rang. "Excuse me." He pulled the phone out of his pocket and put it to his ear as he stood and turned away. "Hi . . . Working . . . I didn't say I was at the station. I'm out at an interview. . . . No . . . We'll talk about this later." With that he ended the call and put the phone back in his pocket. "I should be going." He turned and started toward the door.

"Sam?" I put my hand on his arm. It didn't take a crystal ball to know who'd called. While the spark between us had gone out long ago, there would always be a connection. He was concerned and I owed him something for that. And for other things, long-ago things.

He smiled but said nothing.

"I'd say give her my best, but somehow I don't think my name will come up," I said.

He jingled his keys in his hand. "Tactical omission," he said with a sideways grin.

"There is one thing," I said.

Sam turned to face me, his hand on the doorknob, his face expectant. I took in a breath. If he was expecting some grand revelation related to Carl Henderson's murder, he was about to be sorely disappointed.

"Yes?" he prompted.

"It has nothing to do with what's happened," I began.

"Let me be the judge of that."

"I've been getting these annoying phone calls."

"What sort of calls?"

"Like I said, it's got nothing to do with your investigation, but Sally thinks you should know."

A raised eyebrow. I didn't wait for another prompt and hurriedly added, "I've been getting prank phone calls."

"What sort of prank calls?" he repeated. His expression grew stony.

"Just annoying. Hang-ups mostly." I shifted from one foot to the other. "And the occasional barely audible whisper."

"What did they say?"

"Nothing much. My name. Once, 'get out.'" I looked up at him.

"Anything else?"

I shook my head, then added, "A couple of hang-ups on the answering machine."

"Were they all from the same number?" he asked.

"I don't know. It's not like I can check."

He glanced at the rotary dial phone and the answering machine beside it on the desk.

"I know," I said. "I'm an anachronism. Or at least my phone system is. But I like my grandmother's phone and the old answering machine."

"And you've gotten none of these calls on your cell phone?"

"No. That would have been too easy."

He let out a slow breath, no doubt considering what to do

next. "Let me ask you this. Are you feeling threatened by these calls?"

I considered that. "No. I mean, the whispered calls freaked me out a bit, but I'm not afraid. It's probably just some kid playing games. Like I said, annoying. I wouldn't have bothered you with this at all, but Sally thinks it's something you should know about."

"Your friend is right. It's hard to say what's relevant to an investigation and what's not. That's why it's always best to provide any information to me."

I tried to keep my face neutral, but I'm sure he could see I got his message.

"That said, if you're sure you're not feeling threatened by these calls, what I would suggest to begin with is that you replace that old phone with something that will provide caller ID. As it is, we don't know if the calls are all being placed by the same person. It's possible the hang-ups are simply telemarketers."

I nodded. That sounded reasonable.

"How many of the whispered calls and messages?" he asked.

"Not many. Most of them have been hang-ups."

He nodded. "Okay. So once you get a phone number, you may recognize who it is. Either way, we can determine if it's an attempt at harassment or just random calls. And if anything changes or you feel threatened, let me know right away."

I agreed and promised to bring my phone service into the twenty-first century.

"Be safe, Mags," he said as he stood at the door. "Please."

"I'll do my best," I said. And for that I didn't need to cross my fingers.

He nodded and left without another word.

I didn't watch Sam drive away. I did dead bolt the door and slip the security chain into place.

I hadn't made it halfway across the room when a knock sounded at the door.

Chapter Fourteen

I retraced my steps, peered through the peephole, undid the locks, and opened the door.

Sally stood on the doorstep holding out a large box.

"What's this?" I asked.

"Darned if I know," she said. "I found it on the porch. Family didn't hear the delivery guy when he knocked—all busy playing some new video game down in the family room. Anyway, it's not ours. See for yourself." She pushed the box into my arms.

I took the box, flipped it to check the label. "Ah, my I'm a Gardener order!" I moved back into the room. Sally followed. I set the box on the desk and grabbed a box cutter from the desk drawer. "So why did he leave it at your house?"

Sally reached over and tapped the label. "A simple typo. They transposed the house number."

Sure enough, the label read 86 West End Lane rather than 68 West End Lane. This wasn't the first time it had happened. Still each time it did, I was glad I had a neighbor who redirected my packages promptly. Of course, I did the same when I received Sally's packages and mail. Tit for tat.

I pulled the flaps back on the box. And stopped.

"Something wrong?" Sally asked. "Not what you ordered?"

I stared at the box, but my thoughts were far away. About twenty-four hours away. "What if this package wasn't the only confused delivery?" I said slowly.

"Are you missing something else? I can ask Denny and the kids. I suppose it's possible they forgot to say if there was another package."

"No." I shook my head, turned to look at her. "That's not the kind of delivery I mean. What if"—I took a deep, shaky breath, gathered my thoughts. I didn't like where this particular train of thought ended. I hesitated a moment as though saying the thing would make it so. "What if the person the police were after Sunday night, the one they used the dog to track to your mulch pile and the bloody shovel hidden there, what if that person got mixed up and thought your yard was mine. Eight-six or sixty-eight. One house next to the other. An easy mistake."

Sally stared at me unable to say a word.

"What if the shovel was meant to implicate me in Carl Henderson's murder?" There it was. I'd said it out loud, and it didn't sound nearly so paranoid or far-fetched as I'd expected. It sounded plausible, real. It sounded like a threat.

"There has to be another explanation," Sally said.

"Like what?"

Sally shook her head. "How should I know? It must have been random. A convenient place to hide a shovel. I've been racking my brain trying to figure out why someone would choose my yard of all the places in town to stash that thing."

"And now we have a reason," I said softly.

"Maybe you're wrong."

"I don't think so." I ran my hand over the open flaps of the box. Life in the garden was so simple and straightforward. Well, most gardens anyway.

"You could leave town for a while," Sally suggested. "Go visit some of your friends in Boston."

"And maybe I'd be safe there and maybe while I was gone the police will catch whoever killed Carl Henderson and find out what happened to Violet. Or maybe they won't. Then what? How long do I wait? Do I come back and hope he's forgotten about me?"

Sally stared at me blankly.

"Or maybe while I'm away he plants some other evidence against me, only this time he gets the address right and the police find it and suddenly I'm not just paranoid thinking I'm a suspect and there's a knock at the door and I'm being questioned a whole lot more intensely." I was babbling, a sure sign I was losing focus. I seemed to be doing that a lot lately.

"And maybe being read your rights by that cute detective?" Sally quipped, showing a lot of teeth, trying to lighten the mood.

"Will you stop with the cute-detective comments?"

"I'm just trying to loosen things up a bit. You are really starting to freak me out, you know."

"Misery loves company," I said. "Look, I'm sorry. I'm freaking myself out, too."

Sally reached over and gave me a hug. "It's going to be okay, you know. We'll get through this together."

I smiled and gave her a hug back. Tit for tat and all that.

"So, what's in the box?" Sally asked, suddenly very interested in my order.

"Just a few pieces of gardening gear. And I've decided to try something new." I pulled a plastic-wrapped package from the box. "Gauntlets."

"And that would be?"

I pulled a pair of long suede gloves from the plastic bag. "Rose gloves. Also, very handy in working with other thorny things like blackberries." I slipped one on and then the other. They covered my arms from fingertips to elbow. I held my arms out so she could admire my new garden gear.

When I moved in and began going through things Gramma had left behind, I discovered an old pair of hers, so worn that the tips of the fingers had been patched. I hung them in the garden shed where I can look at them and feel her presence every time I walk inside. It's comforting to know there are things she loved around me every day.

Sally studied them for a moment. "Now that I see them, I remember seeing your Gram wrangling the roses wearing something like these."

"Those roses were her pride and joy," I said. And they'd be mine, too. "She told me these saved her from having to wear long sleeves all summer to cover the scratches. The roses look like they're in good shape this year, but that unruly quince is threatening to take over the south side of the porch. Have you seen the thorns on that thing? I swear they're an inch long." I pulled the gloves off and folded them in half and set them on the table.

"I hadn't noticed them, but the flowers on it are gorgeous," Sally said.

That they were. I'd given the plant to Gramma five or six years before. We'd been scouting out witch hazel at a nursery in Great Barrington when I spotted the flowering quince. Its branches had been naked of foliage, but bloodred blossoms covered it. And thorns. Very nasty-looking thorns. I instantly dubbed it Beauty and the Beast and brought it home for Gramma as a welcome-spring gift.

Memories grew around this house faster than the weeds. There was no way I was retreating to some friend's guest room in the hope of avoiding a threat to me that might or might not be real.

I gathered up the packaging the garden gauntlets had arrived in and carried the box with the rest of its contents to the back porch.

"So, did you tell Sam about the mystery calls?" Sally asked as she followed me.

"Yes, I did. No follow-up nagging needed."

"Just looking out for you." She flashed a grin. "And you're convinced that someone planted that shovel in my mulch pile in an effort to implicate you in Carl Henderson's murder?"

"Yes. It makes more sense than running through town carrying the shovel used to kill someone and randomly finding a mulch pile to hide it in." I stared out at the backyard. The thought of a killer setting one foot in Gramma's garden beds made me grow cold inside. But it wasn't just fear. There was anger, too. Anger like I hadn't felt before, not even when I'd found out about Bryce's fling. Or the fling before that.

"And you're going to keep on poking around in this, aren't you?"

"Yes, I am." I turned to face Sally. "But that doesn't mean you have to have anything to do with it."

Sally smiled and said simply, "Someone's got to keep you out of trouble."

A few minutes later, she had left on a mission to find her backup phone.

Once I was alone in the house, I paid a visit to the phone company via my laptop. It didn't take long to sign in and sign up for its caller ID service.

Back downstairs, I sat on the sofa to unwind for a few minutes. Television didn't offer much of an escape, but I left a rerun of *Murder, She Wrote* playing in the background as I dined on spinach salad with a side of gnocchi and pesto from the fridge. My mind kept circling back to Carl Henderson's body in the garden bed. Had Violet been there? I pushed the plate aside. What happened at the community garden on Friday night?

Sally, phone in hand, came back around the time I'd stacked the last of the dishes in the drainer to dry. Her family was fed, her children in bed, her husband making sure all remained safe and secure. She'd brought the remains of a bottle of red wine and helped herself to two glasses from the cupboard.

She poured us each a glass and asked, "Where do we begin?"

I thought about that as we made our way to the comfort of the parlor. I settled into one of the wingback chairs and put my glass on the coffee table. Sally did the same.

"I'm not sure," I confessed. "I know I don't want to sit idly by and wait for someone else to figure out what happened, especially if whoever's responsible is trying to point the police in my direction."

"We could start with what we know," Sally suggested.

"I know for sure that Violet was alive and well and among the not missing on Friday morning when we met concerning last-minute details for the opening," I said. "We know she was fine until sometime Friday afternoon. But I don't see how that's helping."

"Maybe looking further into Violet's day will help. You know, finding out when she crossed paths with Carl Henderson."

"That's assuming she did." Before Sally could object, I held up my hand. "I know, her disappearance and his murder must be related. I really wish I knew more about him. I can't just ask random people if they saw him on Friday."

"Well, there's a couple of things we could try," Sally said. "We could ask Catherine about her brother."

"Yeah, not happening," I said.

"Or we could follow up on Violet's afternoon and see where that leads. Maybe Carl and Violet were at the same place at some point. That could be where something happened. Or it might have happened right afterward," Sally suggested.

"But Carl was found inside the community garden."

"Doesn't mean that's where he was killed."

I had to admit she was right. "But that opens up another slew of questions."

"One slew of questions at a time, please." Sally picked up the remote and clicked off the television. "If only we had a clear line of clues to follow like Jessica Fletcher," she mused.

"Lacking that, I think I'll start with a bit of multitasking tomorrow. I totally forgot to go to the copy shop today. I was supposed to get copies of the handouts from my talk Sunday and bring them to Howie at the hardware store. Violet was supposed to stop at the copy shop on Friday, so I can ask some questions while I'm there. Maybe I'll get lucky and Carl will have stopped there, too."

"We can only hope." Sally toasted me with her wineglass.

I raised my own glass to her. And to my absent friend.

"With Violet's family away until Saturday afternoon, no one realized she'd disappeared. I wish I'd kept the note Violet left." A little light bulb went on over my head. "Wait," I said. Of course. I'd already locked the door when I found the note. I smiled. By the time I got to the garden on Saturday morning, I was so distracted I'd forgotten about that piece of paper. I ran upstairs. "I'll be right back," I called over my shoulder. My laundry basket sat in the hall closet. Inside were the jeans I'd worn on Saturday. And inside the right front pocket were the crumpled remains of Violet's note.

I brought it back downstairs and spread it out on the coffee table, carefully smoothing away the wrinkles.

"You found it!" Sally exclaimed, leaning closer to get a good look at it.

Too late I thought of the possibility of fingerprints. I sighed. If anyone else's fingerprints had been on the note, they were long gone now; though truth be told, they probably were gone when I crumpled it up and shoved it in my pocket on Saturday morning.

I stared at it, too. White paper, lined, about four by six

inches, with a ragged edge where it had been torn from a spiral-bound notebook. I turned it over. Blank on the back. I picked it up and examined the hastily scribbled block letters.

May be late—start without me. V

The words were written in black ink, not Violet's usual purple. But then, she'd been known to borrow a pen from time to time. I dropped the note back on the table.

"Doesn't look like Violet's usual careful penmanship. She won an award back in grade school, you know," Sally said.

"Of course she did," I mumbled.

"Do you think someone else wrote the note?" Sally asked.

I cocked my head to the side, not taking my eyes off the hen-scratched words. Had Violet written it? I sure as heck didn't know. I shrugged. "Maybe I'm naive because I don't want her to be involved in Carl Henderson's death. Maybe I'm just being paranoid. But I don't think so. Something just doesn't seem right."

"Well, if she did write it, then Violet was around on Saturday morning and whatever had delayed her might be related to her disappearance," Sally said.

"And if she didn't write the note, then it's an obvious attempt to hide her disappearance. Or at least blur the timeline," I said. Which meant I'd likely crossed paths with a killer. Probably more than once.

I closed my eyes and tried to clear my head.

"The police must be considering all this," Sally said as she refilled our glasses.

"I have one bit of information the police don't. Whatever they may think about the note, I know the note was real because I found it on my door." I took a sip of wine. "Make that two pieces of information. I also know I wasn't involved in either Violet's disappearance or the murder of Carl Henderson and the attempt to hide his body. Without those facts, the police could be pursuing their investigation in the wrong direction, investigating me rather than pursuing other suspects."

"Maybe we can come up with a lead the police might have overlooked."

The fact that someone may have planted evidence in Sally's yard had upped the stakes all around. With any luck, the next time I spoke to Detective Quinn—or Sam Whitacker for that matter—it would be to report what we'd found. In the meantime, I'd drop the note at the police station in the morning.

Sally was giving me a quizzical look. I'd been woolgathering again. "That would be the plan," I agreed. Like *The A-Team*'s Hannibal Smith, I really do like a plan. "Tomorrow I'll call Frank Wellman in the morning and find out when he saw Violet on Friday afternoon. Maybe I'll get lucky and Carl was there at the same time."

Satisfied that we had a starting point for the next day's inquiries, Sally and I called it a night.

I'd barely pulled the coverlet over my shoulders when I fell asleep.

Chapter Fifteen

Sometime after midnight the phone rang. I glanced at the alarm clock on the dresser across the room, but my sleepy eyes refused to focus, leaving the numbers a red blur in the darkness. I listened in the nighttime quiet of the house for the sound of an identifiable voice to justify getting out of bed. But there was no voice, apparently no message, only the silence of the sleeping house around me. I lay there waiting for the phone to ring again. When it didn't, I rolled over and fell back asleep without much more than a passing thought about who might be calling at that hour.

On Tuesday morning, I added the final touches to my to-do list for the day and hooked up the phone Sally had loaned to me and connected it to the answering machine. I stowed the old phone in the desk drawer, reluctant to commit to its removal.

Before she left the night before, Sally had made me promise to carry my cell phone with me, just in case something unexpected happened. I suspected she also wanted to be a part of my inquiries since she had appointments scheduled that morning and wouldn't be able to go with me.

I grabbed my organizer notebook and flipped through the pages to find Frank Wellman's number. Violet and I had been going over the task list for what she called countdown week. She had wanted to be very hands-on as far as the preparation of the garden was concerned, so there was no reason for me to speak with him. I never thought I'd need to call him, but I'd jotted his name and number down. Just in case. Good thing I had.

I dialed the number. On the first ring an answering machine picked up. Of course. I should have known it wouldn't be that easy. I left my name and number and asked him to call me. Whether he would or not, time would tell.

I stared at the phone for a moment after putting it down. I considered calling Sam to tell him about the mix-up in house numbers, but I suspected he'd simply tell me to stay out of it, that the state police would take care of it. I didn't want to hear that. And I didn't want to call Detective Quinn directly. What I really wanted was to dig deeper. The truth was out there, as Fox Mulder used to say every week on my television screen when I was growing up. If I could connect the dots, I would find it.

In the end, my conscience won out and I dialed Sam's number. It went straight to voicemail. I left a message telling him I'd found the note and would drop it off at the station this morning. That should ratchet down his reaction to my continuing to snoop. At least a little.

I'd done what I could at home. I grabbed an envelope from the desk and put Saturday's note in it. I'd drop it off when I went to the copy shop to get copies of the handouts from my talk on Sunday. Then to the hardware store to drop them off, only a day late. Maybe I'd find a lead there. Howie usually had some juicy piece of gossip to pass on to those interested. I just had to ask the right questions.

I picked up the phone and began to dial Sally's number to report in, then hesitated. If I called, Sally would likely assume I was asking for help rather than a sounding board for my ideas. She'd probably insist on canceling her appointments and go with me on today's quest. But was that fair? I put down the phone. I could handle asking a few questions on my own at a store in the middle of the day with other customers coming and going. I'd consulted Howie numerous times while fixing things around the house. Today's questions would just be a tad different. No backup needed.

There was no need to distract Sam or Detective Quinn from their investigation with my plans. There'd be plenty of time to call the professionals with an update once I'd learned something they'd consider evidence. And of course I'd share whatever I found—significant or not—with Sally when I got home later in the day.

I dropped my organizer and the envelope in my bag, slung my purse over my shoulder, and headed for the back door.

The copy shop was a ten-minute drive on a slow day. A stone's throw away from the community garden. When I started out, I had no intention of going near the garden. In fact, I wondered if I'd ever have the courage to set foot there again. I didn't want to be reminded of the boot sticking out of the soil or the foot attached to it, or the body attached to that. In fact, I'd decided to go out of my way to avoid the small side street where the lot containing the garden was located.

That changed as I entered downtown Marlowe. The red light ahead paused traffic long enough for my curiosity to take hold. What was I so afraid of? Bad memories were just that: pieces of the past that were emotionally distressing. But I wasn't in any danger from memories, even if they were so fresh. The sunlight streaked through the trees and across the sidewalks and street, bouncing back from storefront windows. People went about their business all around me. And whatever had happened in that lot behind the hardware store had happened days ago. Whoever was responsible was long gone. Confronting my memories of what happened there was a good thing.

Instead of turning left at the traffic light, I drove straight ahead down the street, through the town's business district, and left onto the small street running past the hardware store and parked next to the fence enclosing the portion of the lot behind the store where we'd built the community garden. The remains of yellow tape, which had been stretched across the gate by the police on Saturday morning, remained tied to the fence, but someone had torn it. Its ends flapped in the breeze.

I sat in my Jeep with the motor running, my hands gripping the steering wheel. A part of me wanted to take one more look at the location of the crime. The rest of me wanted to drive on by and not come back. But I knew I needed to come back, particularly with Violet's inexplicable absence. Decisions would need to be made soon concerning the future of the community garden; and, as Violet's second-in-command, it would fall to me to get the ball rolling if Violet didn't reappear. So, I reached down and slowly turned the key and pulled it from the ignition.

I sat there another minute or two before opening the door and walking slowly toward the fence. I could see the garden perfectly well without walking through the gate. The ground between the entrance and the place the body had been buried was trampled with the footprints of police and crime scene investigators. The offending plot had been thoroughly dug up, and apparently much of its soil taken away, to be examined for evidence, I assumed. And of course, Carl Henderson's body had been removed.

I stepped closer. My fingers gripped the crisscrossed wires of the fence.

"I don't think you're supposed to be here," a gruff voice behind me announced.

I jumped back and spun around.

Roy Hansen stood on the sidewalk a few feet in front of my Jeep, hands in the pockets of his khakis and a smirk on his face. Of all the things that had been turned upside down over the past few days, why did Roy's bad attitude have to be the champion of consistency?

"Roy, you startled me!"

"Didn't mean to."

"It's okay—I just wasn't expecting anyone to be here."

"I was passing by and wanted to make sure there wasn't anything funny going on." His head turned in the direction of the ends of the broken tape. "Going inside? You shouldn't waste much time getting things back in order if we're going to get our gardens in this year. They've made quite a mess."

"It's going to take some work once we're allowed back inside."

We stood there looking in at the garden, the weight of what had happened here making the work needed to get it up and running daunting. The silence between us became anything but companionable.

I glanced at Roy. I glanced down the street. Ghost-town empty. Not a surprise at this time of morning. I knew I wasn't really alone. Lights gleamed in the café at the end of the street where diners enjoyed breakfast. People worked inside other buildings. When else would I get the chance to question Roy?

"I didn't know Carl well," I said. "Did you?"

Roy made a face like he'd eaten a sour grape. After a moment he said, "Too well and not by my choosing." When I didn't respond, he went on. "I own a chunk of the woods in back of your grandmother's house. Did some timber harvesting a few years back. She was one of the abutters we had to notify. She was concerned with the effect on water runoff; but since we were cutting selective trees, not clear-cutting, she didn't object. Anyway"—he took a long breath—"Henderson had his eye on my property. I told him no. The past six months he'd been after me again. Relentless."

I knew the feeling.

"I hear you're asking questions around town. You probably heard we got into it at the diner the other day," Roy said.

I hadn't but made a mental note to ask around about it.

"It wasn't the first time we had words, but it was the first time I gave him a fist in the face." He shrugged and gave a self-satisfied nod. Odd, considering Carl Henderson's subsequent demise.

I must have looked shocked because he said, "The police have already talked to me about it." As if that settled the matter.

But I knew there could always be more questions from the police.

"Were you able to answer their questions?"

"Do you mean do I have an alibi for Friday night?" The trademark smirk returned. "I'll save you the trouble of calling your old flame Sam Whitacker at the PD. I was at home with my wife all night."

With his wife? Very convenient. I wondered what the detective thought of that.

"Let's hope they find who's responsible sooner rather than later," I said.

"In the meantime, what are you doing about this?" He nodded toward the upturned soil and trampled plots.

I turned back toward the garden. It was true the police had left a mess, but my bigger concern was when we'd be able to gain access. I wasn't at all sure that torn crime scene tape meant we were being invited back inside. "I hadn't planned on doing anything here today. I think we need to get official permission to go back inside."

"Well, I hope you intend to do that soon. I'd hoped Violet would have returned from wherever she's gotten to by now. I hear the police are looking for her. I got the impression she's the one they really want to question. Looks like she's out of the picture one way or another." His grin was anything but reassuring. He pointed a finger at me. "That means you need to deal with this and pronto," he said and abruptly turned and continued on down the sidewalk.

I stood there awhile longer, trying to come to terms with what I'd seen on Saturday. Everything appeared so harmless now. Nothing at all to be afraid of, but still. I'd about decided it was time to go when I heard footsteps. I turned to see a familiar face. After my conversation with Roy, the gruff love of the diner's owner would be a welcome relief.

Bill Button headed across the street. He was dressed in his usual white tee shirt and pants, though he'd left his cook's apron back at the diner. He walked straight toward me, a man on a mission if ever I saw one.

Bill wasn't a tall man, but his general roundness and his abundant personality made him seem formidable. At the diner, you could hear his booming voice cracking jokes or chewing out someone from the kitchen all the way to the last booth. Yet he'd shown me more than once what a sweetheart of a man he could be.

Once, years ago, I'd stopped in for a quick lunch while doing errands for Gramma. One of the two waitresses had called in sick and Bill was running around bussing tables between prepping orders. I hesitated at the door and he'd waved me in, pointing at the table he'd just cleaned. He slapped a menu on the table and barked at the harried waitress as he headed back to the kitchen. The waitress took my order, but it was Bill who brought out my meal. With my check he'd brought a foil-wrapped piece of carrot cake, saying it was in honor of my birthday—which happened to also be his anniversary. When I got home, Gramma explained he often did things like that—but only when they weren't expected. He liked to surprise people.

"Hi, Bill," I said. "What's up?"

"Nothing much. The world seems to have taken a step back toward normal today. Just taking a break before the noontime crowd arrives. Took a walk, saw you on my way back, and ended up here. How you doing after your little run-in with Cathy Whitacker?" He stepped closer to stand beside me.

"About as well as can be expected," I said.

"What a waste," he continued, shaking his head.

"Yes," I agreed. "No matter what the reason may have been, such an untimely death is always a waste."

"Wh—oh, right. Henderson. Right." He smiled. "I don't suppose they've got a lack of suspects for that one."

"What do you mean?" I turned to look at him. He was staring straight ahead toward the hole in the ground that had been Roy Hansen's plot.

"Just what I said. There won't be much wailing and moaning at his demise. Henderson left a whole lot of unhappy people behind him where those real estate deals of his were concerned." He turned his head to look at me. "Would you want him as your neighbor? I sure as hell wouldn't. Didn't even care to have him in the diner. Didn't want people to associate the place with his wheeling dealing. But with him being Cathy Whitacker's brother, well, didn't want to ruffle her feathers too much. I seen what she does to people she thinks crossed her."

I cringed at his referring to Catherine as Cathy. I wondered if he did that to her face or if the slight was for my benefit or if he just really didn't know better. Somehow, I doubted it was the last one. Not much seemed to get by Bill. But I didn't bother to ask. Instead, I said, "Did you ever have any dealings with him?"

Bill shook his head, again looking through the fence at the garden. "Been living here long enough to know better than that. I saw that boy grow up. He always had something or other going on behind someone's back. Smart people steered clear."

I recalled the stories my grandmother had told me while we chatted on the phone—the ones that I'd half listened to about the real estate developer at odds with the mayor. Gramma was a real fan of Marlowe's multi-term mayor, which, even if the developer's actions had not been reprehensible, would have put him on Gramma's blacklist. If I'd paid more attention to the stories, I might have connected Henderson's name with them sooner. As it was, I could have become just another cautionary tale if—and it was a big if—I'd been willing to discuss selling Gramma's house in the first place. Which I hadn't.

"Did you ever have a run-in with him?" I asked, my curiosity piqued. I couldn't help but wonder what it would take to cause Bill to feel so negative about anyone, even if that someone was less than admired by what seemed to be everyone he met.

"Me? No reason to. My little diner is hardly prime real estate. But it's mine and that's what's important to me. Henderson had bigger fish to fry." He half laughed, then deadpanned, "Looks like someone ended up frying him."

Ouch. I looked up and down the sidewalk, across the street, then back into the garden and the rest of the empty lot beyond. "I don't suppose there's anything around here to develop."

Bill stared back at the garden. "'Cept this lot, of course," he said.

I thought about that for a moment. "If that were the case, Howie would have sold it rather than offer it for the community garden," I said.

"Maybe so," he said. "You never can tell what people are gonna do."

"True," I said. Time to dive in. "I heard Roy Hansen and Carl Henderson had a disagreement at the diner the other day."

"So you heard about that. Humph. I heard you've been asking around."

Had everyone heard about the questions I'd asked? I needed to get an improved tap into the local grapevine. He looked like he was considering whether to share this tidbit with me or not.

"I'm used to all the talk around town ending up at my place," he began, "but the last week we've been churning out the drama. First Roy Hansen, then you and Cathy Whitacker. Folks were so busy chewing on what happened I thought I was gonna have to shoo 'em out to make way for the dinner crowd."

Not exactly what I wanted to hear about myself, but Roy and Carl Henderson, on the other hand, that I definitely wanted to hear about.

"So what happened with Roy?" I prompted.

"Henderson was having his usual solo steak and eggs platter when Hansen walked in. Henderson stops Hansen before he has a chance to sit and starts talking up some deal he was working on. Hansen turned his back on him. Henderson grabbed his arm and it looked like it was gonna get rough. I had to come out and suggest they take it outside."

I suspected "suggest" wasn't quite the way it went down. But this wasn't the time to comment on Bill's choice of words. "And?"

"And they did. I called the cops when they started in on one another in the parking lot. I could see it was gonna turn into a brawl. By the time they got here, both of 'em were gone. Hansen hit Henderson with a right hook. Henderson went down like a rock. Hansen left. So did Henderson. End of story."

Or was it? What if Roy had stopped by the garden on Friday and crossed paths with Carl Henderson? Could they have come to blows again?

"Doesn't matter anyway, him being dead and all." He turned from the fence. "Gotta get back to work."

"Hey, Bill, you didn't happen to see anyone around here, maybe while taking a break on Friday over this way while getting some fresh air, did you?" I asked.

"Friday? Nope. Fish 'n' chips night. Customers start piling in around noon and there's not much time to think, let alone take a walk between then and closing."

"Oh. I was hoping you might have seen Violet. I'm trying to retrace her steps on Friday afternoon."

"Sorry. Can't help you." He shoved his hands in his pockets and started to walk away, then turned back. "Why do you want to know what she was doing on Friday? Do you think she was involved in what happened here, too?"

I shrugged. I really didn't know what I thought despite all my questions and snooping around. I admitted as much to him.

"I know what you mean." He glanced at his watch. "Well, break time's over." And with that he was off, cutting diagonally across the street toward the diner.

I watched him go, then glanced over at the bulletin board mounted on the shed door. The notice advertising the community garden stared back at me, as did the schedule I'd posted Saturday morning before all hell broke loose. So Violet had indeed stopped here on Friday and posted about the available plots. Not a surprise.

The schedule would take some serious fixing if the garden project was to go forward this year. A relaunch, maybe, when all this was settled. Maybe sooner. Time had become muddled in my mind. Saturday morning seemed so very far in the past.

I walked over, unlocked the shed's door, and pulled out one of the brochures from the box inside. Violet had suggested keeping a supply here to have ready to hand out to anyone who might be interested. More evidence she'd been here sometime on Friday afternoon.

Violet had finished the design just before the printing deadline and had delivered it to the printer before I'd had a chance to see it. As I opened the trifolded, double-sided sheet, I could see Violet's handiwork. The text was brief and to the point and well designed—large enough to be easily readable, yet small enough to fit all the necessary information in, along with pictures of the project so far: the fenced-in, neglected lot behind the hardware store, the community cleanup day when trash and debris were banished last fall, the ribbon cutting when the snow had retreated around the first day of spring with a smiling Violet and Howie Tucker standing beside members of the garden club and town council and mayor. All the information a prospective gardener could need in one handy place. Violet had a way of knowing just what was needed. I folded the brochure and put it in my pocket and frowned. *What happened here on Friday night?*

With a last look at the community garden, I headed down the sidewalk.

The entrance to the hardware store was a stone's throw away around the corner and beyond that was the copy shop. The walk would give me time to think.

The one thing that the police had glommed on to (and which made me feel they—well, Detective Quinn specifically—suspected me) was the fact that only two people were known to have a key to the lock securing the community garden's gate: Violet and me. If Violet had multiple copies of the key made as backups, that knowledge would lead to the conclusion that at least one other person might have had access to the garden when the body was disposed of there. And that was something I bet Howie Tucker could tell me. I added that to my list of questions to ask him when I dropped off the compost handouts.

As I passed the hardware store's entrance, I spotted a hastily scrawled note stuck to the front door. It read simply BACK IN A FEW scrawled in black ink. A few what? I wondered. Presumably minutes, but that still left the question of when he left, which would, of course, determine when he would be back. Or even if he'd be back when he intended to be. My luck with good intentions lately, my own and other people's, had not been good. I hoped he'd be back by the time I returned from the copy shop.

Chapter Sixteen

The copy shop sat on a quiet side street two blocks down and around a corner. Violet likely had stopped there to pick up the brochures and then run by the garden to drop them off sometime on Friday afternoon.

A bell above the door jingled as I entered. Voices coming from the workroom at the back of the store paused.

The shop was housed in a surprisingly small space. The front of the store was only as wide as the two plate glass windows and the door between them. By one of the windows a comfortable-looking sofa had been placed. An array of brochures and advertising material was spread out on the small coffee table in front of it. By the other window a table with three chairs had been placed with more promotional materials displayed there. Samples of the print shop's wares—brochures, business cards, digital prints, menus from local restaurants, and so on—covered the walls on either side. Directly in front of me sat the counter, and a few feet behind that a wall separated the public space from the work area in the rear, the door in its middle open barely an inch. I could hear a printer running somewhere out of sight.

The door opened and a young man emerged. He asked,

"Can I help you?" His tone was distracted but his expression welcoming. He wore wire-rimmed glasses, blue jeans, and a bright yellow tee shirt that read THINK INK in a rainbow of colors.

"Hi. I'm Maggie Walker," I replied as I stepped up to the counter. "I'm assistant director at the community garden. I think you did some work for Violet Bloom. Promotional brochures?"

"Something wrong with them?" he asked, a crease forming between his brows.

I pulled the brochure out of my pocket. "No, actually they're beautifully done."

"Oh." He sounded surprised. I hoped it was because people were more apt to complain than to compliment and not because this example of the shop's work was an exception rather than the rule. "So, what's up?" He took the brochure and turned it over in his hands. "Did you want to order more?" He sounded hopeful, his hand reaching for the order pad on the counter. "What can I do for you?"

"Well, you can help me with a couple of things." I pulled the compost handout from my bag. "I need fifty copies of this packet, please."

"Sure. Did you want to wait for them?" He jotted my order on the pad.

"If you don't mind."

"No problem. You mentioned there was something else?"

"Actually, I was wondering if you could tell me what time Mrs. Bloom picked up the brochures."

"You want to know when she picked them up?" he echoed. Now he looked at me like I had three heads.

"Yes," I said and painted on my sweetest smile. I hoped I looked like I was asking the most usual of questions.

The sound of the printer stopped. Footsteps approached from somewhere in the back room. A moment later, a gray-headed man about thirty years older than the clerk appeared.

"Good afternoon," he said. "Anything I can help with?" His eyes darted between the clerk and me.

"She needs some copies made. And she wants to know what time Mrs. Bloom picked up her order on Friday."

"Is there a problem?" the older man asked.

"Nope." I smiled again and shook my head. "I'm assisting Mrs. Bloom with the community garden and I'm just following up on a few things. Do you recall what time she was here?"

He gave me the you've-got-three-heads look, too, but stepped up to the computer behind the counter and nodded at the clerk and said as he began tapping keys, "You go ahead and make this lady's copies. I'll check on Mrs. Bloom's order. It looks like the order was logged out just before five o'clock. Of course, she wasn't able to get the entire order."

"More brochures?"

"Ah, no." He looked a bit embarrassed. "She'd placed an order for some photo enlargements through our website. She uploaded the photos earlier in the day with a request to pick them up that afternoon. Unfortunately, she didn't specify which of our locations she wanted to pick them up at. We're a satellite store here. The main shop is in Pittsfield, so it's the default pickup location. When she got here on Friday, she was quite upset that her enlargements weren't here. We offered to have them brought up so she could get them on Saturday. I told her we'd even be glad to deliver them to her home, but she said she wanted them right away, so she'd drive there to get them. She was so very upset. I offered her a discount, she paid for the brochures and the pictures, and she headed off to get her enlargements."

I thought about that for a minute. That proverbial light bulb clicked on above my head.

"Did she pick up her enlargements?" I asked.

He tapped a few more keys. He frowned. He blew out a breath through pursed lips. "That's curious," he said. "You know, she didn't pick them up on Friday. Says they sent them back here since that was her original intention." He reached under the counter and took out an interoffice envelope. He opened it and withdrew an envelope the right size for a set of photo enlargements. "You said you're working with her?"

I nodded.

"Seeing how important it was to her to get these enlargements, do you think you could give them to her?"

The photos were important to Violet, but were they related to what happened at the garden? I wouldn't know that until I saw them. But they might have something to do with the garden itself, and if they were important—

"I'd be happy to," I said.

Looking relieved, probably at not having to confront Violet's wrath a second time, he handed over the envelope. "Would you let her know that if she needs any more copies, the website retains the images, so she just needs to enter the order number and she can request additional prints. And let her know again we apologize for the delay."

I assured him I would the next time I saw Violet, fervently hoping that would be soon. The clerk returned from the back room. I paid for my copies, thanked them both, and was on my way, headed to the hardware store. Hopefully, Howie had returned and I could drop off the handouts and ask him a few questions.

It was a good plan, I thought. Until I reached the hardware store's door and found a paper sign bearing a new hand-written message, saying he'd be back in an hour, taped to the inside of the glass. Damn. My curiosity would have to wait for any attempt at satisfaction. I banged on the door in frustration, channeling Cousin Simon no doubt, hoping Howie was inside and would open the door. I started to turn away but stopped.

Had he forgotten to lock the door when he left? The impact must have jarred the old latch loose and the door opened a few inches. Oops. Or maybe it was already open. I pushed at the door with my index finger and stepped inside, the familiar jingling of an above-door bell announcing my arrival. No one stood behind the checkout counter to my left and only about half the lights in the store were on. Those were in the rear near the garden center and storeroom. Maybe someone was here at the store after all.

I stepped onto the worn wooden floor, closing the door behind me, and walked along the double-wide center aisle past the weekly specials toward the back of the store. Behind a display of shiny new hoes, shovels, and rakes, I spotted my quarry.

Howie looked up from the magazine he was reading behind the worn wooden counter.

"Hey, Howie," I called out. "Are you open?"

He stood up and dropped the magazine on the counter. "For you, Maggie," he said, "absolutely."

"I brought those handouts from my talk on Sunday. I know I promised them Monday, but I totally forgot. I'm sorry they're a day late." I put the box on the counter.

"Not to worry," he said with a sad smile. "I've had a couple of people ask about them, but they said they'd check back. How's it going?"

"Not so good," I replied. "No one's seen Violet since sometime on Friday."

"You're kidding." He looked shocked. "I'd heard rumors, but figured she was just lying low after what happened. I heard the police are looking for her. What do they call it? A person of interest?" He shrugged. "You know how things get exaggerated."

"Not this time. At least the part about them looking for her. Her husband filed a missing person report. Did she stop by here on Friday afternoon?" I asked.

"Actually, she did. Didn't stay long. She said she just wanted to thank me again for my part in the community garden. She really is such a nice lady. I suppose you tried calling her. Oh, of course you did." A chagrined look crossed his face. "She's such a busy person. Always on her way somewhere else whenever she stopped in here. Though she always had a minute or two to say something nice. I hope nothing's happened to her."

I nodded in agreement, though I found myself wondering about Violet, considering the story related to me by the men at the copy shop. I wondered how much of it was mere drama. I didn't know them and, while I called Violet my friend, how well do we really know anyone?

"Did she mention where she was going after she left here? Pittsfield maybe?"

"Nope." He shook his head. "She was practically gushing in her enthusiasm for the project. Said how much she was looking forward to finally getting the gardeners working in their plots because all their efforts so far had been preliminary stuff."

I could relate to that. As much as I enjoyed the planning and organizing, I'd so been looking forward to literally digging in the dirt with fellow gardeners and getting started. All that had come to a screeching halt on Saturday morning when I'd discovered Carl Henderson's body. I tried to push the image out of my mind.

"What time was that?" I tried again, concentrating on Violet.

He scratched his head and made a face. "I really have no idea. It was later in the afternoon, but I honestly can't say what time. One of my clerks went home sick and the hours just kind of blurred together until around closing. I'm really not much of a clock-watcher on the best of days. The traffic gets lighter a little after five. I start to do my end-of-the-day chores around then before the last rush of people. But anything before that was just one thing after another. Of course, this time of year I stay open a little later. You know how it is. As the days get longer, people are cleaning up their yards after the long winter and brown days of early spring. They're likely to stop in on their way home, so I stick around just in case. So, I really have no idea."

I nodded as though appreciating the logic of retail sales.

"I don't suppose you heard Frank Wellman when he came by on Friday to till the plots," I said.

"Actually, I did." He smiled at me as though pleased to have something useful to say. "It was a little before Violet stopped in. It was such a warm, sunny day that I'd opened the rear door to let the fresh air circulate throughout the store. One of my clerks was arranging a new display in front and I was working in the back of the store. Nothing like a perfect spring day and some fresh air to lighten the spirits."

"Very true," I agreed. That very afternoon I'd opened every window in the house to let the breeze blow the last vestiges of winter out and the fresh air of spring in. That day held the promise of a perfect weekend for our gardening plans. I shuddered at the thought of just how wrong those plans had gone.

"Anyway," Howie went on, "I heard the tiller going at it back there for the better part of an hour. I looked out a couple of times out of curiosity. I think he finished up while I was waiting on a customer because the next time I looked, he was gone. Does it make a difference?"

I shrugged. "I'm not really sure. I'm just trying to retrace Violet's steps."

"You think she was there when he was tilling?" he asked.

I thought about that for a moment. "I don't know. I haven't had a chance to ask him."

"Yeah, he can be a little hard to get ahold of." He laughed. "Have you left a message on his answering machine yet?"

"I have," I said. "I haven't heard back from him, though. I guess he's just been busy. Probably taking advantage of this beautiful weather."

Howie laughed again.

"Did I say something funny?" I asked, confused by his reaction.

"Oh, no," he said. "It's just that he hates answering machines. His daughter insisted he get one and use it so that she could leave messages for him. She just can't make him listen to the messages or return calls." He laughed again. "Every once in a while, the messages reach their limit, and she storms in and deletes them all and it begins all over again."

"So how the heck is someone supposed to get ahold of him if he doesn't listen to his messages?"

"Keep calling, of course." He grinned. "He'll answer the phone if it rings and he's there. Otherwise—" He shrugged.

"Otherwise, you're out of luck." I finished the sentence for him.

"Exactly." He smiled broadly.

"Well, that's not very helpful," I said a bit indignantly.

"Now you sound like his daughter. Besides, look at it from his perspective. You see, if you know him, you know to keep calling until he answers. If you don't know him, you leave a message and call back and leave more messages when he doesn't call back. Odds are you'll stop after a while."

I shook my head. "That's ridiculous."

"Hey, he figures that just because you leave a message doesn't obligate him to return a call—or even to listen to the message. Can't say I blame him. I'd probably do the same thing if I didn't have a business to run. Can't escape technology when you're running a business."

"I can't say it makes much sense to me."

"To each his own," he said and began to busy himself straightening a cardboard display box containing plant tags at the end of the counter. When I made no move to leave, he asked, "Something else?"

"Well, yes," I said. "I believe Violet purchased the locks for the garden here."

He nodded.

"Do you recall how many keys there were?"

"Sure, each lock comes with two keys. Oh, and the locks she bought were keyed the same."

That I already knew. "Just four keys, then? Did she have any duplicates made?" I asked.

"Nope."

"You're sure?"

"Positive. I think I'd remember cutting extra keys."

"Of course you would. I'm sorry. It just seemed strange."

"Nothing strange about it. She was always one to be in control of things. No point in having a lock if you're going to pass keys out to everyone and anyone."

"One more thing," I said. "Did you by any chance see Carl Henderson on Friday?"

Howie blanched. "No, of course not. Haven't seen him since I don't know when. Horrible business what happened back there. Didn't care for the guy, but I wouldn't wish that on anyone."

"No, I suppose not." I thanked him for his time. But I was hardly convinced. As I returned to my car, I thought about how Violet was always prepared, always had a backup plan. Of course, she kept a spare key for herself. The other spare she gave to me with my key. Maybe she didn't have any other keys made, but that left Violet and me the only ones with access to the garden. I didn't like where that thought would lead the police at all.

Back in my Jeep, I dialed into my answering machine to check messages. Nothing. On the upside, my mysterious caller had taken a break. On the downside, Frank Wellman hadn't returned my call. I tried his number again but didn't bother to leave a message on his answering machine. My questions regarding Friday's tilling at the garden would have to wait.

I opened the envelope containing the photos and emptied its contents onto the passenger seat beside me. A half-dozen enlargements fell out. More pictures. Could these have been part of what Violet picked up at the post office earlier on Friday or were they unrelated? More questions. When was I going to start finding some answers?

Whatever I expected to find, the enlargements proved disappointing. The photo on the top of the pile looked innocent enough. Certainly nothing to warrant Violet getting upset about it. The simple outdoor scene could have been taken in the woods somewhere around Marlowe or, for that matter, pretty much anywhere else here in the Berkshires. Or it might have been somewhere else entirely. There just wasn't anything distinctive enough to tell. I reached over and fanned out the remaining photos. All similar outdoor scenes, though some seemed to feature a close-up of some tree or rock. There were no people in the pictures, no recognizable human habitations, though evidence of a human presence was there—a shovel propped against a tree in one picture, a dirty knapsack with a broken strap, and paper coffee cups and other trash in another. Bits and pieces. But was there any significance to them?

I slipped the photos back in the envelope. It was a puzzle for later. I should call Sam and let him know I had them. But did I need to do that? I certainly had no reason to suspect the photos had anything to do with Violet's disappearance or Carl Henderson's death. Heaven knew Violet had enough irons in the fire and the pictures might have to do with any one of them. Or perhaps none of them. Maybe she just liked walking in the woods with her camera as her only companion. But if it was as simple as that, why was she so upset when her pictures weren't at the Marlowe copy shop to pick up? Ultimately, there was always the possibility they were related to Carl Henderson's murder. And that meant I needed to turn them over to those investigating his death and let them try to figure out what they meant.

As I turned the key in the ignition and the Jeep's engine roared to life, I wondered about the keys to the garden. It seemed unlikely there were more than the four original keys.

I doubted she'd go elsewhere to have another key made. If Howie had made one or more spares, why lie about it? No one had access to my keys on Friday. That led me to wonder if Frank Wellman had Violet's spare key. Or had someone taken it from her? And most important, the question I most needed to answer: Who had used one of Violet's keys to bury a body in the community garden?

Chapter Seventeen

I had no answers to my bumper crop of questions, but I could check one item off my ever-evolving to-do list. I flicked on the Jeep's directional signal, checked for oncoming vehicles, and moved out into traffic. Five minutes later, I pulled into a vacant parking spot in front of the Marlowe Police Department. Before I went inside, I pulled out my phone and took a quick photo of the envelope I'd been given at the copy shop. There might be some useful information on the receipt stapled to it. I grabbed the envelope with the photos and the one with Violet's note and dashed inside.

It didn't take long to drop off Violet's note and the envelope of enlargements for Sam. As soon as I pulled back on the road, my mind started going over the events of the past few days.

"Friday," I said out loud. "Violet. Meets with me for final prep before Saturday. Her husband and kids are on a trip to visit his mother. She went to the post office early in the day. Grocery shopping. Hardware store. Maybe saw Frank Wellman. Copy shop. She was supposed to go to Pittsfield to pick up her photo enlargements, but she never got there. Why?"

I rode in silence for several minutes as the possibilities for Violet's Friday afternoon rolled around in my mind. Halfway home but nowhere near an answer. Not even one.

"Friday, Violet supposedly sent a text to her husband saying she was going to stop by my house." My guess was she didn't send that text. She never made it to the Pittsfield copy store despite being very insistent that she needed to pick up the enlargements that day. Either she changed her mind or something prevented her from getting there. As far as I knew, no one had owned up to seeing or hearing from her on Friday night. If she left the Marlowe copy shop around five, she should have been at the Pittsfield shop well before it closed. But she never got there. Something happened between the time she left the copy shop and the time she should have gotten to Pittsfield.

And that thought led me back to Carl Henderson and how he managed to end up in the community garden. I was almost certain he and Violet had crossed paths. How else would he have ended up in the garden? Her key had been used to open the gate. But was that before or after he'd been killed? Perhaps Frank Wellman could shed some light on that part of the mystery. Surely he'd seen something while he was tilling the garden plots. I had to talk to him.

If I still had the photo enlargements, Sally might be able to help me make sense of those pictures. I found it hard to believe they'd shed any light on what happened to Violet or Carl Henderson. And then I smiled. What had the man at the copy shop said? The photo scans were online. All I needed was the order number.

A few minutes later, I pulled into my driveway, around the house, and into the old garage. I pulled the door closed and headed into the house.

As soon as I got inside, I checked for messages. There were none. I was disappointed but decided that on the upside, the mystery caller hadn't left another message and the hanger-upper, whoever it might be, had refrained from doing so.

I headed upstairs and once I'd settled in at my desk, I picked up the phone and dialed Frank Wellman's number.

The phone rang several times. Unlike prior calls, the answering machine didn't pick up. I wondered whether it had reached its message capacity and was about to hang up when a man's voice answered.

"Yup." He sounded as though he couldn't care less who might be calling.

"Mr. Wellman? You might not remember me, but this is Maggie Walker. I'm working with Violet Bloom on the community garden project here in Marlowe."

"I remember. If you're calling to have the tilling redone after what happened down there, I'll tell you right up front, I'll have to charge you again if you want me to do it again."

I was caught off guard. This was the last thing I'd expected. Well, maybe not the last. But pretty darned close.

"No, that's not why I'm calling. I've been trying to reach you since the weekend."

"Yeah, I know. Sorry. Didn't get around to returning your call." Well, at least he'd checked his messages. Maybe things were looking up.

"That's okay," I said. "I just wanted to ask you something."

"Sure. Ask away."

"Did Violet stop by the garden on Friday afternoon when you were working there?"

"Course she did. She's a funny one. Kept asking questions. How long was I going to be, would I wait till she got back. If she'd just let me get on with it, I'd've been done sooner."

"So, what did you tell her?"

"I told her 'bout how long it was going to take and that I wasn't about to sit around in a vacant lot waiting for her to do whatever it was she was going to do and get back there."

"And?"

"And she held out her hand and told me to give her the key she'd given me the day before to get in and to lock up after myself if she wasn't back by the time I was done."

"And did she come back?"

"Nope. I finished what I was paid to do, put the padlock back in place, and left. Oh, and in case you're wondering, no, there wasn't no boot sticking up out of the dirt when I left."

"And you didn't see her come back?"

"Nope."

"While you were there, did you see Carl Henderson by any chance?" I kept my fingers crossed. This could be the link I was searching for.

"The dead guy? Nope. Not dead or alive. Last time I laid eyes on him was a day or so before. That big black SUV of his was parked in the fire lane in the parking area off Center Street. I stopped in the hardware store and there he was, giving Howard Tucker a hard time. Man hasn't had enough grief over the last year, Henderson had to add to it."

"Did you hear what it was about?"

"I don't eavesdrop and don't gossip." From the tone of his voice I thought he might hang up the phone, but no telltale click followed.

"Mr. Wellman, maybe you overheard part of their discussion. You wouldn't be able to help it if their voices were raised."

A long pause left me wondering if he might not have hung up the phone after all. Then the sound of an exasperated breath came over the line. "Something about buying Tucker's property."

That was news. So Carl Henderson wanted to buy the hardware store. Or maybe the lot the community garden was on. Interesting, but it didn't get me anywhere.

"One more question. When Violet was at the garden, did she fill the holder by the message board with the brochures she brought with her?" Maybe I could narrow the time Violet dropped off those brochures. If she came back later, she might have run into Carl's killer.

"Brochures?"

"Yes, brochures promoting the community garden."

"Didn't see no brochures. But I wasn't paying much attention. She wasn't there more than five minutes, though she was flitting around the place. Didn't pay much attention to what she was doing. Asked her questions, then went on her way like her tail was on fire."

"Did she say where she was going?"

"Nope."

"Did you happen to see what direction she headed?"

"Nope. Didn't see her drive off. Car must've been around the front of the building."

I thanked him and hung up the phone. Our much-anticipated conversation didn't seem to have helped me any more than Violet's photos had.

I turned on my laptop and brought up the copy shop's website and entered the order number. There they were. I saved the images and a few minutes later, my printer had produced copies of the photos in Violet's order. They still looked like a lot of nothing to me. Maybe Sally could make sense of them.

I put the copies in a folder and headed to the pantry to find something to eat. I also needed to give Sally a call. I sure wasn't getting very far on my own. But before I picked up the phone, there was a knock at the front door. Sally stood there, a towel-covered tray in her hands.

"Well, this is a surprise," I said as I opened the door and motioned her inside. "You must be psychic."

"Not sure about that," she said, "but we'll see. I decided not to come empty-handed this time. I'd intended to invite you to breakfast, but you snuck out on me this morning. So, I figured afternoon tea would work as well."

I followed her to the sofa, where she set the tray on the coffee table.

"Voilà!" Sally pulled the towel aside with as much drama as she could manage without sending the tray's contents flying. The tray held an insulated pitcher, two mugs, two small plates, utensils, napkins, and a plate heaped with pastries.

"Wow" was all that I could manage to say.

"Chai?" Sally asked, obviously pleased with my reaction.

"Home-brewed?" I asked incredulously.

"But of course." Sally grinned. "Just call me Martha."

"Okay, Martha, to what do I owe this feast?"

"I wanted to get on your good side," she replied.

"What's that supposed to mean?" I asked as I broke off a piece of a scone and popped it in my mouth.

"I know you and you're planning to satisfy your curiosity, and I figure you've decided to do it without me."

"What makes you think that?" I tried to hide my guilt behind another, larger bite.

"Because of the way I reacted the other night. Scared for my family."

"You have every right to be," I insisted. "Someone killed Carl Henderson. Someone left a bloody shovel—probably the murder weapon—in your mulch pile. I'd say those are pretty darned good reasons to be concerned. Heck, I'd be shaking in my shoes if I were you. I'd lock the doors with my family inside and not leave until this was over with."

"Would you really?" Sally didn't sound convinced as she poured us each a steaming mug of chai. "I don't see you hiding. In fact, you weren't home when I called this morning. Running errands? Or snooping?"

"Same difference," I conceded.

"Then why would you think I'd hide?"

"To protect your family."

"I think the best way we can protect ourselves is knowing what's going on. So don't even think of trying to do this alone. We stick together and we'll come through this and get back to the real world, okay?"

"Okay," I agreed, though it was my turn to be less than totally convinced. Still, she had a point. There was safety in numbers, after all. And how could I shut out my best friend? Sally clinked her mug against mine.

"Deal." Sally took a sip, then grabbed a raspberry scone. "So, what were you up to when I arrived?"

"I was going over what I know—and don't know—about what happened Friday."

I gave Sally a rundown of my trip to the copy shop and my various conversations that afternoon, ending with the CliffsNotes version of my call to Frank Wellman and my conclusion that Violet returned to the community garden after the tilling was completed and somehow ran into Carl Henderson there, likely after the hardware store had closed for the day.

"So, you think Carl's killer did something to her?" Sally asked.

I shook my head. "I hope not. But I can't think of any other reasonable explanation for why she hasn't reappeared. If she was hiding, I would think she'd have contacted her family by now."

"Maybe she has," Sally suggested.

"No, I don't think so. Vic is worried sick about what might have happened to her. If he'd heard something I'm betting the news would spread like wildfire."

Sally took a sip of her tea.

"What about those photos Violet picked up at the post office on Friday? Do you think they have anything to do with all this?" Sally leaned forward, obviously hoping I was about to share information that was, unfortunately, still a mystery to me.

"I don't think they're related at all. I picked up the enlargements she ordered from the copy shop," I admitted, "but there's nothing identifiable in them. I dropped them off at the police department along with the note Violet left me." Sally's eyebrows shot up and she put down her mug. I tapped the file folder with the printouts lying on the coffee table. "Duplicates from what she uploaded for the enlargements. I think these are enlargements of the ones she picked up at the post office. I just don't think they tell us anything."

"If they are the same pictures, when did she order the enlargements you've got there?"

"My guess is she did that before I arrived for our meeting. She scanned the photos and then uploaded them to the copy shop's website and ordered enlargements—a rush order to be picked up later that afternoon."

"Why?"

I shook my head. "I have no idea. The enlargements are just scenery. Nothing special."

"Okay, so, assuming, like you said, she did that while she was waiting for you, after your meeting she runs her million errands and gets all mad that her pics are in Pittsfield, not at the Marlowe shop."

"Right, then she stopped at the hardware store. Or she went there first." I frowned. "Either way, something about that bothers me. I mean, she stops in to see Howie just to say thank you? Seems odd considering she was running around doing all these errands and low on time to get them done."

"Yeah," Sally agreed. "Violet is more the multitasking type. She'd save her thanks for later if she didn't have another reason to be there." Sally chewed thoughtfully on the rest of her scone. "Maybe she did have another reason to be there."

Did she? Something someone said was just out of reach in the back of my mind. I should have written it down.

"But Howie didn't mention anything else when I talked to him."

"Maybe he had a reason for not saying so."

Ah, suspicion, I thought, frowning more deeply. Was this what it had come to? Suspecting people I knew and thought I trusted? Niggling little doubts creeping in about anyone and everyone? Well, not everyone. I looked over at Sally. Never everyone.

It felt like I was making progress, but the pieces still weren't fitting together. With Sally's help I just might turn up something worth contacting that detective from the state police.

Sally nodded, following my train of thought. "So, you think she stopped at the garden, spoke to Frank, then went to the copy shop, got the brochures, and came back to the garden to drop them off and check up on what Frank did? But this was after he left, right?"

"Maybe. Or she went to the copy shop, then to the garden. The timeline is kind of muddled at that point. Howie didn't mention seeing her come back, but that's what I think must have happened. Either way, she's at the garden late in the afternoon. And I haven't found anyone who actually spoke to her after that and no one saw Carl Henderson there."

Chapter Eighteen

We'd gone around and around, trying to make something of the little information I'd been able to turn up and had only come up with more questions about what happened Friday night at the community garden.

"Now what?" Sally started putting our empty plates back on her tray.

"Ah," I said, pointing at Sally, "that's the ten-million-dollar question. I think it would be far too big a coincidence if something happened to her while she was on her way to Pittsfield. It had to have happened at the garden."

"But what? Did she see something she shouldn't have while she was there?"

"Well, she never picked up the enlargements, so yes, I'd say she never went to Pittsfield." I tapped on the folder.

"May I?" Sally made a grab for the envelope. "My curiosity is killing me. I know you said they're nothing special, but there must be some reason Violet was so upset when they weren't ready."

Sally pulled out the photos and flipped through them.

"Recognize anything?" I asked. "Nothing looked familiar to me. Nothing stands out. Nothing looks wrong. Nothing, nothing, nothing," I said, my frustration growing with each word. "I don't see how these are related to Violet's disappearance at all."

She fanned them out across the tabletop, a half-dozen glossy eight-by-tens showing lots of trees and bushes. Green. Brown. The occasional rock. A path. A couple showed hanging pink ribbons tied to branches or stakes in the ground. And trash. A plastic bag snagged in a tree. Beer cans and the remains of a campfire. Nothing that would mean anything.

"Maybe not. But maybe you should take a walk in your own backyard," she said simply.

"What's that supposed to mean?"

Sally laughed. "Nature Girl, you need to get back to nature. When was the last time you took a walk in the woods?"

"I have no idea what that has to do with anything, but I'll bite. The last time I took a walk in the woods, any woods, was about five or six years ago when Bryce and I did the Mount Greylock Ramble. That was his first and last nature excursion, and he made it clear he didn't approve of me rambling anywhere without him."

"That explains it." It was Sally's turn to tug on my curiosity.

"Explains what? Come on, Sally, if you've got something here, give it to me."

"This"—she pointed to the top picture, a toppled pile of stones that might have once been part of a stone fence—"is in the woods behind your house, about two minutes from your back door. This"—she flipped to the next picture showing a path cutting through the trees—"is the old wood road that runs along the back of our properties."

I took the pictures from her. "Are you sure? This just looks like trees and brush to me."

"You need to get away from cultivated spaces for a while. We've still got some daylight left. How about a walk in the woods?"

"Okay," I agreed with more than a little reluctance. "Maybe actually seeing these places will give me some idea about why these pictures were important to Violet."

I drained my mug, then walked it to the kitchen. Sally followed with the tray. By the time she'd rinsed the cups and put them in the sink, wrapped the remaining pastries, and put the last of the chai in the refrigerator, a face had appeared outside the back porch door. Sally's nine-year-old daughter was tapping on the glass to get our attention. Sally let her in.

"Hi, Maggie. Hey, Mom, did you forget I'm supposed to bring cupcakes to school tomorrow?"

By the look on Sally's face, she had indeed forgotten. "Oh, Maggie, I've got to go. I have to make thirty cupcakes tonight."

"No problem. Give me a call tomorrow. I've got to stick around the house to finish up a review I'm writing and email it in by noon, so I'll be ready for that walk in the woods when you are."

"Sounds good. I'll give you a call when lunch is ready, okay? We'll have a bite to eat and take a nice, long, hopefully informative walk afterward."

That night I tossed and turned and moved from one side of the bed to the other, trying to find a position comfortable enough to rest. I'd doze off and dream of trees scratching on the windows of the house, jolt awake, only to doze off again in the silence of the night to dreams of a dark and foreboding jungle beyond my backyard. When I finally did sleep more deeply, I wandered endless paths that led nowhere. I couldn't find my way home out of the once familiar woods. No one answered my calls for help, and trees crowded in on either side of the path until there was nowhere left to walk and no way to turn back.

In the morning I was tempted to sleep in, feeling more tired than when I'd gone to bed. But the echoes of the past night's dreams and countless unanswered questions haunted me. I forced myself to set them all aside and work on writing reviews of several gardening books I'd added to my bookshelf and could easily recommend. It went well and I finished far sooner than I expected. Once I'd sent the article on its way, I spent a few minutes checking online for anything new about Carl Henderson's murder. What I found rehashed what I already knew. It looked like I wasn't the only one whose questions weren't being answered.

I sat back in my chair and looked out at the woods behind my house. I probably wasn't the only one whose house had made it on Carl Henderson's must-have acquisition list. I'd seen him coming from Sally's house on Friday morning. But who else? Surely he wasn't trying to buy every house. So which ones?

If his plan was to develop the property behind our homes, mine made sense since my property included about five acres of woodland stretching behind Sally's, my, and my other next-door neighbor's houses. That included a part of what had been a dirt road 150 years ago. I supposed that might prove useful to him. It would certainly be easier to put a new road in along the course of the old road where boulders had been cleared and the terrain somewhat leveled.

If I remembered correctly, the old, now-overgrown wood road ran perpendicular to Elm and Spring Streets on either end, petering off in the woods behind the backyards of houses there. It must have been a connecting road in the days before those houses were built.

Libby Sheridan from Just Food lived right around the corner on Elm Street. I found myself smiling. I wondered if Carl Henderson had approached her about buying her house. Even if he hadn't, she might have heard about his acquiring property in our neighborhood.

I glanced at my watch. Nine thirty. Libby would probably be at work at Just Food. I had enough time to make a quick trip there to catch her before the noontime crowd arrived.

I grabbed my bag and was on my way.

Another sun-dappled morning greeted me as I drove the familiar streets to Just Food.

Luck was with me when I arrived. Libby was filling the self-serve pastry case as I walked in the door.

"Libby! Just the person I was hoping to see! Do you have a minute?"

She looked up from the container of individually wrapped pastries remaining in her cart. "Sure. But I need to get these stocked and get to work on some hazelnut tarts for this afternoon."

"This won't take long," I said and grabbed two ginger scones from her cart. "I was just wondering whether anyone's asked about buying your property."

She paused, her hand midway to the cart. "The store?"

"No, your house."

"Oh. Funny you should ask that." She began placing scones in a basket on the shelf. "Carl Henderson—may he rest in peace—made an offer a month ago. I told him no. He came back and spoke with my husband who also told him no."

I nodded. "Seems he was hot to purchase more than my house. Did he tell you why he wanted to buy your house?"

She shook her head and wagged a scone at me. "Nope. Very mysterious he was, so he must have had one of his schemes hatching."

"I heard it had something to do with the woods."

She popped the last package in place and leaned closer. "I heard he had some big project planned. Luxury condos, someone said. Can you imagine? Our beautiful woods traded for condos and manicured lawns?"

I shook my head.

"I also heard there were those in town hall who want the woods preserved, so he'd have needed some support to get past the zoning board."

"Any idea who?"

"Ms. Walker."

Drat! At the sound of the detective's voice I swung around, feeling very much like a squirrel caught at the bird feeder: I regretted being caught, not what I'd been doing.

Libby's eyes darted from the detective to me. "Those tarts aren't going to bake themselves," she said with an uneasy smile. "I'll catch you later," she said to me and escaped down the aisle toward the prep area in back of the store.

I had no such escape route open to me. Caught in the act of actively snooping, I turned to the detective and met his scowl with a smile.

"I see you've discovered one of our local treasures," I said. "Is it the farm-fresh eggs or the bakery goods?"

"Ms. Walker," he said again.

Either he was having trouble deciding what to say or knew exactly what he wanted to say but hadn't decided whether to do so here or haul me to the lockup. I'd won no brownie points being caught in the act.

"Look, Detective," I said, trying to look contrite. "I know what you said, but it occurred to me that—"

"That you could ask just a few questions."

What could I say? He had me there.

"Ms. Walker—"

"It's just that if Carl Henderson was set on carving a development out of the woods, it may not be just my property he was trying so hard to buy. He annoyed me, but maybe he was harder on someone else. I've heard his business practices were not always the most ethical."

"We are aware of Mr. Henderson's business practices and his latest venture. It might surprise you to know we're well versed in conducting these investigations." He held up a hand.

"You need to stop before you put yourself in danger or"—he paused—"legal difficulties."

"Right." I took a step back. Glanced at my watch. "Got it. I'm going to be late for an appointment." Without waiting for another word, because I was sure there would be further recriminations to come, I dropped the scones in the display basket and made for the door and home.

At a few minutes after twelve, the phone rang. Lunch was about to be served.

I hurried over to Sally's house, where the two of us made quick work of BLTs and iced tea.

By twelve thirty Sally had clipped on Dreyfus's leash, and we'd started into the woods by following a well-worn path from Sally's backyard. I'll admit to being a bit apprehensive despite the presence of Sally's golden retriever dancing along beside us. I know bad dreams are just a manifestation of our fears, but the woods seemed to close in around us as we followed the old wood road. Our houses and those of our neighbors were close by, but the newly leafed-out undergrowth blocked much of our view. In a few weeks, they would seem a world away.

Sally was perfectly at ease, reminding me that the path led in both directions past other backyards in neighborhoods similar to ours. In fact, she came here several times a week during warmer weather for some pleasant exercise for herself and Dreyfus and as often as she could during the winter months.

As soon as the peace of the woods closed in around us, I felt the tension begin to drain from me. I found myself wondering why I hadn't done this before. The trepidations of last night's dreams evaporated like an early morning mist. The sounds of birds in the trees around us calmed my nerves. At the unexpected streaking of a rabbit across our path, my sharp inhale of breath released in a wave of nervous laughter.

A pink ribbon fluttered from a branch a dozen feet off the old road in the direction of my property line. A short while later I spotted another one.

"What's with the pink ribbons?" I asked.

Sally stopped for a moment. "Those weren't here a week ago when Dreyfus and I walked this way." She looked back at the one we'd passed. "Looks like someone's doing a land survey. Those ribbons would show where the property line runs. The corners are marked by iron pins." She pointed into the woods. "There are more markers over that way. I wonder who would be surveying this area."

"Maybe the owner is planning on selling or subdividing," I suggested. "Rumor has it Carl Henderson was buying."

"I can't imagine anyone would try to build here. It's full of huge rocks. You can see some of them through that break in the trees. And there are dozens of springs in this area. Most of it would probably never pass a perc test to build on it today. The ground's just too wet in places or doesn't drain properly." She laughed. "Not to mention it's mostly landlocked—no way to access it from the street except across someone else's property."

What had Violet called Carl Henderson's new venture? Marlowe Estates? It sounded impressive. Big. Maybe the size-of-these-woods big?

We continued on along the overgrown road as it narrowed to little more than a path. Sally had taken possession of the envelope of photos and was leading the way to our first stop.

"Over there," she said as she pointed to a stack of stones visible behind a bunch of shrubs leafing out. The discarded beer cans visible in the photo were still present. "We'll have to make a trip back through here to pick up all the crap somebody's left behind," she said. "I wish I had thought to grab a trash bag on the way out the door."

I agreed. Even if it hadn't been near my property, I would have wanted to remove the trash. Its presence was offensive. Beside me, Dreyfus sniffed at the ground, straining at his leash.

"What's with him?"

Sally shrugged. "Anxious to chase a squirrel, I suppose. Everything fascinates him out here. I usually let him off his leash in the woods. He's very good about coming back when I call. On our way back I'll let him go."

"So, what do you think the point of the picture is?" I asked. "Why was Violet so hot to get enlargements of them?" I spotted a handful of bottle caps on what remained of a tic-tac-toe grid drawn into a patch of cleared ground. I picked them up and stuck them in my pocket. The larger pieces of trash would have to wait, but bits and pieces like this were easy enough to take back with us.

Sally shrugged. "Maybe she's as bothered as we are by people leaving their trash behind. You know, documentation of man's footprint in nature—the nonbiodegradable kind."

"Maybe," I said. Sure, Violet was adamant about the environment, but this? She'd be more likely to lie in wait and confront the offenders if she thought she could catch them. Violet was never shy about voicing her concerns, but I didn't believe that's what happened here. And what did any of this have to do with Carl Henderson? It must have been very important to her to have been so upset about the delay in getting the enlargements. What was she looking for that she couldn't see in the smaller prints? I walked up to a fallen wall and peered over it. A few of the larger stones had been pulled forward to serve as seats around a makeshift firepit. Disposable coffee cups with their plastic sippy caps and beer cans littered the ground. "Kids?"

"Who knows. There's no age limit on apathy." She glanced at the next picture in her stack. "We follow the deer path to the right. Up over that rise we'll find the remnants of a cellar hole."

"Is that what that is?" I asked, leaning forward to examine the picture more closely. "Are you sure? Doesn't look like a cellar to me."

"Not now it doesn't. But a hundred fifty years ago there were two or three houses back in these woods. Did you think people built these old stone walls among the trees?" She grinned. "This whole area was cleared and farmed all those years ago. Farms eventually got sold and the land broken up for housing. What's left was off the beaten path. No town water or access roads. Too rocky, too hilly, or too much ground-water from springs to be usable as building lots. Eventually the few houses that were here either burned or were torn down or fell down after being abandoned. The cellar holes—just big old holes with piled rocks for walls—began to fall in. Trees grew up and took over. Mother Nature doesn't let the land lie fallow for long."

"I had no idea," I said. "Watch out for that tree branch."

"I see it," Sally said, pushing it aside. Dreyfus tugged on his leash and danced beside us impatiently. Sally pointed to our right. "There."

We stood at the edge of the old cellar hole. Near the bottom among the discarded soda and beer cans and several plastic shopping bags captured by the branches of the trees and shrubs growing there, a blue tarp was snagged on something. Dreyfus began to whine. I stepped closer. Something was almost visible in the shadowy area beneath the tarp. Something partially concealed by its folds. I jumped back. An arm twisted at an odd angle peeked out from the edge of the tarp. My eyes followed the line of the sleeve of a muddied, all-too-familiar teal jacket to a shoulder.

Dreyfus barked furiously and bolted. His leash jerked from Sally's grip, and the dog leaped down the sloping side into the cellar hole. Dreyfus paced back and forth, now whining. The edge of the tarp slid to the side in the commotion, revealing a woman's body. She'd landed facedown, her arms and legs spread as though she were trying to stop her fall. Dark hair obscured her face, but somehow I knew.

I swallowed back the bile in my throat. "I think we've found Violet," I whispered. My vision blurred.

Sally stepped forward as if she intended to go down the banking into the hole. I caught her arm. "We have to get the police," I said.

"She might be alive," Sally insisted, pushing my fingers from her arm. I grabbed at her again and shook my head.

"Look at her. She hasn't been alive for a while." I took a step back from the edge, nudging Sally to come with me. She called Dreyfus to her side. "I left my phone at home. Do you have yours?" She shook her head, still staring in the direction of the body. "You go call the police. I'll wait here with her." I wanted nothing more than to be the one to run back to the house, but I was afraid Sally would go down there, try to help where it would do no good at all. The only thing we could do for Violet now was to preserve whatever evidence might be here. And that meant leaving her alone at the bottom of the cellar hole for a little while longer.

Sally agreed reluctantly. "Keep your eyes open. Not that I think anyone will come back here, but you never know." She pushed the leash into my hand. "Dreyfus, stay," she said firmly. And when the dog complied, "Good boy."

My breath caught in my throat. Could whoever did this still be around? I told myself it was unlikely. After all, Violet had been missing since Friday. Whoever did this had to be long gone by now. Dreyfus leaned against my leg. I reached down and clenched his warm fur in my fingers as though he were an anchor and I in danger of drifting off in the storm brewing inside me. My knees gave way. I sank to the ground and wrapped my arms around him, holding on for dear life. Kneeling there, I stared down at Violet Bloom's remains, listening to the harried crunch of last fall's leaves as Sally took off through the woods for home. The sound grew fainter and fainter until there was nothing left but the sound of the breeze rustling through the trees. And the birds. Somehow, they still felt the need to sing.

Chapter Nineteen

I heard sirens in the distance. I looked around, trying to determine the direction but failing miserably. Dreyfus shifted against my side. I grabbed his collar and rose to my feet, staring at breaks in the trees. I couldn't see a thing to indicate help was on its way. For all I knew, the sirens were headed toward some fender bender at the other side of the woods. My heart beat faster, drowning out the sounds around me. Dreyfus shifted nervously. I could barely hear the whining low in his throat. My pulse pounded in my ears; my breath came in ragged gulps. Was help about to come into view or was Violet's killer returning to the scene of his crime? I clenched Dreyfus's collar until my knuckles hurt.

I whirled around as a four-wheeler crested the rise on the old wood road. The uniformed officer riding it skidded to a stop as I ran to meet him, Dreyfus still at my side. The cavalry had arrived. I turned again at the sound of cracking branches and pounding footsteps. Two uniformed officers burst from a side path from the woods onto the road.

It took mere minutes for the officers to confirm what Sally must have reported, first listening to me babble a few incomplete and likely incoherent sentences while gesturing up the embankment to the cellar hole. One of the officers took a look into it.

As when I found Carl Henderson's body at the community garden, I was removed from the vicinity of the cellar hole and escorted down a path through the trees to a waiting cruiser, Dreyfus trotting by my side. The drive home was in silence; I was lost in my thoughts and the anonymous officer had nothing useful to say. He couldn't, or wouldn't, confirm it was Sally who'd called for help, and she was now safe and sound at home. I closed my eyes. Of course it was Sally. How else would they have known to come? I was letting my imagination run wild. I opened my eyes and watched the comforting sight of the oh-so-familiar front yards of my neighbors pass by. I nearly cried when we pulled into my driveway.

To my surprise, Sam himself waited there, along with the always concerned Officer Sinclair. Two police cruisers sat at the curb in front of my house. Sally came running as soon as I opened the door and stepped out. She wrapped her arms around me, and we followed the officer to the house, leaning into each other as we'd done as children.

We waited in my kitchen under Sinclair's watchful eye. The rest of the police presence had gone elsewhere. If Sinclair knew what was going on from her brief communications outside our earshot, she didn't let on.

The light outside was fading when Sally asked, "They aren't going to leave her out there all night, are they?"

Sinclair shook her head. "I'm sure we'll hear something soon. They'll have secured the scene and are gathering what evidence they can. They would have moved the remains as soon as they were able."

A few minutes later, I heard a car pull up out front. I wasn't sure I trusted my legs, so I stayed put. Whoever it was, the news couldn't be good. There was a sharp knock at the door. Officer Sinclair opened it and let in Detective Quinn. He wore a dour expression. I looked up at him, bracing myself for the questions to come. But it wasn't me he spoke to, not directly anyway.

"Ladies," he said to the room in general by way of greeting. He spoke to Officer Sinclair first. "Jan, could you take Mrs. Kendall back to her house? Her family is concerned, and I'd like to speak with Ms. Walker alone."

"Sure. Shall I stay there, or would you like me to come back here?" she asked as she waited for Sally by the door.

"Stay there. I expect to be there shortly."

A few minutes later, I sat on the sofa, my hands clasped tightly in my lap. A cup of now-cold tea sat untouched on the coffee table in front of me. As the door closed behind Sally and Sinclair, the detective moved the chair from the desk to the opposite side of the coffee table, its back facing me. He looped one leg over the chair and sat, crossing his arms over the back of the chair. An oddly casual posture for someone in a suit and such a don't-mess-with-me scowl on his face. I had no idea what was coming next, but I knew I wouldn't like it. I knotted the fringe on a pillow between my fingers.

"So, what the hell were you two doing out there?" he said softly.

I raised tear-filled eyes to meet his. I'm not generally into drama and I absolutely hate shedding tears in front of anyone, particularly someone who made me feel so vulnerable. But there they were, threatening to spill out, run down my cheeks, and take with them the last of my composure.

"Look, Ms. Walker," he said, his voice softening, "I know you've been asking questions around town. You need to understand—and I hope you do now—just how dangerous that can be. Someone has killed two people."

"I know that," I said, my voice barely a whisper. "Don't you think I know that?" I pulled in a ragged breath and clutched the pillow as though it were a life preserver.

He nodded. He sat quietly for a moment as if deciding the best way to approach me.

"We just wanted to find Violet," I said.

"Well, you did that."

I shook my head. My cheeks burned and I felt the tears begin to slip down them. "Not like this."

"I know this is hard," he said, his voice soft, concerned. "I need to know what you've done. Who you've spoken with. And how you happened upon that spot in the woods."

"I don't know where to begin." I shook my head and swiped a hand across my face.

He leaned over and pulled a handful of tissues from the box on the end table and held them out to me. I took them and blotted my face, then blew my nose.

By the time I'd composed myself, Quinn had pulled out his notepad and pen. "Let's start from the beginning. The last time you saw Violet Bloom was when?"

I couldn't believe he was back to that, but I answered the question, along with each of the others he asked, despite how many times or ways he asked each particular question.

When the subject came up of the missing photographs and the enlargements that had led us to Violet's body, his jaw clenched.

"You do realize that collecting those photos and then tramping through a crime scene might be considered tampering with evidence in an ongoing investigation."

I gaped at him. My cheeks burned again, but this time with anger and frustration. "We didn't know they were evidence at the time. We were just trying to retrace Violet's steps to figure out why she didn't show up at my house on Friday night like she said she was supposed to do. And I did leave the enlargements at the police station for Sam." He didn't look impressed by my argument. Maybe nothing I could say would matter to him, but I plowed on anyway. "The original pictures—at least what I think are the original pictures—we never saw them, but I think they'll be at Violet's house. As I said, I think she went home on Friday after she picked them up at the post office and scanned them to have the enlargements made. The originals might be at her house if she didn't have them with her when . . ." My voice faded to silence. All this time we'd been looking for her and she'd probably been there, cold and alone at the bottom of an old cellar hole in the woods a little more than a stone's throw from my back door.

"When she met the killer."

I nodded, unable to say the words.

"And what did you think the significance of the photographs was?"

I shook my head. "We didn't know. They seemed to be generic nature pictures. Sally recognized the places. So, we decided to take a walk in the woods and look at the locations where the pictures were taken. We thought by doing that we might figure out why Violet would want enlargements so urgently."

"And did you?"

"Figure out why they were important? No. Of course, we didn't get far. We found Violet at the site of the second photo."

He nodded, jotted in his notebook.

"And Mrs. Bloom's enlargements that you picked up at the copy shop, you gave all those photos to Chief Whitacker?"

I nodded. "I left them at the police station."

"How did you obtain the copies you referenced today?"

I could see no way to avoid the proverbial iceberg ahead. "I downloaded them from the copy shop's website, then printed them."

His face didn't turn red like Sam's would have, but his jaw tightened. I steeled myself for his response, but he simply asked, "And where are they now?"

"I think Sally has them. She was taking us to the locations in the pictures. They weren't familiar to me at all. But she walks her dog in the woods and recognized some of the places in the pictures." I blew my nose again and willed away the next wave of tears. "I remember she was holding them when we saw Violet down in that old cellar hole, but I can't remember what happened to them after that. I guess they just didn't seem important anymore."

"Had you been there, the old cellar hole, before?" he asked.

I shook my head. "I don't think so. If I've been there, it was a long time ago. I haven't been in the woods since I moved back here. There was always something else to do."

"And Mrs. Kendall, how often does she take walks in the woods?"

"I'm not sure. Often enough, I suppose. I know she takes her dog for walks along the old wood road. I've seen them cutting across the back of my yard sometimes to get to the path heading south toward the old quarry. I've never really paid enough attention to be able to tell you how often."

"Okay," he said, flipping back through the pages of his notepad. "Let's go back to Sunday."

And so it went on for another half hour. More questions, going over answers I'd given before. And nothing from him. Near the end of this latest interview, my wits began to return and so did my own questions. I asked them. He ignored them. Right up until he closed that annoying little notebook of his and slipped it in his pocket along with his pen. "What I'd like is to get your reassurance that you will refrain from any further amateur investigating in this case."

"I don't think you have to worry about that."

"But I do worry. I've now got two murders to investigate. I don't want to add any further complications. Do you understand?"

Oh, I understood all right. And I told him so. "I have no

intention of poking my nose anywhere near your investigation. I just want this over with."

"Good. Because there's nothing I'd like more than to be done with this, too."

When he left, I wandered from room to room, checking the locks on the windows, then checking to be sure the dead bolts and security chains were set on all the exterior doors. I tried to settle on the sofa but couldn't find anything to watch on the television. I went to the kitchen to fix something for dinner, not because I was hungry—I wondered if I'd ever be hungry again—but because fixing something to eat would give me something to do and it was the next best thing for comfort besides gardening. I stood in front of the open refrigerator until the chill reached my toes and sent a shiver through me. I closed the door and left the room. It was little more than an exercise in frustration. What I really wanted to do was go outside and pull some weeds. Maybe prune one of the slightly overgrown shrubs I'd put off. Or plant something. Or—or nothing. I shivered despite the warmth of the day. Gardening wasn't likely to be the calming influence I could usually count on. I'd probably spend more time looking over my shoulder or staring at the greenery at the edge of the woods than at my garden. Going outside was off the agenda for today at least, like it or not.

With nothing to do downstairs, I went upstairs and splashed cold water on my face. My reflection studied me from the bathroom mirror.

"How the heck did we get here?" I asked it. But mirror me

provided no more answers than the detective had. I turned away with a sigh.

I paused at the hall window and pulled the sheer curtain aside. Quinn's cruiser still waited patiently at the curb. I wondered how Sally was holding up under his questions. Would Dreyfus ever get to take a walk in the woods again? Or would Sally forever see it as the place Violet had been found and never go there after this? Would I feel comfortable enough to go back into the woods? I'd carefully avoided the street corner where my husband had been killed, never again going within a half dozen blocks of the place, and I hadn't been a witness to what had happened there or its aftermath.

I pressed my forehead against the cool windowpane. Of all the things to be thinking about. Why had my mind settled on Sally's dog's pleasure? Or Bryce's accident? Maybe because they were the least threatening thoughts I could find regarding all that had been going on lately outside the protective walls that surrounded me.

A movement caught my eye next door at Sally's house. The detective exited the front door and walked toward his vehicle. Before he got inside, he glanced in my direction. He spotted me in the window and nodded. A moment later he was gone. A moment after that, the phone rang.

I grabbed the upstairs extension. "Sally?"

"No," the whiny voice coming through the telephone said. "It's your cousin Simon Gleason. I'm calling to inquire as to what you intend to offer to settle my case."

You have got to be kidding me. I held the phone at arm's

length, gave it a dirty look, then carefully replaced the handset on the base. I shook my head and turned away. It began to ring again. I grabbed the receiver.

"Look, Simon," I began through gritted teeth.

"Hey, it's not Simon, so there's no need to snap at me," Sally said.

"I am so sorry," I pleaded. "Simon just called. I thought it was you because I saw that detective leave, but it was Simon asking about a settlement, of all things. I hung up and when the phone rang again, I thought it was him dialing back. I—"

"Okay, okay," Sally said. "You're forgiven. Actually, I needed that."

"You needed me to yell at you?" I said, thoroughly confused.

"No, silly, I needed a laugh, so I guess I have to thank your cousin Simon for that."

"Well, he has to be good for something."

"True enough." Sally laughed.

"So how are you?" I asked. "You looked white as the proverbial ghost. I thought you were going to keel over earlier."

"I felt like I was. I'm better now. A little anyway." I heard the sound of ice against glass. "Denny's across the room watching me like a hawk. As soon as Detective Quinn left, he sat me down and poured me a little liquid fortification."

"Brandy?"

"Nope. A little gin and tonic. Which is, by the way, the reason why I wasn't the person on the other end of the phone line when you picked up. So, why don't you come over and I'll have him make you one, too. I'm sure you could use it."

I considered the offer. A part of me hesitated to walk out the front door. A part of me said how silly that thought was. "Sure," I said finally, cutting off the internal argument. "I'll be over in a minute."

I locked the door behind me, started down the front walk, then went back and checked the door to make sure it really was locked. All this was getting under my skin and uncertainty had joined the paranoia I'd been feeling. I looked back at the house. I'd left lights on in the kitchen and parlor. To a passerby it would look like someone was home. At least I hoped so.

Chapter Twenty

Sally's teenaged daughter opened the door when I rang the bell and ushered me into the den, where Sally and her husband waited for me. So did a tall gin and tonic.

"I'll leave you two to chat," Denny said as he offered me his chair. "Just do me a favor and make it about what kind of tomatoes you're going to plant in the garden this year or the health benefits of dark chocolate and red wine, okay?"

When he'd left the room and I'd taken a long swallow of my drink and leaned back in the overstuffed chair, I smiled sadly at Sally.

"We kind of made a mess of things, didn't we?" I asked, taking another sip.

"How do you figure that?" she asked.

"We walked smack-dab into a crime scene today, in case that fact escaped you," I said, a bit more harshly than I'd intended. "At best, the police think we're meddlesome idiots; at worst, I'm a suspect in at least one murder. For all I know, maybe two now."

"And how is any of this our fault?" Sally said.

I stared at her in disbelief. I'd expected to find Sally shaken, as scared to venture outside as I was. Instead, she appeared almost defiant. Surely, she couldn't be considering continuing to poke around as we had been.

Sally went on, echoing my thoughts. "I know you're shaken up. I am, too, but I don't think this changes anything except to answer the question of where Violet was. All the time we were looking for her, she was there in the woods."

"Behind our houses."

"Maggie, it's not like she was in our backyards. Someone took her in the woods and hid her body there. Like they tried to hide Carl Henderson's. Only this time they did a better job of it."

"Do you think someone brought her body there to hide it or did they bring her there to kill her?"

"That's a very good question," Sally said as she leaned forward, picked up her glass, and swirled the ice and remaining liquid around as she thought about it.

"No," I added quickly. "Never mind. I don't want to know unless I can read about it in the paper. We can't help Violet anymore. I don't want to look into this. I don't want to skulk around behind Detective Quinn's back. I just want to go back to my life like it was a week ago."

"Not going to happen," Sally said as she finished her drink.

"Promise me," I pleaded, "that you'll let this go. I'm afraid for you as much as I am for me. Maybe the killer was just trying to scare us off leaving the shovel here, and if we stop asking questions, he'll leave us alone."

"And if he doesn't? I for one want this SOB put away. I want my children safe. I want to be able to walk the dog without

bringing pepper spray with me just in case we come upon someone else while we're out walking in the woods."

"You'll go back in the woods?"

"As soon as they tell me I can. Detective Quinn warned
us they'll be doing a search for evidence around the area and
where the other photos were taken. And he said it would be
prudent to stay out of the woods until they'd found whoever
did this. Which is fine with me, I guess, though I think ban-
ning walks in the woods in general is a bit much." She held up
a hand as I started to protest. "But once they tell me it's okay
to go back in the woods, Dreyfus and I will be back to our
routine."

Try as I might to dissuade her, Sally's resolve remained in-
tact.

As for me and my resolve to keep my nose out of the investigation into Violet Bloom's and Carl Henderson's deaths, it
remained firm as I returned home via the well-lit sidewalk and
front door to my house.

I couldn't get comfortable in bed that night, tossing and
turning as the moon rose and its reflected light cast discon-
certing shadows across the room. More than once, I got up
and looked out the windows toward the woods, wondering if
danger lurked there or if it had already finished its business.

By morning, clouds had moved in. I looked out at a decidedly
gray day. A heavy breeze rippled through the trees, and when I
opened the window, it felt like rain. Probably just as well. The
garden could use a deep drink of water, and I couldn't settle

on a single task that appealed to me. Too many dangling loose ends, I supposed. I needed to do something.

I sat at my desk, picked up the phone, and dialed Victor Bloom's number.

"Thank you for calling," he said after I'd offered my condolences. "They told me you'd been retracing Violet's steps, trying to find her. Thank you."

A chill rippled through me. The air around me felt cold as dusk on a winter's day. "I wish it would have done some good," I said.

"I know. But I'm glad you found her. I don't know what we would have done if this had gone on much longer. I kept hoping that she'd just walk in the door with some explanation about where she'd been, why she'd been gone without calling, but I knew there was such a small chance—" His voice broke. "I was so afraid something terrible had happened to her."

"I know," I said, not sure what to say. "Violet was a good friend. I'm going to miss her. She was the first new friend I made when I moved back here."

"I can't help but wonder about all the people she worked with," he continued softly as though he hadn't heard a word I'd said. Maybe he hadn't. "Who could have done this? She was involved in so many things. You know, everything interested her. People interested her. She always wanted to help, to be involved."

"Violet was a good person."

"She cared. Like you. I'm afraid that's what got her killed."

That sent a shiver down my back. Normally I would have been honored to be compared to Violet, but something led her to that spot in the woods. Something I didn't want to have in common with her. And yet by my actions, I did.

"We don't know that," I said. "We won't know why it happened until whoever did this to Violet and Carl Henderson is caught."

Silence on the phone line. For a moment, I thought he might have disconnected the call.

"Strange thing," Vic finally said, drawing out the words. "We'd been talking about Carl just a few days before she disappeared. He's buying—or I suppose I should say he was buying land on the other side of town—near your place, I think. Violet knew where. I don't remember where she heard it. I wasn't paying attention to the details, I guess. I told her I heard some of his dealings were a bit further into unethical territory than usual. Violet told me he'd been sniffing around the community garden, and she sent him packing. You know, Violet could be a handful when she wanted to be, though most of the time she preferred honey to vinegar to get her way. She just had no use for him. None at all."

"So it seemed," I said. "Do you think he had a particular reason to be there? Or if Violet had notes or documented anything? I'm sure the police are trying to put all the pieces together."

"Yes, they are," he said softly. "Sam Whitacker and that detective from the state police have her computer and files."

"I'm sure they're doing everything they can."

"Yes. Thank you," he said. "Thank you for working with her. She enjoyed it, you know. She said you stood up for what you believed without being a stubborn ass." He sniffled.

I said my goodbyes and sat back. I'd meant what I said about the police putting the pieces together. They were, after all, the professionals, as I'd been reminded on more than one occasion. But it was Sally and me who had found Violet. Maybe that would have to be enough.

I could feel last night's resolve crumbling. There were too many unanswered questions for me to do nothing.

I grabbed my bag. Maybe I could find some answers where it all began. Or at least clear my head. I got in my Jeep and drove to the community garden.

It looked more forlorn than ever. I got out and walked over to the fence. The yellow DO NOT CROSS tape had been removed. I could see a piece of it fluttering out of the top of the trash bin a few feet away. A car drove by on Center Street, but otherwise the downtown was eerily quiet. A few cars were parked at the end of the road by the diner. The neon light in the window was lit, so I knew Bill was on duty and it was open for business. Life went on in Marlowe, injured somehow by what had happened to Carl Henderson and now Violet Bloom, but life went on. I wondered how long it would take for things—to all outward appearances at least—to return to normal.

At the sound of approaching footsteps, I turned. Normal, it seemed, now included far too frequent run-ins with Catherine Whitacker. She, Rita Merchant, and Joyce Bellows were engaged in an animated conversation. Catherine paused a dozen paces away. Joyce jerked to a stop, but it took Rita a few moments to adjust her stride, and she ended up standing in the middle of the sidewalk several yards ahead of the other two. Whatever the topic of discussion, it had been put on hold.

"Hello, Margaret." With the forced grin that spread across her face, Catherine looked like the proverbial Cheshire cat. Too bad the grin wasn't the only part of her that remained. "My husband tells me that you've finally agreed to stop your amateurish efforts at investigating our recent unpleasantness."

Recent unpleasantness? Who was she kidding? With two murders and a killer on the loose, that had to qualify as the understatement of the year. I just looked at her without saying a word.

"Come on, now," Catherine cooed. "Nothing to say?"

"What do you want me to say, Catherine?" I was in no mood to be pleasant, though I still had sense enough to know anything I might say would definitely be used against me, even if she had to twist it like a pretzel to make it work.

Catherine shrugged. She was playing with me, like a cat with a captured mouse. Maybe if I played dead she'd go away. Or maybe she'd just yell "off with her head" and be done with it.

"It's really for the best, you know," Catherine said to her companions. "We've seen this before. People who think they know as well as the authorities and who just end up mucking up an investigation." She looked back at me. "It's good that you've decided to let common sense prevail." Catherine shook her head like she was the voice of reason dealing with a recalcitrant child. I half expected her to tsk-tsk next.

"Well," Rita said to Catherine as though I were nowhere to be seen, "some people think they know best. They think they have some right to meddle where they don't belong. But, tell me, isn't it a crime to interfere in an ongoing police investigation? Perhaps Margaret should think twice before indulging herself again." Rita droned on, but I wasn't listening.

"Well?" Catherine said, her tone sharp enough to cut through to my thoughts.

"Ah, what?"

She waved her hand toward the fence and the plots beyond it.

"I said, what are you going to do about the community garden? People have been calling and asking about it. I want to know who is taking over for Violet. I'd like to speak with them."

"Them would be me, of course," I said, more than a little irritated that she'd assume anyone but Violet's second-in-command would be managing the garden now. I took a step forward and was pleased to see Catherine take a small step back. I must have caught her off guard. "What you should do if someone inquires about the status of the community garden project is to refer them to me."

Catherine stood there with her mouth slightly open as if she wanted to speak but couldn't find the words. Rita had no such trouble.

"Really, Margaret, haven't you meddled enough?" Perhaps Catherine practiced ventriloquism.

"Meddled? This is hardly meddling. I worked with Violet on the project. I assisted her in the planning and coordination of the project. For the time being, at least, I will deal with getting the project back on course."

"Don't you think there might be some hesitancy to deal with you after what's happened?" Rita suggested. She placed her hand to her throat as though shocked at the thought of me taking charge.

"What? Why?" I could feel my face redden. *Be careful*, I warned myself silently, *don't let her bait you.*

"Well," Catherine said, looking ever so much like a barracuda about to order lunch. "You can't deny your rather unsavory encounters of late. It just casts the project in a poor light."

"The fact that I found a body—"

"Two bodies," Catherine corrected.

"I happened to be there when a body was uncovered at the community garden and was unlucky enough to come across Violet's body where it had been abandoned in the woods. And neither one has anything to do with the continuation of the community garden project. To suggest the entire project should be shelved is a disservice to the people who signed up to participate and an outright insult to Violet's memory. She worked hard to give this gift to our town and I for one intend to see it go forward. Now, if you'll excuse me, I have work to do."

With that I turned and stalked off toward the entrance to the garden. I half expected Catherine to follow, but instead I heard her say, "Let's go." As I looked back, the three of them were setting a good pace away from me.

I pulled my key ring out of my jacket pocket, then realized the padlock was gone. Of course it was. The police likely took it as evidence. Slowly I opened the gate, half expecting a nonexistent alarm to go off or to hear a voice behind me.

"Hey!"

I nearly jumped out of my skin. I whirled around to see Howie Tucker standing there.

"Sorry if I startled you," he said.

I put a hand to my chest and laughed. "Just a little jumpy, I guess."

"Busy place back here today," he said.

I looked around again at the now empty street. "Really? Seems awfully quiet, except for—" I nodded in the direction Catherine and her cohorts had taken.

"I mean relatively speaking. Once the police cleared out, not much of anyone has been back here. A few curious passersby. Chased them off. Don't need anyone mucking around in there. This morning three cars so far. Last night I saw Victor Bloom parked out here for nearly an hour. Called the police station and had them come over to make sure he was okay."

"What did they say?" I asked.

He shrugged. "Cruiser stopped over behind his car. Chief got out. They talked awhile. Both drove off."

I wondered what Victor Bloom was doing at the garden. Maybe he was just saying goodbye at a place she was happy, and it had nothing to do with Carl Henderson's body being found there.

"So, who else stopped by today?" I asked, then half wished I could take the words back. Why was I asking this? I knew better. A little curiosity led to a few questions led to . . . meddling. I could hear Catherine's voice in my head, see the smirk on her face. Margaret Walker couldn't control her urge to meddle.

"You, of course," Howie said, "that old couple, the Goodmans, I think their name is. And Bill from the diner, though he may have been just taking a walk. Oh, and a few other cars drove by real slow. Roy Hansen was in one of them. Must be anxious to get going again."

I glanced at the garden and its tilled soil, now trampled down in many places. And the plot Carl's body had been in, a gaping hole where its soil had been removed for examination. Beyond that, the rest of the vacant lot, and beyond that a backdrop of brick buildings, including the hardware store.

"I didn't realize you had such a bird's-eye view of the comings and goings here."

"I don't really. Usually, I don't notice unless the back door is open. I leave it that way sometimes to let the fresh air circulate. It's just that today has been so quiet I've been doing busy work around the store. Only so many shelves to be restocked and dusted. So, I read a bit, and I'll confess to staring out the windows now and then. Especially if it sounds like someone's passing by and might stop in." He laughed. "The exciting saga of a small business."

"Right. I hear you." I thought for a moment, then said, "I don't suppose you noticed Carl Henderson here on Friday."

"Nope." He continued to look straight ahead at the garden.

"Any other time?" I asked. "Did he come by, maybe pay particular attention to the work going on here?" I had a hard time believing Carl Henderson's death had anything to do with the community garden, but why on earth would he have ended up here?

"Nope," Howie said again. "Happy to say I rarely saw the guy. Didn't much like him."

"That seems to be a lot of people's reaction."

"Yeah. Thought about nothing but himself. Someone told me he got into it with Roy Hansen at the diner the other day."

"So I heard. It's funny you should mention that. Frank Wellman told me you had a disagreement with Carl Henderson recently." Maybe the nudge would get Howie to tell me something he'd seen or something useful about Carl Henderson. I just hoped he couldn't hear the air quotes in my voice when I said the word *disagreement*.

Color rose in Howie's face.

"I'm not proud of losing my temper with him. Carl had a way about him. Knew how to push people's buttons all right. Truth is, I didn't like the man. I know we're not supposed to speak ill of the dead, but there you have it. I avoided him and he knew it."

"What did he do to get under your skin that time?"

Howie turned to face me. "Not important anymore, is it?" He let out a huff. "Frank doesn't know what he's talking about. It was a disagreement is all. Look, I gotta get back to the store."

I led the way back out of the garden, closed the gate, and drove off. I looked back at Howie standing there, staring after me.

As I turned down the street leading to my house, I passed Sally and Denny's van heading out. I paused as their vehicle slowed and Sally's husband rolled down the driver's side window. Sally leaned across from the passenger side.

"We stopped at Vic's earlier to see if there was anything we could do to help, but it looked like an overflow crowd. I don't think he needs more people there at this point. We were feeling a little claustrophobic at home and are heading out to do some shopping. Care to come along? It might distract your thoughts for a while."

I shook my head. "I think I'm going to go over my notes. If we're going to get back on track and have a functional garden this year, we're going to need to get started real soon."

"Okay. I'll give you a call later. Good luck. Let me know if you need anything before then."

As I turned into my driveway, I decided that my first task would be to review all the information I had regarding the community garden and see what was missing. Once I had a list, I could check with Victor Bloom and ask to go through any of Violet's notes the police hadn't taken. Maybe I could ask the detective for a look. Nah. That wasn't likely to happen.

I'd gathered folders containing the various information Violet and I had collected for the garden project and had them spread across my dining room table when there was a knock at the door. Reluctantly I left the paperwork behind and answered it. To my surprise, a Marlowe police cruiser was parked in my driveway. Sam Whitacker stood at the door.

"May I come in?" he asked.

I hesitated.

After my most recent run-in at the garden with Catherine, I wasn't particularly interested in a chat with Sam, but there he was. The question in my mind at that moment was whether he was standing there because he had more case-related questions or it had something to do with Catherine. It turned out, neither was on his mind.

"Come on in," I said and waved him inside.

"I just want you to know that I know how difficult this has all been for you," he said as he took a seat on the arm of the overstuffed chair by the sofa. I settled in the other chair. "Since the day you got back into town, it seems like it's been one thing after another."

I stared at him. What was he up to?

"You make it sound like I'm living the life of Job."

He laughed and ran a hand through his hair. "Biblical references? I get that from Catherine and her friends. I didn't expect it from you."

"And you haven't heard it now. I couldn't quote you chapter and verse if my life depended on it. Catherine on the other hand is really good at that as I recall."

He nodded. "That she is." His eyes grew serious. "She's a good woman. She means the world to me. But she has a blind spot where you're concerned."

"So why are you telling me this?"

"Because you're a friend and I care about you. You know I've been worried about your involvement in this investigation."

I stood up, ready to argue.

"Wait." He held up a hand. "Let me finish. I've been worried. I don't want anything to happen to you. I know you have this need to know the answer when a question pops into your head. I remember all those hours you spent at the library in the summer, checking out what the camp counselors told us. The simple explanation was never enough for you. And God forbid you found out something that didn't jibe with what they'd said. I remember one time when a camp counselor was talking about moss growing on the north side of trees and how the slaves had used that to point their way north when they were escaping to freedom before the Civil War."

I nodded. "I spent hours at the library that night. They had to ask me to leave when the library closed. I started research-ing moss, then just went on from one subject to another. I had an entire table covered with books I'd pulled."

"And the next day you challenged him with a few tidbits you'd picked up doing your research. I can still remember the look on his face when he challenged you back and asked for your sources. You rattled off a half-dozen books and authors. Never saw anyone shut down so fast. Changed the subject at the speed of light." We both laughed at the memory.

"But you have to admit, it was interesting, and it just might have saved someone from getting hopelessly lost in the woods. Moss does grow on the north side of trees, since conditions are likely more favorable, but it doesn't grow only there. Imagine it on the east or west or south side of some trees and how turned around someone believing that myth might get." I shrugged. "I like to think I've developed a bit of tact in the years since then."

Sobering, he said, "Now you just go ahead and keep look-ing for those answers without always passing on what you know." He stepped closer and put his hands on my shoulders. "Look, we appreciate you turning over that note and the pic-tures, but next time just call and we'll take care of collecting evidence. It's what we do, remember? We will find out who did this, and you will know eventually."

"You mean I'll read it in the papers," I said dryly.

"No, I mean someone with inside knowledge, who will remain nameless, will let you know when we have some answers and you can let your guard down again. For now, just keep the doors locked and be careful. You've lived in the city. You know the drill."

"That I do. And you can rest assured I intend to play it safe from now on."

He held me at arm's length and gave me a long, searching look. "So, can I ask what you intend to do instead of questing for answers?"

"Gardening, of course. It's more than enough to keep me occupied this time of year. Between getting my own yard in shape and getting the community garden back on track, I've got more than enough to occupy my waking hours."

"Good," he said and gave me a peck on the forehead. Before he closed the door behind himself, Sam turned back and added, "I'm glad to hear that you've decided to stay out of police work and play it safe. Stay safe, Mags."

I sighed and put my palm against the closed door.

I wasn't trying to deceive him. I never intended to pursue a murderer. My friend was missing and a suspect in Carl Henderson's murder. Now I knew why she was a no-show at the garden on opening day. The answer wasn't one I wanted, and it left other unanswered questions. Lots of them. Questions that could prove dangerous to pursue. No, it shouldn't be difficult to keep my promise, knowing that there was someone out there who had killed twice. I had no doubt he—or she—could do so again. And I had obligations I needed to attend to.

But before I could get to any of that, my phone rang. I waited for the answering machine to pick up, then did a slow burn as I listened to—nothing, then the click of the phone. Before I could check the caller ID and solve the one mystery likely within my control, the phone rang again. I grabbed the phone, ready to give my mysterious caller an uncensored piece of my mind.

"Back door," Sally said. Before she severed the connection, I heard the rustling of leaves. She was taking the shortcut through the gap in the lilac hedge.

"So?" she asked when I met her at the back door.

"So what?" I countered, more than ready for a distraction as I put the kettle on and she settled in at the kitchen table. "How'd the shopping go?"

"Never mind the shopping. What was Chief Whitacker doing here? What did he have to say?"

"Not what you're hoping for," I said. "He's worried about me and my snooping."

"And?" Sally asked, sitting on the edge of the chair.

"And I told him I was done snooping. I mean it. I've had enough of dead bodies," I said, trying to convince myself as much as Sally. "I just want to return to something that feels normal." On cue, the kettle began to whistle.

Sally grabbed two mugs from the cupboard, added tea bags and hot water. "Sounds good to me. I'm not sure it's going to be that easy to do, but I'm with you." She raised a mug in mock salute. "Here's to the banishment of stressors large and small."

I nodded my agreement. "That includes my cousin Simon and whoever is leaving those mysterious messages on my answering machine, right?"

"Totally."

"Good, because they called again."

"It's probably a wrong number," Sally said. "At most someone's playing a stupid joke. Did you take care of subscribing to caller ID and installing the phone I gave you? It'll set your mind at ease."

I stared at the old rotary phone on the wall. Sally was probably right. I was letting this bother me way too much. Finding out the calls were just random nonsense would do me good. But what if it was more than a prank?

"I did. It's on the desk in the living room by the answering machine. But I love that old rotary phone. The sound it makes takes me back to all the time I spent here growing up."

"Look, I know you love the old stuff. But at least the next time you get one of those calls you'll be ready."

"There was one just before you called."

Sally was halfway to her feet. "Who was it? Did you check?"

"Not yet."

"Well?" prompted Sally. "Come on!"

As we reached the desk, the phone rang. I glanced at the display and picked up the handset. "Hello?"

Nothing.

"Hello?" I said with a bit more annoyance than I intended. Click.

"You've got to be kidding me," I said, giving a dirty look to the receiver but not putting it back in place.

"What's wrong? Didn't it work?" Sally looked confused.

I hoped I didn't look as angry as I felt.

"Oh, it worked all right. And I know that number by heart. It's been on my answering machine more times than those stupid anonymous calls."

"What number?" Sally asked, stepping closer. "Who?"

"Cousin Simon," I said through gritted teeth as I dialed the number. I had no idea what I was going to say, but whatever his reason, that was the last prank call he was making to my phone.

The line rang. And rang. I could picture him looking at his undoubtedly technologically relevant phone with its caller ID and trying to decide whether he should answer a call from me following so closely after his latest hang-up. Then the ringing stopped. A moment later his outgoing voicemail message kicked in.

"I'm currently not available to take your call. Leave a message. I will return your call if necessary."

I took a deep breath. "I know what you've been doing. This ends now. No more hang-ups. No more creepy voicemail messages. Nothing. If you call again, you'd better identify yourself and leave a proper message—though if you never call again, I'm just fine with that. If you pull another of these stupid pranks, I'm going to the police to pursue a criminal complaint. Got that? Criminal complaint for harassment. And another thing: I know you knew Carl Henderson. I don't know what you two were planning, but it better stop. Got it?" Then I banged the handset onto the base much harder than I intended, making a sound that had me checking for cracks in the plastic.

"Easy, girl," Sally said. She took the handset from me and carefully put it in its proper place. "I'm glad that message wasn't for me. Simon's probably shaking in his shoes."

I retraced my steps, let out a huff, and sat down hard on a kitchen chair. "I hope he is. Maybe now he'll leave me alone."

"I wonder what he was trying to prove?" Sally said from the stove, where she was putting on the kettle to reheat the remaining water.

I shook my head. "Not a clue. Maybe trying to convince me to sell so he could claim a part of the sale price? I don't know where his twisted train of thought led. I just hope now that he knows that I know, it's over and done with."

That night, to my utter amazement, I managed to contact Frank Wellman on my first attempt and arranged for him to rework the garden plots before the coming weekend, replacing the missing soil when he did so. I'd decided not to get a new lock for the garden gate, so he could complete the tilling at his convenience. Then I got back on the phone and contacted all the gardeners who'd signed up for plots at the garden and re-scheduled opening day for the next Saturday. My last task was to call the nursery and add to the delivery of my own seedlings and a few yards of bark mulch on Friday.

That done, I couldn't resist the urge to go online and check for updates on finding who killed Violet and Carl Henderson. I found articles with little to say. No news was definitely not good news. Frustrated, I headed off to bed, hoping for an un-interrupted night's sleep.

Chapter Twenty-One

Saturday arrived full of sunshine and possibilities. I headed out the door with my backpack in hand and a smile on my face. I had my to-do list completed and felt pretty good about abandoning my own garden for the day. Mother Nature was certainly in the mood to christen the community garden. There was enough of a breeze to keep things from getting overheated (not to mention keeping annoying insects at bay). Showers were predicted for later in the afternoon, which suited me just fine. If Mother Nature would water the newly planted beds, all the better.

As my front door closed behind me, I waved to Sally, who was weeding the rose bed in front of her house. Sally's golden retriever, Dreyfus, rolled on the grass and thumped his tail in greeting. I hoisted my backpack on my shoulder and grabbed a tray of tomato seedlings delivered by the nursery the day before. I took it around back and loaded it in the Jeep. It didn't take long before everything I'd need was stowed and ready to go. As I retraced my route from that dreadful Saturday just one week before, I flashed back to that morning. It seemed so much longer ago. Funny how the mind could play tricks.

Maybe relegating traumatic events to the distant past made them more bearable. Maybe.

As I neared Tucker's Hardware Store and the turn to the community garden, my stomach clenched but, as I'd seen during a brief stop on Thursday, it all looked normal. Fresh soil replaced that removed from the plot where Carl Henderson had been found and all the plots had been freshly tilled. All signs of the police presence had been removed. Everything should be fine today, yet that nagging concern lingered.

When I arrived at the garden, anxious gardeners waited in small groups along the fence line. Some of them were well-known to me, some I'd spoken to only in passing. Violet had been their contact when signing up for the project. Roy Hansen waited, uncharacteristically quiet, in the background. This time no one crowded by the entrance gate. I couldn't say I blamed them. If I hadn't been here since the police had removed the crime scene tape, I'd have hesitated a bit, too. I made a point to say hello to the less familiar faces first, then offered a quick greeting to the others before opening the gate.

"Well, what do you say we get started," I called out to the group a few minutes later when my watch read nine, our designated start time for the day. In twos and threes, they pressed forward and through the gate. I handed out the plot assignments again. No one grumbled that it had been done before. No one commented on the circumstances that necessitated planting the garden a week late. Not even Roy Hansen. He took the sheet of paper from my hand and proceeded through the gate with the others.

Some pulled garden carts with tools and plants. Some traveled more lightly with seed packets and rakes and shovels. Everyone got to work as I planted some colorful annuals in the bed Carl Henderson had been found in. I suspected Roy was a bit relieved I'd assigned him a different set of plots.

Before long, things changed as the gardeners relaxed into their planting tasks. I tended my own plot, kneeling at the edge of the garden bed and using a trowel to dig trenches. Next, I gently stripped the bottom leaves off each tomato seedling and laid one down in each trench, carefully bending the top of the stem so that only a few leaves on the top of the plant were exposed. I scooped the rich soil in my gloved hands and carefully tamped it in around the young plants. Soon roots would sprout from the segment of stem I'd buried, providing a stronger foundation for the plants. With five different heirloom varieties of tomato in the ground, I inserted a spiral stake beside each one. I stood back and smiled, admiring my handiwork. The tall stakes looked pretty funny with the tiny tomato plants reaching for the first twist of the spirals, but I knew it wouldn't be long now that the weather had warmed until the tomatoes spurted into growth. I could almost taste Mortgage Lifter sliced into a salad with other veggies on my planting list.

I spent the next half hour working my way around the edges of my plot planting marigolds. I'd started them from seed during late winter. Now the young plants were covered with buds. Soon their flowers would attract pollinators and other beneficial insects to my nearby veggie plants. As an added bonus, the flowers were edible. Though I hadn't added them to my salads yet, I'd give them a try this year. I'd grown them organically and avoided sprays of any kind, so I wouldn't need to worry about any chemical residue on the petals.

I stood up to stretch my legs and unkink my back. I was searching my backpack for my phone to snap some photos of the garden when I felt a hand on my arm.

I must have started because Joyce Bellows, vice president of the Marlowe Garden Club, pulled back her hand as if she'd been burned.

"I'm so sorry," she sputtered. "I didn't mean to startle you." She looked as shocked as I felt. Her white curls were covered with a flowered bandana today and she wore an oversized button-down shirt over a tee shirt and white jeans.

"It's okay." I adopted a neutral expression, unsure what to expect. "Something I can do for you?"

She hesitated, glancing down at my patchwork of plants. "Nice garden," she said.

"Yes, it is," I replied. I tried on a small smile. She was flying solo today, and if she had something to say, it might be worth hearing.

Joyce shuffled her feet. "I'm here to pick up my daughter and give her a ride home. I was hoping to get a chance to talk to you." She sighed. "Look, I just wanted to say I'm sorry." She reached out her hand again and laid it on my arm.

I was confused by her apology and said so.

"But I do have something to apologize for. I should have said something, but I didn't Sunday at the picnic. Then at the diner. And here."

She looked as though she expected a response, but I didn't have one and I had no idea where this conversation was headed.

"I just stood there. Sat there. As she said those terrible things to you."

"Catherine?"

She nodded.

"It's okay," I said, even though I couldn't recall a single occasion when *okay* applied where Catherine was concerned.

"No, it's not," she insisted, giving my arm a little squeeze before releasing it. "I was taught better than that. When I saw you here I had to talk to you."

"Away from Catherine?"

She nodded. "And Rita. I'm ashamed to say it, but—"

I waited for her to continue.

"Could we sit down for a few minutes and chat?" Joyce nodded toward one of the benches along the edge of the garden where fruit trees would be planted.

We took a seat and sat in silence for a minute or two, watching the gardeners at work, apparently neither of us sure what to say. She had, after all, apologized. I'd accepted. End of story. Or was it?

"I don't think I've really had a chance to say how sorry I was when your grandmother passed. She would be so pleased you decided to stay."

"There never was any question about that," I said.

She smiled and nodded. "I'm glad to hear that. You've done some nice work on her garden, at least what I've seen driving by. I remember how lovely the gardens in back were. You should think about joining the garden club."

Well, that was unexpected. Before I could think of a polite

response, she continued. "Rita isn't the entire club. We have quite a few new members. You might be surprised at what you find." She laughed to herself. "We love our gardens, but there's no shortage of tasty snacks and local chitchat. There was even talk at the last meeting about possible development of the land behind your house."

"The woods?" I asked, very interested in this particular topic of local chitchat.

Joyce nodded.

It seems everyone in town knew about Carl Henderson's plans. But why my house? The woods had to be thirty or forty acres at least. Had he purchased other parcels in the area?

"Do you know who?" I asked.

Joyce shook her head. "There were a few names tossed about, but no one seemed to know anything for sure."

"Was Carl Henderson one of those names?"

"Oh, yes, he was indeed. There was quite the discussion about whether he'd actually get his plan off the ground since it was so grand, though I expect it wasn't grand at all but grew with people's speculation."

But it didn't need to be grand to draw pushback, especially from those whose homes he was trying to acquire, perhaps by less-than-scrupulous means.

"Who else did they mention?" I asked. "Anyone who might want to stop him?"

"Oh, I don't recall. Once his name came up, there was so much talk about what he might be planning, it was hard to keep track. I do recall Lillian Button said her husband—you know Bill from the diner, don't you? Anyway, she said he said someone was going to squash Carl like a bug if he dared bring his project before the planning board."

"Did she say who that was?"

Joyce thought for a moment. "No, I don't think so. If she did, I don't recall. Like I said, there was a lot being said." Across the way, one of the gardeners waved at Joyce. "Well, it looks like my daughter is ready to leave. She has to work this afternoon but wanted to get some planting done here this morning. It's been lovely talking with you, Maggie. I do hope you'll at least come to one of our meetings. I think you'd find some kindred spirits in the garden club."

I told her I'd think about it. I had to admit I'd been judging every member by Rita's and Catherine's attitudes toward me. Maybe once Violet and Carl Henderson's killer had been found, things would quiet down and I could take in a meeting of the Marlowe Garden Club.

Around noon, boxed lunches arrived from the diner (a surprise arranged by Violet as a gift to the first of the community gardeners). I passed them out and we set up a makeshift picnic area in the pathways between the garden beds with various folding chairs the gardeners had brought with them. Soon they were recounting their experiences with Violet not only during the planning stages of the community garden but in other projects in years past as well.

"I remember the day Violet and Vic got married," Mrs. Goodman said. "Do you remember, Jacob? We were on our way to pick up our granddaughter at the bus bringing her back from summer camp and we got a flat tire when we were about a half mile away. We had a spare but hadn't gotten a hundred feet further down the road when we realized a second tire was going flat."

"Must've run into a bad patch of something," her husband added. "I was fit to be tied and Helen was worried Rachel would be left standing there alone at the bus stop."

"Then along comes this beautiful white limo. It drives past, then stops and backs up. Back window rolls down and there's Violet all decked out like a princess."

"Driver says he'll call a tow truck when they get to the church. Not everyone carried a cell phone in those days," Jacob said, "but when Helen told Violet why we were so worried, she invites us into the limo."

Helen continued. "Jacob sits up with the driver and there I am sitting with all these pretty girls in their frilly dresses drinking champagne on the way to pick up our granddaughter. Violet was a tad late for her wedding, but she earned a place in our hearts that day."

Jacob nodded. "And a beautiful wedding it was," he said. "Never expected her to pick up Rachel and invite us along for the wedding. But she did."

"She was like that," another gardener observed. "And she didn't much care what people thought either. If something needed to be done, she found a way to do it. I remember when funding was cut for the food pantry. The lease was up and there was no money to renew it and the landlord—good old Carl Henderson—not meaning to speak ill of the dead—wouldn't give an inch to help us keep it open. He said it was just business. Violet worked like crazy to find a new location and organized volunteers to get what little food was left at that point packed and moved. She headed the committee that held all sorts of fundraisers and food drives to keep the food pantry afloat. She was an amazing woman."

Heads bobbed in agreement.

"Wouldn't want to cross her, though," Roy Hansen said from his chair at the edge of the group. "She never forgot any wrongs."

"Yeah, I heard Sue at the post office has been avoiding her. Violet's been after her to keep a permanent donation bin for the food pantry there. Sue said no but Violet keeps asking every time she's there, so now Sue is never in when Violet stops by. Well, I guess that's all in the past now," one of the gardeners added.

"Come on," another said, "you're making Violet sound vindictive. Violet was not vindictive."

"No, but she had the memory of an elephant."

More nodding heads.

"I don't understand," I said. "Surely you're not saying Violet would deliberately go after someone for some kind of revenge if they did or didn't do something in the past that annoyed her."

"Violet Bloom had a great sense of what was right and what was wrong," Jacob Goodman said. "Carl Henderson is the perfect example. He wanted to be on the town council in the worst way. Never got elected even though he ran for a seat in every election for more than ten years. But Violet made sure no one forgot that he put profits above people when the food pantry almost went under. Once she was really obvious about it when there was just one extra candidate for the counsel and the odds were he'd get in. She wrote a letter to the editor asking people to vote their consciences and remember the importance of supporting the community on projects like the food pantry rather than pursuing individual interests at the expense of the community. Anyone who didn't know what she was doing heard about it when people passed along those juicy tidbits as the election grew closer. Usually, though, she just worked for someone else's election rather than against him."

There was bad blood between Violet and Carl Henderson. Wasn't it ironic that the same person probably killed both of them? Who that was remained a mystery. The police certainly were still investigating, but that didn't stop me from silently speculating.

Howie Tucker had come out of the store's back door earlier to watch the goings-on at the garden. He'd emerged again and sent a wave in our direction. I waved back, wondering what he'd seen. He claimed nothing, but I found that hard to believe. But why would he keep quiet? He would if he wasn't just an observer. He'd argued with Carl Henderson. If Carl had come back while Violet was there, she might have seen something more than verbal jousting. The logistics of it all escaped me. Violet was unlikely to be at the garden after dark. Perhaps she'd crossed paths with Carl elsewhere. But then why come back here? And how did Violet end up in the woods?

"Do you think Carl had anything to do with Violet's death?" one woman asked.

"Or the other way around," Roy added with a chuckle.

"Humph. Wouldn't put it past him," Helen said.

"Now just because he snookered you in that land sale a couple years ago doesn't mean he'd hurt anyone," Roy said, tongue firmly in cheek.

"There are many ways to hurt someone," Jacob replied.

"You know what I mean," Roy muttered.

And then there was Roy. He'd come to blows with Carl. It wasn't difficult to imagine something similar happening at the garden. He claimed to have been home with his wife, but was he?

"I heard he was after your property, too," Roy said in my general direction. "Whatever he had planned, be glad it's not going to happen now that he ended up dead. You might want to thank whoever put a stop to him."

Heads turned in toward Roy. There was silence as everyone chewed on those thoughts and the last of their lunches. One by one they went back to their plots and returned to work.

A few hours later, I stood outside the garden's gate, waving goodbye to the last of the gardeners. I stored my tools in the shed and closed the gate.

Behind me twenty plots had been planted, each to its owner's preferences. A few used square-foot gardening techniques while others utilized more traditional rows. Others didn't seem to have any plan at all. Many of the gardeners had applied some sort of mulch on their plots to combat weeds while, despite my suggestions, others had not. The latter, I knew, would be spending a lot of time pulling weeds if they wanted to keep the uninvited plants at bay. It was all a grand experiment with each gardener ready to give it his or her best efforts. I smiled at how they'd all come together and wished fervently that Violet could have seen this. Then again, Violet was there in spirit as she'd left a piece of herself behind in its planning even if she couldn't be there for its planting. And just maybe she was watching us and smiling at the crop of gardeners she'd grown.

Chapter Twenty-Two

I took my time on the drive home. I was tired and sweaty and feeling thoroughly fine. Nothing like a day digging in the dirt to make the world feel like a better place. I was taking it on the run, singing along to REO Speedwagon as I turned onto my street.

My mood evaporated at the sight of the state police cruiser parked in front of Sally's house. Now what?

As I crossed the yard, Sally's door opened, and Detective Quinn stepped out and began to walk toward me. By the time I'd reached the driveway, Sally's husband had run out of the house and passed the detective.

"Where have you been?" Denny grabbed my arm. "I've been calling for hours. Your cell's going directly to voicemail."

"Hey!" I said, pushing his hand away. "That hurts! What the heck is the matter with you? I forgot my phone this morning. What's going on?"

"Have you seen her?"

"Her who?" I looked at the detective who now stood behind Denny, his hand resting lightly on the other man's shoulder. My stomach lurched.

"Ms. Walker, would you come inside?"

I took an involuntary step back, fear welling up inside me. "What's happened?"

"Sally, she—she—" Denny sputtered to a stop.

"Sally!" I cried. "What's happened? Tell me!"

"Inside, please." The detective motioned to Sally's front door. "I'll explain everything once we get inside."

I followed them, dreading what was to come. Officer Sinclair was waiting there, all police business today. As usual, her expression gave nothing away. I looked around the quiet living room. Everything was in its place. But no Sally. My stomach clenched. A television was playing somewhere upstairs. Must be the kids. Sheer curtains fluttered in the breeze through the open dining room windows. Somewhere on the block, someone was mowing his lawn. So normal. So wrong.

"Where's Sally?" I asked quietly.

"Why don't we sit down?" the detective suggested, gesturing to the dining room table. So, we sat around the table, facing one another. Denny had the same harrowed expression in his eyes that Violet's husband had worn. My heart beat so hard I could hardly think through its insistent rhythm. I clenched my hands together on my lap. And I asked again, forcing myself to be calm. "Please, tell me what's happened. Has something happened to Sally?"

"I wish I had something to tell you," the detective said. "We—"

"She's gone," Denny blurted out. "She's not answering her phone. She just disappeared."

"But I just saw her this morning," I said. Maybe there'd been a mistake. *Please let there be a mistake.*

"Did she say where she was going today?" Detective Quinn asked.

I shook my head. "We didn't really speak. I was on my way to the garden. We had our planting day today."

"You were there all day?"

"Yes, of course I was there all day. I left around eight thirty this morning. I drove to the garden, spent the day working there, and drove home."

"Who else was there?" he asked.

Laughter drifted down the stairs and into the dining room. At least the children weren't aware yet that something was terribly wrong.

"What difference does that make?" Denny demanded. "Who cares who did what at that damned garden. My wife is missing. You've got to do something." He stood up, pushing his chair back so suddenly it fell over, bounced, and slid across the floor. Upstairs the laughter abruptly stopped.

"Denny," I said, reaching out for him. "Please, sit down. You'll frighten them."

The anger seemed to drain out of him as he glanced toward the stairs. He picked up the chair, righted it, and sat down. "Please," he said simply, looking between the two of us. "Do something. Find her."

"We don't know that anything's happened," the detective began.

"Of course we do," Denny said, this time controlling the emotional discharge.

"Could someone please tell me what you do know?" I said.

"We don't know much so far," Detective Quinn began again. "Mr. Kendall left early this morning to take the children fishing at the lake."

"About seven."

"Mrs. Kendall was cleaning up the breakfast dishes at the time and mentioned taking the dog to the dog wash. No one there remembers seeing her, and her car was in the driveway when Mr. Kendall and the children returned home. Mrs. Kendall and their dog were gone."

"Are you sure she didn't say where she was going?" Denny asked me.

I shook my head. "No, we really didn't talk. Just a wave. I was in a hurry to get to the garden. Sally was in the front yard weeding. Dreyfus was keeping her company."

Denny looked crestfallen. The detective pursed his lips and tapped on the notebook. Behind him, Officer Sinclair remained silent.

"Wherever she went, she either went on foot or someone else drove," he said. "Can you think of anywhere she might have gone? Was she expecting any visitors?"

Denny looked up, panic in his eyes. "You don't think that whoever killed Violet came here?" He turned accusing eyes at me. "She said you'd sworn off doing any more snooping."

My eyes darted back and forth between the men. "And we haven't. After we found Violet, we even avoided talking about what happened. Honestly, I don't even want to let myself think about it."

"Okay, so you've kept out of it, but can you say the same

for Mrs. Kendall? Are you sure she didn't pursue it on her own?" the detective asked.

Denny answered for me. "Sally wouldn't, not without Maggie. She always says Maggie is insufferably curious, then she laughs and says she means that in the nicest possible way. There is no way she would even consider doing anything on her own." He stared at me, his face expressionless. Except for his eyes. There were unspoken accusations there.

Once again, I felt myself accused, but this time, I wasn't concerned with defending myself. All I could think of was how to find my friend. And that meant letting my need for answers out of its box.

"She must have left on her own," I said, thinking out loud. "If she didn't, there'd be some sign. Everything looks normal." I glanced around the room, waited for a contradiction to my assumption.

"That's true," the detective said. "There's no sign she left involuntarily. Normally, we wouldn't be concerned that a grown woman went out without telling anyone. It's just that under the circumstances, we're being particularly cautious."

I nodded. Caution was good. In fact, it was Sally's caution that led me to believe this must be some kind of mistake, because she wouldn't go out alone after all that had happened. "Unless she didn't go out alone." I finished my thought out loud. Silence hung in the air as the room closed around us.

"You think she's with someone. Someone who maybe took her," Denny said in a low, controlled voice.

"No, no. I mean where would she go with Dreyfus?" I asked.

Denny shrugged. "I don't know. His leash is gone. Sally must have taken him somewhere."

"It's quite possible Mrs. Kendall simply took the dog for a walk," Detective Quinn said. "Perhaps she met someone and has been delayed." He was obviously trying to sound reassuring but failed miserably. From his expression, Denny wasn't buying being sidetracked as a plausible reason for Sally's absence. Neither was I.

"The local police are keeping an eye out for her. With any luck, she'll walk in the door and ask what all the fuss is about," the detective continued.

I bit my lip. I might as well say what I was thinking. There was no time to hope for the best. "You might want to have them do more than that."

"And why's that?" Denny looked more worried than before. "Like he said, maybe she'll just walk in the door anytime now and we'll all have a good laugh over this." His forced chuckle fell flat.

What I was about to say would probably make it worse for Denny, but he wasn't my primary concern. Finding Sally and making sure she was safe was. I plunged on. "Is the area where Violet's body was found still restricted?" I asked.

A crease formed between the detective's eyebrows. "No. We've got everything we need. Why?"

"Because Sally made the comment that once she was allowed back in the woods she intended to go back to her usual routine."

"Which would be?"

Denny brightened. "She used to walk the dog in the woods

two or three times a week. She said it made for a more interesting walk for both of them. She probably really is just walking Dreyfus." He looked hopeful. I wasn't.

"Well, then, that's probably what happened," Detective Quinn said. "Still, it wouldn't hurt to take a look around." Whether Quinn was trying to calm the distraught husband or buying into the idea, I couldn't tell. He started to get up as one of the children came down the stairs.

"Hey, Dad," nine-year-old Polly said. "Dreyfus is barking out by the woods. Mrs. Peterson is going to complain again." We all turned our attention toward the back door. Sure enough, I could hear the golden's insistent bark.

"See, she's back. It was all a mistake," Denny said, smiling, and headed for the door.

But Sally wasn't back. Dreyfus stood at the edge of the woods, doing a doggie dance, alternately barking at the house and the trees. Patches of dirt and bits of leaves and twigs clung to his fur as though he'd been rolling around on the forest floor, something Sally had tried to discourage during their walks. I hoped that's all this was, that Sally had taken Dreyfus for a walk, twisted her ankle, and was waiting for us to help her home. I sprinted toward the tree line.

Detective Quinn reached Dreyfus first. He grabbed for the leash flopping on the ground behind Dreyfus just as he started to dart away back toward the woods. Quinn put a stop to that with a quick tug and a low command.

I reached them, breathless, Denny a few yards ahead of me. He stood staring at the leash the detective held in his hand.

Half its length was missing. Quinn held up the ragged end, staring at it. He cursed under his breath.

"What the—" Denny began.

Detective Quinn turned the end of the leash over in his hands as Dreyfus danced at his side, anxious to go—somewhere. "Looks like he chewed through it," he said half to himself.

"Sally!" her husband shouted toward the woods. "Sally! Answer me! Are you all right?" He took a lunge forward, but the detective caught his arm. Dreyfus whimpered at his side.

"Wait," the detective said in much the same tone he'd used on the dog a few minutes earlier. He handed Denny the leash. "Don't let him get loose. We need to do this right. If your wife is in there somewhere, perhaps injured and unable to make it back on her own, we need to be sure we don't obscure her trail. Let me get a search team in here so we can find her as soon as possible."

"But I can help," Denny pleaded. "I can start now."

"And maybe there will be two people we'll be looking for. No, please, wait here and help us get to her as soon as possible."

Denny obviously didn't like it, but stayed put, Dreyfus's leash wrapped around one hand, the other fisting and flexing at his side. I understood his frustration. My first instinct was to head into the woods, too, but my better sense told me that I'd been away a long time and would be wandering aimlessly. Search and rescue had a much better chance of finding a trail and finding Sally.

Detective Quinn had stepped aside and was quietly talking

into his cell phone. I stood beside Denny and Dreyfus at the edge of the woods, afraid of what would come next.

"Are they coming to search for her?" I asked when he ended his call.

He nodded. "Search and rescue is coming in," he said to Denny. "We'll follow your dog's trail and find out where he left the rest of his leash. From there we'll track Mrs. Kendall."

It sounded like a good plan. Dreyfus strained impatiently at what remained of his leash, ready to head back into the woods. All I wanted to do was run in the woods after him and find Sally.

Denny returned to the house to check on the children and brought back a replacement leash. Neither Dreyfus nor I was particularly satisfied with waiting for the arrival of the search and rescue team and whoever else Quinn had summoned to aid in the search for Sally. While he spent his time either on the phone or trying to calm Denny, I paced the backyard staring into the woods, trying to calm myself and Dreyfus, who now followed obediently at my side.

"It won't be long now," Quinn said as he joined me.

I absently stroked Dreyfus's head. "We're both anxious to get started," I said.

The detective shook his head. "Not you. I need you to stay here. Keep an eye on Mr. Kendall and listen for the phone, in case Mrs. Kendall calls in or comes back." He handed me a business card. "Just in case you didn't keep the other one. My cell number is on the back."

A few minutes later, what I hoped was the cavalry arrived. It looked like half the Marlowe Police Department pulled up along the curb in front of our houses, Sam Whitacker and Sally's cousin Robby among them. A K-9 handler and a German shepherd, wearing an orange vest, emerged from a cruiser and headed across the lawn. I watched as Denny gave the K-9 handler a crumpled shirt I recognized as the one Sally had been wearing the day before. I couldn't overhear what was being said but watched as Detective Quinn pointed to the area where the dog had exited the woods. Quinn and the officer studied a folded map, then walked over to where Dreyfus and I were waiting impatiently. Dreyfus began to dance around as two men and their K-9 companion approached.

The taller of the two put out his hand. "Ma'am, if you'll let us take that leash, we'll see where he leads us." I bent down and hugged Dreyfus and relinquished the leash. He said a few words to Dreyfus as he stroked the golden retriever's fur to calm him. I thought Dreyfus knew it was time to find Sally. They headed toward the woods with Robby and another officer following.

I brought a folding chair to the edge of the woods and spent the better part of an hour pacing more than sitting. Officer Sinclair kept watch near the back door. Denny retreated to the play area behind the house, where he was trying to keep the girls occupied. At the first sound of footsteps heading in our direction, he froze in place. I spun around to face whoever was headed our way.

Robby alone emerged from the trees with Dreyfus.

"They asked me to bring him back," he said as he handed me the leash. "He led us to an old tree where someone had tied him. We found the remains of his leash. Went in circles after that. No sign of Sally." He turned back toward the woods. I caught his arm.

"Wait. What now?" I asked.

"We keep looking. I'm sorry, but I've got to get back." He glanced at Denny, who was headed in our direction, Sinclair a few steps behind him. "Don't say I told you, but it looks like there was some kind of a struggle. Like Sally was dragged off by someone. This is no time for heroics on anyone's part."

I gasped.

"Stay here. And keep him with you. I've gotta go," Robby said. This time I didn't try to stop him. He disappeared into the woods as Denny and Sinclair reached me.

"Well?" Denny said. "What did he say? Where's he going?"

Sinclair slipped her cell phone into her pocket. "They finished with Dreyfus. As soon as there's more information about your wife's whereabouts, they'll let us know. Until then—" She glanced back toward the house. The girls had stopped playing and were looking in our direction.

Denny hesitated, then said, "As soon as you hear something."

Sinclair nodded. Denny pasted a good imitation of a smile on his face and headed back toward the house.

"How are you doing today?" Sinclair turned her attention to me.

"Not so good," I said.

"Most of the time it's nothing," she said. "I'd bet Mrs. Kendall walks up any minute now."

I glanced back at the woods. Was it already starting to get

dark in there or did it just seem more foreboding? "I wish I could believe that."

Dreyfus danced at my side, vying for attention.

"Easy, boy." Officer Sullivan laughed as she rubbed the dog's head. "He's sure affectionate."

"I guess it's a trait of the breed," I said.

"Yeah, I've heard goldens are like that." Jan Sinclair nodded, giving the woods a sideways glance. "Why don't we go inside and get some coffee?"

"I don't drink coffee."

"I'm sure we can scare up a mug of hot water and a tea bag or two." She smiled.

The tension inside me lightened just a bit. This cop was good at putting people at ease, suspect or bystander. I stroked Dreyfus as we headed back to the house, picking burrs from his fur and a bit of debris caught in his collar. I absently stuck it in my pocket intending to toss it in the trash once we got inside.

A little over an hour later, as the sun was headed down below the surrounding hills, I heard a sound coming from the woods. Denny had heard it, too. Dreyfus beat both of us to the door. The beams of their flashlights preceded the search party out of the darkening woods. Detective Quinn and Sam Whitacker emerged moments later. There was no sign of Sally.

My fears were confirmed when Denny ran up to the detective, who spoke softly and shook his head. I ran across the lawn as fast as my feet would carry me.

"What do you mean you lost the scent? How could you lose the scent?" Denny shouted. Fists clenched, he stood inches from the detective. "She was there just a few hours ago. Dreyfus was, too. You had her shirt. How could you not find her?" The detective didn't flinch.

Sam came up behind Sally's husband, put a hand on his shoulder, and spoke softly to him. "Easy, Den," Sam said.

For a moment I didn't know if Denny would stand down, but then he began to tremble. He staggered back, and Sam caught him, guiding him back toward the house where Officer Sinclair waited. Denny was in good hands.

The search and rescue guys and their K-9 companion walked up to Detective Quinn where I stood beside him. "I'm sorry," the dog handler said. "She must have been all over those paths back there. We were able to follow the scent, but it didn't take long for Molly here to get pulled in multiple directions. She led us back to where the golden had been tied to the tree. Looks like he gnawed through the leash trying to get loose. Couldn't tell from the way it was looped around the branch whether it was tied there deliberately or the dog just got himself tangled up, though I'd bet he was tied there to keep him from following wherever Mrs. Kendall went. The area is pretty torn up, and it looks like there was a struggle, but again we can't say for sure. Goldie there could have been responsible for disturbing the scene." He shrugged. "Could be why he was tied up."

"And there was no sign of Mrs. Kendall?" I asked, waiting for the detective to shut me down. He didn't.

The dog handler shook his head. "Nothing. We tried to

find a trail and had a good lead heading north on that old overgrown road but lost it. It might have been from a recent walk they took together. Hard to tell. The weather's been so agreeable the trail could have been set days or hours ago. As it is, just too many overlapping trails."

"Thank you for trying," I said as he walked away.

"I wish we could have done more."

"So, what now?" I asked Detective Quinn.

"Now you go home and get some rest," he said. He had to know that would go over like a lead balloon.

"What about Sally? You can't think I'm going anywhere until we find out where she is."

"I think you've got to let us do our jobs," he said. "Get some rest. That's what we'll advise Mr. Kendall. To take care of his children and try to rest."

"That's it?" My voice rose in pitch and loudness.

"Ms. Walker. Maggie," he said, nodding toward Denny, who had stopped on the doorstep and was looking back at us. "He's barely hanging on. If you lose it, you'll do nothing but make it harder on him. We can't do our best jobs if everyone around us is falling apart. You'll make it impossible if you try to 'help' us."

I did my best to regain control. But how could I simply go home as though nothing was wrong? "I have to do something. Please."

He shook his head. "There's nothing you can do that won't get in the way. We've searched the area between here and around where we found the dog's leash and began to expand the search area. As you might guess, it's difficult to do in the dark. Come daylight we'll get back on it if she hasn't returned home on her own. In the meantime, we've been contacting people she might have been in touch with today. For all we know she's out visiting a friend."

I opened my mouth to protest, but he waved me into silence. "I know," he said, "you don't believe that. But right now we've got to look into all the possibilities. Now, Maggie, please, go home. Get some rest or don't. Your choice. But keep in mind, Mr. Kendall may need your help tomorrow, and it would be best for everyone if you weren't exhausted."

I didn't like what I was hearing but nodded mutely and turned to go home. Once there I checked my phone, hoping—in vain, I knew—that there would be a message from Sally. The red light on the answering machine stared at me unblinking. No messages. I checked my cell phone again. No missed calls.

My stomach growled. How could I think of food at a time like this? I couldn't. I compromised and made myself a cup of tea, swallowed some aspirin for the headache threatening to erupt, took a shower, and went to bed. I tried to sleep, then I tried to read for a while, but my eyes were tired and refused to focus. I put the book down and got up to pace the room. I turned out the light and stared out the window at Sally's house and the woods behind it. Somewhere out there my friend was lost. Maybe hurt. Maybe worse. I scrunched my eyes closed against the burning tears that threatened. I turned away from the window. I wouldn't consider the possibility that something had happened to Sally. She was alive. Maybe hurt, but alive. She had to be. So, where the heck was she?

By the time light began to streak across the darkened sky, I still had no answers. But I was determined to at least be with the people who would find them first.

I pulled on a hoodie over my tee shirt and grabbed my jeans from the chair beside the bed. As I pulled them on, I felt something sharp. I shook my head as I pulled it from my pocket. Trash. At least it hadn't ended up in the laundry.

I stared at the wad of yellow dog hair, fragments of dried leaves and twigs, and something else. Something shiny. I pulled the bit of painted metal loose and turned it over in my hands. It was circular in shape and snapped off where a hole had been punched near one edge. There was something familiar about it. Was it part of something I'd seen recently? But what and where? And what was it doing snagged by Dreyfus's collar?

I looked out the window again. Lights were on next door in the kitchen and parlor. The police cruiser that had been there all night had been joined by a second one. A changing of the guard or had something happened? I picked up the bedside phone and dialed. Denny picked up on the first ring.

"Hi, it's Maggie. I just wanted to check to see if there's any news."

"No, nothing. They're getting ready to go out looking again."

"Is there anything I can do?" I asked.

"Not at the moment," Detective Quinn's voice cut in. Had he been listening on the extension? "We'll call you if we hear anything. Thank you."

And the line went dead. I stood there with my mouth open. I'd been shut out, just like that. What did they think I was going to do, head off into the woods with my own search party? Maybe upstage them? I slammed the phone back onto its cradle, clenching the metal bit in my other hand.

Pain stabbed at my palm. Great. I opened my hand to see a drop of blood where the sharp metal edge had punctured the skin. Damn.

In the bathroom I rinsed off the cut and, satisfied it wasn't deep and was no longer bleeding, I wiped my palm and dabbed on a bit of antiseptic cream. Then I picked up the offending fragment and held it up to the light. It was thin and only a little over an inch long, painted pewter gray on one side and glossy orange and black on the other. And I knew where I'd seen it.

One night when we'd spent the evening in the early stages of planning the community garden, Violet had suggested we take a break. While we chatted about everything but the project at hand, Violet mentioned her love of photography and how it had led her to the idea of the community garden. Violet loved gardens, though she proclaimed herself queen of the brown thumbs. I had laughed and Violet had pulled out her inspiration for the community garden—a scrapbook containing photographs she'd taken of gardens around town and in nearby communities. She explained that once she'd compiled the photos and heard about how much people's gardens meant to them, she knew there had to be someplace for people without their own land to have a garden.

We'd perused the photos for far longer than we'd intended to take our break, but I had enjoyed hearing the stories of the various gardens as much as Violet had enjoyed telling them. In one of the gardens, there were unique metal sculptures and ornaments. All made, Violet told me, by one of her neighbors. Among the sculptures was a monarch butterfly. Its colorfully patterned wings were composed of spangles painted glossy black and orange on one side, gray on the other. Each had been lovingly attached to the framework by hand. The fragment I held could have broken off from that sculpture. If not that one, one very much like it.

If I was right, there was a connection. A man who'd lost his wife so recently. A man who made sculptures for her garden. A man who might have killed the person trying to take his home and his beloved wife's garden from him. Howie Tucker.

I reached for the phone. I should call and tell the detective what I'd discovered. I hesitated. Tell him what, exactly? That I'd picked up a metal fragment that was wedged in the fur at the dog's collar? They'd all probably just dismiss it as of no significance. It could have come from anywhere and Dreyfus could have picked it up at any time. And maybe it really wasn't important. Maybe it meant nothing at all. And what if they accepted my conclusion about where Dreyfus and maybe Sally had been the day before? And what if that conclusion was wrong? The answer to the last question was simple: if I sent them on a wild-goose chase with my found evidence and conclusions, it would be valuable time wasted that might have gotten them closer to finding Sally.

I should just leave the search to the professionals. I pushed the fragment across my palm with my index finger. I couldn't just ignore this. It *was* evidence. It was a clue. And it just might lead to Sally.

I stared out the window. The search team had arrived and

was getting ready to head back into the woods. They'd find Sally today now that it was daylight again. But what if the answer lay not in the woods but at a house on the far side of the woods? Would their search lead them there? I had to believe eventually it would—if that was where Sally was. In the meantime, I could do a little reconnaissance and, if I discovered my suspicions were correct, I'd call Detective Quinn and this time I wouldn't let him shut me out.

By the time the searchers had entered the woods, I'd grabbed my purse, tucked my cell phone in my pocket, and headed out in my Jeep on a search of my own.

Chapter Twenty-Three

I parked down the street from the house I had in mind. Vicky's Victorian, as Violet had called it, sat on a large lot surrounded on two sides by a wide border of flowers and shrubs, and on its back by the woods—those very same woods bordering my backyard a half mile or so away as the crow flies.

The house looked sad and a bit neglected. The paint had faded and started to peel in places. The front walk had heaved from winter's freeze and thaws. The mailbox listed drunkenly to one side. But the landscaping was meticulous. A border of pansies lined the front walkway. Hostas had poked through the neat strip of mulch running along the edge of the sidewalk. The lawn and shrubs were precisely manicured. Roses anxious to bud climbed trellises affixed to the wide front porch. All a testament to the gardener who no longer lived there. Contrary to what he'd told me, Mrs. Tucker's garden was doing just fine.

I sat there for a few minutes, trying to decide what was best to do. Obviously, I couldn't walk up to the door and ask its owner if he'd had a hand in Sally's disappearance. Even a knock on the door and a simple inquiry if he'd seen her could raise his suspicions.

Maybe I could take a look around without being seen. Confirm this was indeed the house with the colorful sculptures. A lot of people slept in on Sunday mornings. But if he caught me, it would be embarrassing if I was wrong, downright dangerous if I was right. And no one knew where I was. Like Violet when she disappeared. And now like Sally. I didn't want to go down that road. But if I called Sam or Detective Quinn, I was sure they'd just tell me to go home. Instead, I dialed my home phone and waited patiently for the answering machine to pick up. Just a little insurance that I'd probably laugh at later when I listened to the message.

"This is Maggie Walker," I said, "and if you're listening to this message, I'm missing and you're trying to find me. It's seven A.M. on Sunday and my Jeep is parked at the corner of North and Spring Streets. I'm going to take a look around at number one oh three." I finished the message with why I was there, ended the call, and put the phone back in my pocket. My hand was on the door handle when Howie Tucker's car pulled out of the driveway. He drove by without a glance in my direction. This was my chance.

I slipped out of the Jeep and walked quickly down the sidewalk. I crossed the neatly mown lawn, passed the rose garden at the side of the house. There, just ahead of me, stood a large metal scarecrow, just like in Violet's photo except that the forsythia in the photo had been in full bloom. This year's blooms had passed and now only a cascade of green remained. Behind it, if I remembered correctly, was a bed of perennial flowers that featured a flock of metal butterflies. I rounded the house and there they were.

I stopped short. Several of the ornaments had been torn from the ground and lay scattered about. A bent and broken monarch butterfly was among them. A few steps away stood a weathered toolshed, its scarred door padlocked. I inched closer. The door was marked with long scratches. Fresh ones. Like something had been trying to get in. Dreyfus? I tried to pull open the door, but it held firm.

I moved to the shuttered window on the west side of the shed. I grabbed the shutter and, despite creaking hinges, it pulled aside to reveal a filthy window. I rubbed at the dirt with my sleeve and put my face closer to the glass. There was more dirt on the inside of the pane and little light entered the shed. I couldn't see a thing.

I wiped furiously at the glass, changed my angle of vision a couple of times, and pressed my face against the glass. Inside I could make out gray and black shapes. Barely. I squinted. Had something moved over by the door? It looked like a tarp had been thrown over something. It might be a trick of the light or just my nerves. My heart beat faster. No. It moved. Maybe mice? Some other animal? Maybe not.

I ran to the door, yanked at the handle. The padlock held firm. I yanked again, harder this time. The lock held, but the hasp wiggled where it was attached to the door. I looked around for something to wedge between it and the door for leverage. Several long-handled tools lay strewn on the ground nearby, apparently knocked from their perches as they leaned against the shed. I grabbed a shovel, upended it, and shoved the blade behind the hasp and pulled on my makeshift lever. Again. The nails holding the hasp creaked in protest, but they started to give way. I pulled harder. Just a little more. With a loud *crunch!* it gave way.

The nails released their hold and the hasp flew aside. I dropped the shovel and lurched backward, landing on my behind. I scrambled to my feet, scanned the yard around me. Nothing moved. I yanked the shed's door open. Light flooded into the interior. In front of me, the tarp moaned. I pulled it aside. Lying beneath the tarp, Sally began to struggle against the cords binding her hands and feet. A gag muffled her attempts to speak.

With shaking hands, I pulled her to a sitting position. What looked like a large, bloody bruise marked the side of her head. Her clothes were torn and dirty. But her eyes were opened and alert. Tears welled up in my eyes and my vision blurred. I pulled off the gag.

"Thank goodness," Sally whispered. "I thought—I thought I was going to end up like Violet. All I could think of was my kids and Denny. Maggie, he—"

I wrapped my arms around her. "I need to get you out of here," I said and stood to do a quick search of the shed. I found what I was looking for and a minute later I'd cut the cords at her ankles and wrists and dragged Sally to her feet.

"Dreyfus! Is he all right? Howie Tucker said he tied him to a tree. But I heard him outside, then I heard him yelp—"

"Dreyfus is fine. You can tell me what happened later. We need to get back to my Jeep. Come on," I said, leading her into the sunlight as I reached for the phone in my pocket.

I dialed the detective's number. It went directly to voicemail. "I've found Sally. We're at Howard Tucker's house. We're headed to my Jeep now." I left the address and disconnected.

For good measure I dialed 911. Sally's eyes opened wide.

Standing a few feet away was Howie Tucker, his usual congenial smile nowhere to be seen.

"I should have known," he said quietly. "I thought that Jeep down the street looked familiar. Good thing I decided to come back and check it out."

"It's over, Howie," I said with all the bravado I could muster, hoping the 911 operator was on the line and listening. "I'm taking Sally home." I took a step forward. Howie didn't budge. I took another step, reaching back and taking Sally's hand.

"I know what you did. I know you killed Carl Henderson and Violet Bloom. Did you fight on Friday night? Is that what happened? Did Violet see?"

Howie pulled a pistol from the pocket of his windbreaker.

"Drop the phone," he said in a tone that inspired my fingers to do exactly as he said. Howie moved toward me. As I stepped back, he kicked the phone. I watched as it skidded out of reach into a tangled mass of a rugosa rosebush.

"You don't understand," he said. "I didn't want any of it to happen. He just wouldn't stop. I told him I'd sell him the land out back but not the lot the house is on. He said he needed it all for that project of his."

"Marlowe Estates," I said, stalling, hoping for the sound of approaching sirens.

"Just another of his schemes." Howie waved the gun at us. "I told him no. Kept telling him no. But he wouldn't listen.

Found out I was behind on my mortgage. Outstanding bills at the store. All those medical bills."

"And he wanted to use that to convince you to sell."

"I couldn't. This place"—he waved his arm, taking in the house and garden—"this place is all I have left of her. A part of her is alive here."

"And he wanted to take that away from you," I said softly. Still no sirens. No sounds from the woods behind us. How long could I stall him?

"Friday afternoon, Wellman was out back tilling the garden. Violet came by. Didn't see her after Wellman left. I was closing up the store when Henderson came in. Said he was going to make sure I didn't get the loan I needed from the bank. Said one of the members of the loan committee owed him a favor or two. I'd end up losing the house anyway eventually so I might as well sell now and save my business." He looked from Sally to me and back again. "I was no match for him. We fought. I grabbed a shovel from the display. It was over so fast. You understand, don't you?" The pleading in his voice would have broken my heart—if it weren't for the gun in his hand.

Sally's knees gave way, and she collapsed in a heap at my side. Howie took a step back, perhaps wary of a trick. I seized the opportunity and the shovel I'd used to pry the door open. With my best Little League swing, I brought the shovel down across his arm. The pistol flew into the tangle of the forsythia bushes. He recovered quickly, lunging at me. I moved aside, putting the blade of the shovel between us. Howie stopped short.

"Back off," I said. I dared a quick glance at Sally. She was on her knees trying to stand.

"I'm okay," Sally gasped, not sounding entirely convinced of her own words. "Just need to get on my feet." She pulled herself upright with a grunt. Howie took advantage of my distraction to move closer.

"Back off, I said." I poked the shovel at him.

He looked at me. He looked at the shovel. He looked at the pistol lying under the branches of the forsythia. Stalemate. He turned and ran toward the house, then disappeared around its corner.

"Come on," I said, tugging at Sally's arm. "We've got to get to my Jeep."

"No." Sally held her ground. "That's the way he went."

"I know." I kept my eyes on the house to be sure he wasn't circling back. "But we've got to get to the Jeep. And we've got to do it now."

Still Sally refused to move. "No, I have a better idea."

"I'm all ears, just make it quick."

Sally nodded toward the woods. "The old road is about fifteen feet beyond the end of the lawn."

"You want to run through the woods?" My tone added, *Are you crazy?*

"Come on." Sally pulled at my arm. "Once we get on the road, it'll lead us straight through to right behind your house."

I'd opened my mouth to protest that the woods were the last place we should go, when Howie appeared at the corner of the house—another pistol in his hand—blocking any other means of escape.

"Okay, now would be good."

Together we ran, stumbling, toward the trees at the back of

the lot. As we reached the edge of the grass, my heart pounded in my ears and I was already breathing hard.

Bark flew at us from one of the nearby trees.

"He's shooting at us!" I cried, pulling Sally along faster.

"He's lost his mind!"

We struggled through the undergrowth, pushing aside small branches and tripping over rocks and uneven ground until we reached the wood road. I heard a shot echo somewhere behind us but couldn't tell where it hit. We lurched forward, our feet slapping against the hard ground. Clear of the underbrush, we sprinted toward a bend up ahead in the road. As the ground rose in front of us, I tripped over a rock in the road, gasping for air. Beside me Sally wasn't faring any better. Adrenaline and fear kept us going.

Another shot. Dirt sprayed in the road ahead of us. As we leaped forward, I heard Howie's curse not far behind. I didn't dare look back. A few feet from the bend, Sally's foot caught on a root protruding from the uneven surface of the overgrown road. She fell face-first. I turned to see Howie jogging to a halt, the pistol pointed at Sally.

"Make a move to run and she dies," he said.

"How many more people do you think you can kill?" I called out, spitting out the words with what felt like my last breath. I bent down beside Sally. Her face was streaked with dirt, tears pouring from her eyes.

"Get her up and head back that way." He pointed with the barrel of the gun.

"No," I said simply.

"No?" He waggled the pistol at me. "You forget who's got the gun here. And you know I'm not afraid to use it."

"But will you?" Sally asked. She ran a dirty sleeve across her cheeks. "You've been our friend for years. You've been to my home. I've been to yours. How can you do this?"

"I didn't want to," he said calmly. "Sometimes there's no choice. If Maggie here hadn't come snooping around, I might have had time to figure out what to do. But now I've got no choice."

"Of course you've got a choice," I said softly. "You didn't kill Sally. You chose to look for another alternative. Do that now."

"I really wish I could," Howie said. The gun in his hand trembled. "I didn't mean to kill Violet. She just got in the way. She said she had pictures. She said she knew what we were doing. She didn't, it turned out, but by then it was too late. She knew Carl was up to something. But I wasn't." He thumped his chest with his free hand. "Not me!" He started to laugh, but it came out a sob. When he spoke again his voice was flat.

"I tried to talk to her, but she wouldn't listen. I knew if she told anyone, they'd put two and two together. You know, it's funny. When she showed up at the store on Friday night, I thought she'd heard us. But she just had a fistful of papers. She said she was going to deliver them to the head of the town council on Saturday morning unless I came clean. She thought I was in cahoots with Carl! She had no idea. But it was too late. She saw the shovel by the back door. Then she saw his body." He shook his head. "Always, always too late."

He looked around the woods, seemingly lost in thought. But he recovered quickly, leaving no time to take advantage of his lapse. His eyes focused on me, and he shouted, "Now move!" He pointed the pistol at a spot down the road as he maneuvered to one side so he could get behind us without our passing too close to him.

Sally struggled to her feet, nearly falling again when she tried to take a step.

"We're not going anywhere," I said, standing my ground. No way was I going back to his place, to that shed to be locked up or shot. Somewhere nearby, a search was going on. If I could stall long enough, maybe they would cross our path. If my 911 call had gone through, they were on their way here.

"Then you're going to die right here," Howie said matter-of-factly. He aimed the gun at Sally's head. She whimpered.

Maybe, I thought, we should go with him for a bit, slowly, just to see if some chance of escape would present itself.

I spotted movement among the trees.

"Drop it!" a voice shouted behind us. Howie swung around.

I turned in time to see the police dog leap toward Howie. The gun went flying as the German shepherd's jaws clamped down on Howie's arm.

Chapter Twenty-Four

The early morning's trauma morphed into the drama of Howie Tucker being handcuffed and taken to a cruiser and the paramedics waiting at his house to treat his dog bite. An ATV arrived to chauffeur Sally to a waiting ambulance. I was left to walk back to the house accompanied by the K-9 officer and his canine partner. I'd pick up my Jeep later, maybe tomorrow. I had no desire to set foot near Howie Tucker's house again, definitely not today.

At home, I paced the confines of my kitchen, waiting for word about Sally while Jan Sinclair sat at my kitchen table, drinking a calming cup of chamomile tea. My cup sat cooling on the counter. I'd expanded my route to the parlor, checking out the window and the front door on alternating laps. Sometime before I wore a hole in the hardwood floor or through my companion's patience, Detective Quinn appeared.

He said he'd come to take my statement. Judging from his expression, I was afraid something else had happened until Jan Sinclair filled the kettle and offered to brew another pot of tea. When she asked if he preferred chamomile or peppermint with a hint of a smile and that professional calm I'd come to admire, the detective gave her a questioning look, then shook his head.

"Nothing, thanks," he said. He turned to me. "This won't take long."

"Fine," I said. "Whatever. I just need to know if Sally's okay."

"Mrs. Kendall has a few bumps and bruises from your escape from Mr. Tucker and she suffered an injury to her ankle when she fell. She has a relatively minor scalp wound that apparently bled a great deal, but otherwise is doing fine. Her family were with her at the ER when I left. I suspect they'll be bringing her home soon," he said in a maddeningly clinical tone.

"That's it?"

"What more do you want to know? I'm sure she'll fill you in when she gets here."

"Are Denny and the kids okay?"

He sighed. "I'm sure it's all been emotionally trying. As you might expect, their reunion was rather tearful."

I had no doubt it was. The floodgates were sure to open as soon as I laid eyes on my dear friend. Until then, the knot in my stomach refused to ease.

All the while he took my statement, I kept craning my neck, watching the window for any sign of Sally's return home. Other than an occasional pause of his pen while he jotted down my responses in his notebook, Detective Quinn didn't react to my fidgeting. At the sound of an engine, I leapt to my feet and raced to the window, but it was only the neighbors across the street.

"Sorry," I said by way of apology more due to force of habit than sincerity. There was no way I could focus on this latest interrogation until I saw for myself that my friend was safe. I returned to my seat at the table, grabbing one of the sofa pillows on the way. It wasn't exactly a lifesaver, but it was something to hold on to until I reached solid ground.

He continued to take my statement in that exacting way of his. So far he'd refrained from providing an opinion on how we got into the mess we'd made. Waiting just added to my anxiety.

"And that's when the dog came out of nowhere and bit his arm. A second later, it seemed like the woods were filled with people." I knotted the fringe on the pillow between my fingers. "You know the rest."

I looked hopefully at him. Maybe whatever storm I'd sensed brewing had passed. The look on his face told me daffodils in December were more likely.

He closed his notebook and stood up from the table.

"Thank you, Ms. Walker," he said with clipped politeness. "We'll be in touch about having you sign a formal statement." His jaw clenched. And then the other shoe dropped.

"You're both lucky you weren't killed." There was an edge to his voice I hadn't heard before. He put the notebook and pen in his pocket. "If I could arrest you for interfering in the investigation, I would. But I can't. What I can do is tell you that was an incredibly reckless—no, *stupid*—thing you did. How you managed to get away with only a sprained ankle between the two of you I will never understand."

I jumped to my feet and stood nose to necktie with him.

"Well, if you would have listened to me, I wouldn't have had to go there on my own!"

He took a step back, a look of disbelief on his face. "Listened to you? I have listened to you. And I've cautioned you how dangerous this could be. But you didn't listen to me or to Chief Whitacker. You insisted on conducting your own personal investigation."

Jan Sinclair looked back and forth between us.

"We just asked a few questions," I said, digging in my heels.

"Quite a few," he countered. "That led to Mrs. Kendall's abduction."

I had no argument for that, but that didn't stop me. I was on a roll and nowhere near ready to quit.

"If it hadn't been for those reckless questions, you never would have known about the pictures Violet took in the woods and how important they were to her."

"A simple phone call from you and we'd have retrieved the pictures. We follow up on every lead as part of our investigation. There was no need for your involvement."

"And once you looked at them, you probably would have thought the pictures were a lot of nothing, like I did. If it wasn't for Sally seeing what they were, we never would have found Violet." I drew in a ragged breath and fought back the tears that threatened to spill. I was not going to cry in front of him. Not again. Not now.

When the detective spoke, his voice was low and gruff. "Ms. Walker, contrary to your belief, we would indeed have found Mrs. Bloom's body. A Marlowe police unit located her vehicle that morning, abandoned in a wooded area a street away from Mr. Tucker's residence. Those woods would have been thoroughly searched."

When I opened my mouth to speak, he held up a hand. I ignored it.

"And what about Sally? She was just walking her dog in the woods when Howie attacked her."

"And if you hadn't been asking questions and making him think you'd learned something that threatened him?"

"Maybe no difference," I said, but he'd hit home with those words. Had I put Sally in danger?

Jan Sinclair chose that moment to intervene with a fresh cup of tea for me. Quinn shook his head, said his farewells through clenched teeth, and left.

To my amazement, by late that afternoon, to all appearances life on our street had returned to normal with every indication of a police presence having vanished. An impromptu picnic had ensued in Sally's backyard. Denny was busy manning the grill, though he'd maneuvered it so that he could keep a watch on Sally while flipping burgers.

But Sally wasn't going anywhere. She'd been seated on one of their new chaise longues, her foot propped on a pillow, a large glass of lemonade at her elbow. Between the kids and a very relieved neighbor—yours truly—she was being waited on hand and swollen foot.

Some of the searchers had returned with family and covered dishes to share. I sat in a lounge chair next to Sally, enjoying the late afternoon sun and, for the moment at least, allowing

Sally's children to wait on me. The oldest had just brought me a very tall iced tea with fresh mint.

I marveled at the miracle of their recovery from what could have been the most horrible day of their young lives. Denny had hidden the past day's goings-on as well as he could from them and, judging by the grin plastered across his face, he was enjoying their excited screeches as they ran across the yard, chasing Dreyfus in circles, as much as Sally was.

I'd waited as long as I could to bring up the subject of her encounter with Howie in the woods. "Do you think you're up to telling me how you ended up in that shed?"

"Sure," Sally said. "One more time won't make a difference." She made sure the children were out of earshot before continuing. "Dreyfus and I were having a peaceful walk in the woods. I made the mistake of going all the way to the end of the old road where Howie's property is. He must have seen us there and followed us back. We were almost to my place when he came up behind me. Accused me of spying on him. When I turned to leave he grabbed me. I pulled away and fell and hit my head." Her hand went up to touch her hair. "Next thing I knew he grabbed me by the arm and was pulling me back toward his house."

"What about Dreyfus?" I asked.

"Howie said he'd tied him to a tree. I could hear him whining behind us. Howie'd pulled out that gun of his and forced me to go along with him. When we got back to his place, no one was around. He pushed me in the shed and tied me up and gagged me. Said he had to figure out what to do, how to get away. He said if I tried to attract any attention, he'd shoot me."

"Oh, Sally." I reached over and took her hand.

"I tried to work my hands or feet free, but my head was pounding. I don't know if I passed out or fell asleep during the night, but next thing I knew you were there." She squeezed my hand, and I blinked hard to turn off the tears that threatened to start again.

Sally picked up her glass of lemonade. "To good friends and loving family," she toasted. I leaned over and clinked my glass against hers. As I sat there, enjoying a few quiet moments alone with my friend, I could hardly believe our good fortune. Or maybe dumb luck. Had we run for the Jeep, we would have directly crossed Howie's path as he returned rearmed to confront us. As it was, by fleeing into the woods and following the old road, we'd met the search party led by the K-9 team who had been instructed to head toward Howie Tucker's house. Another contingent had arrived there and were making their way toward us from that direction.

"To search and rescue dogs and their handlers," Sally said, her smile even broader.

I again clinked glasses with her, content to toast the moon when it appeared in the sky. I leaned back in my chair, feeling that all was well with the world. Anything conspiring to ruin my mood was nothing more than minor aggravation and would be appropriately ignored for the time being.

"Hey, look," Sally said, gesturing with her glass. "It looks like you've got mail."

Ron the postman had followed the voices up the driveway and into the backyard and was making a beeline toward us. "Got another letter for you, Ms. Walker. This one's express."

I dutifully accepted the envelope with a smile. Even this couldn't ruin my mood. Not today.

"Cousin Simon strikes again?" Sally asked.

"Looks like," I said.

"Aren't you going to open it?"

I considered tossing it in the outdoor fireplace but that would require getting out of my chair. Besides, I knew my curiosity would never let me discard the letter unread. I slipped a finger under the flap and tore it open. I began to read and frowned.

"Well, what does it say?"

"It says he's decided not to file his lawsuit for now. I guess I finally got through to him. And lots of apologizing. I mean a lot. Very strange. Oh, and he asked that I let the police chief know that his calls were just jokes. A little family fun. Anything else was the dead guy."

"Dead guy? Like Carl? That is odd," Sally said. "You think Sam talked to him?"

"Sounds like. Though I never did get around to telling Sam that Simon was the one behind those calls." I snapped my fingers. "But I did tell him that Denny saw Simon and Carl Henderson together. Whatever's gotten into him, I hope it's for good.

"So, you won't be holding the family reunion here anytime soon?" Sally grinned at me.

"Very funny," I mumbled as I reread the letter on the chance I'd misread it the first time around.

"Something else?"

"Uh, no, just checking. Don't want to miss if trouble's coming back."

"True. You've had your share of bad luck lately. But things have turned around," Sally added hastily. "First, in order of appearance and not importance, that greedy cousin of yours tries to extort money from you even though there is not a single reason why he should be entitled to anything more than what he got. If you ask me, he shouldn't have gotten a red cent, but your grandmother always was one to err on the side of forgive and forget."

I nodded absently. Gramma was nothing if not kindhearted.

Sally continued, "And then there's everyone's favorite witch with a *B*, Catherine Whitacker, who for some reason unbeknownst to mortal man has decided you are the enemy of all that's hers and so will take any and all opportunities—even if she has to manufacture them—to make your life as miserable as possible."

"Is this supposed to cheer me up?" I asked.

Sally scrunched up her face and shook her head. "Why does that woman dislike you so much? I know you were never best friends, but I take back anything I ever said about you being paranoid where she's concerned. So, what gives?"

I left the question hanging in the air. I had my suspicions about why Catherine had it in for me. One possibility was jealousy. Somewhere along the line Catherine had gotten it into her head that I was out to restart my relationship with Sam. I'd tried to tell her once it was all in the past, that we were just friends of the most casual kind, but it had only made things worse. Some things you just can't explain. But Catherine was another item on my list of things not to worry about today.

"And that detective didn't help any," Sally went on. "What

was with him anyway? He should have seen right off you were innocent. But no, he kept dogging you. They probably would have found the real killer much sooner if the so-called proper authorities had stopped hounding you."

"Oh, Sally, he really was just doing his job. If it had been someone else and I was just an onlooker, I would have seen that. Sam was, too, for that matter."

"Yeah, some former beau he was. You would think he would have told that detective you weren't a person who could harm anyone, let alone kill anyone, never mind two people." Sally frowned at me. "You aren't listening to me."

I smiled, eyes closed, enjoying the warmth of the sun on my face. "Sure I am. He just couldn't see the flowers of truth through all the weeds. As for me, I just—I am just feeling so good right now I don't want to spoil the mood thinking about Cousin Simon or Catherine Whitacker or finding a body in the garden or Violet going missing, then turning up dead, or about being a suspect or any of it. I especially don't want to think about what happened—and what might have happened—to you." I paused, sitting up to look Sally squarely in the eye. I couldn't help but smile, just because she was there. "How about we don't talk about this anymore and just concentrate on the sun and the blossoming of spring around us," I suggested. "And having the sound of happy kids in the air and a man to cook a great meal for us. Not to mention some good neighbors."

"Sounds like heaven," Sally agreed.

I watched my friend take a long, slow look around the yard. I wasn't sure what Sally was thinking as she began to smile, but I was certainly grateful for the blessings surrounding us this afternoon.

"Don't look now," Sally said, half laughing, "but I'm not going to be the one reminding you of that list of things you didn't want to think about."

"What?" I followed Sally's line of sight.

Detective Matt Quinn was tracing the path taken by the mail carrier a few minutes earlier. He had a paper shopping bag in his hand. He'd changed since this morning's romp in the woods and was wearing fresh jeans and a khaki tee shirt.

"Ladies." He gave us a nod as he reached our chairs.

"And what can we do for you, Detective Quinn?" Sally said, smiling sheepishly. "I hope you don't need me to add to that statement I gave. I intend to have a bit of amnesia for at least twelve hours if that's the case."

"No threats are necessary," he said. A smile flickered across his face. It occurred to me that it was a very nice smile. But that didn't come close to making up for what he'd put me through.

"Maybe you could answer a few questions?" I asked with a tentative grin.

"I think you're due that much," he replied. "Mr. Tucker has been very cooperative. I'm sure once he asks for counsel, his attorney will regret it, but he's been very talkative so far."

When he paused and glanced around us, I couldn't resist prompting him to continue. "Well, what did he say?"

He shifted the bag he was carrying from one hand to the other. "What I can tell you is that he admits to both murders. Mr. Tucker said he'd met Mr. Henderson in the woods behind his house several times since shortly after his wife's death. He didn't want him in his home or business, and it seems for some reason Henderson didn't want to be seen in public meeting Tucker, though he did stop at the hardware store and they argued in the days before the murder. Henderson had been attempting to, in Mr. Tucker's words, not only force him to sell his home and the adjacent eighteen acres of forested land he owns but to assist Henderson in influencing the approval of a plan to develop this area. Mr. Tucker's brother-in-law is on the planning board and apparently Henderson's plans required variances that would need board approval."

"How could he force Howie Tucker to do anything?" I asked.

"Had to be those medical bills," Sally said. "Vicky wasn't sick for a long time, but it progressed fast. She left her job and then lost her insurance. There were times he closed the store to take care of her. Before we knew it, she was gone. I can't even imagine what a financial mess Howie was left to deal with while trying to cope with his grief."

The detective nodded. "Tucker felt cornered that Friday night when Henderson showed up at his store again. They fought and he bludgeoned Henderson with a shovel from one of his displays. He planned to take the body to the woods behind his house to dispose of it but Mrs. Bloom came in through the rear exit. He panicked. He waited until late that night to move the bodies. Said it was easier to dump Henderson's body in the community garden than to move two bodies to the woods. He used a key he'd previously made for himself to open the lock on the gate. Said he liked being able to take a closer look at what was going on behind his store. After he'd buried Henderson's body, he took Mrs. Bloom's body in her car to the woods. He apologized for leaving her there and causing so much distress to her family."

"But not for killing her?" Sally asked.

"He claims he had no choice. She accused him of conspiring with the man he'd just killed. He hit her with the same shovel he'd used on Henderson as she turned her back. We found her car driven in among the trees off the road near his house." He nodded in my direction. "When he heard someone say you may have been the last person to see Violet Bloom alive, he figured leaving the murder weapon on your property would keep attention on you and away from him. He called in an anonymous tip for good measure."

"But he didn't leave it on my property. He left it in Sally's mulch pile."

The detective shrugged. "Got turned around coming out of the woods in the dark, I guess. Said he used that path through the woods from his house to yours."

"And the note?" I asked. "He left the note on my door on Saturday, didn't he?"

The detective nodded. "He did. Sent the text to Mr. Bloom, too. He figured the more he could muddy when she disappeared, the better. Turns out Mrs. Bloom didn't like dealing with her phone's security lock code, so she disabled it."

"What about Simon?" Sally asked.

"Right. He's your cousin, isn't he?" the detective asked me. When I nodded, he continued. "Chief Whitacker told me he was seen at your house when Henderson was there on Friday morning, so we had a talk with him. Seems he and Henderson had an informal agreement. If he helped convince you to sell, Henderson would make it worth his while."

"Sounds like that's a big lose-lose for Cousin Simon," I said.

"What's in the bag?" Sally asked in a radical change of subject. Nothing shy about her.

"I guess you could call it a garden-warming present," he said. He put the bag on the ground by my lounge chair. "Or a peace offering. My way of apologizing. For my reaction yesterday and before that. I could see all along you were one to follow your nose. I was trying to shut you down to keep you out of harm's way. If I'd responded differently, you might have felt you could trust me enough to call for help when the time came before things got desperate."

I leaned over and peeked in the bag. Inside was a small potted shrub. I reached in and pulled it out. "A reblooming lilac!"

"Yeah. I asked the woman at the nursery for a suggestion. I saw their truck making a delivery at your place the other day, so I thought she could tell me what you'd like."

"Like it? I love it," I said. "Thank you." As apologies went, this one was pretty good.

"She's been wanting one of those," Sally explained, nodding in my direction. "She called it a reminder of spring."

He looked blankly at us.

I laughed. "Lilacs are a spring-blooming flower. This one"—I pointed at the pot in my lap—"will bloom again later in the summer when the days are moving toward winter."

"That's hardly winter," he said.

"Ah, but the days are growing shorter." I smiled. "The garden is winding down toward autumn and the inevitable."

"You don't garden, do you?" Sally asked him.

"Nope. No time, no inclination, and no talent," he said.

I raised my eyebrows.

"Sorry," he said. "Maybe you could give me a few hints for my yard. It's just an unhappy swath of lawn with an overgrown herb garden out back. Used to be my wife's. After she died, I'm afraid I couldn't bear to deal with it. Since then, it's had a lot of time to develop a nice crop of weeds."

"So, what do you want to do with it?" I asked. It was Sally's turn to raise her eyebrows at me, but I could never resist a gardening challenge.

"My daughter saw some pictures of her mother working in the garden. She wants to try her hand at it." He shrugged. "I've been putting her off and not really saying yes or no because frankly I don't know what to do with it. I have a black thumb. I'm amazed the weeds are still alive out there."

He looked so serious, but I couldn't help it. I laughed.

Sally said, "Actually, it's brown thumb."

It was his turn to laugh. "Actually," he said in mock seriousness this time, "you haven't seen the garden. Take my word for it, it's black thumb all right."

"Nonsense," I said, settling back in the chair. "Why don't you pull up a seat and get yourself a glass of something cold. I bet once we take a look at that garden of yours and see what's there under the weeds, we'll find all sorts of possibilities."

About the Author

Deborah J. Benoit was a legal secretary for thirty years before deciding to pursue more creative endeavors. Her debut novel, *The Gardener's Plot*, won the Minotaur Books/Mystery Writers of America First Crime Novel Award. Born and raised in the Berkshires of western Massachusetts, there's no place she'd rather call home, even in winter. Determined to never stop learning, Deborah loves sharing her knowledge of gardening through articles she's written, in person, and on social media. When not writing or digging up plots in her garden, she can be found working on her latest fiber-arts project. Learn more about Deborah at PenPaperPlant.com.